THROUGH THE BOOKSTORE WINDOW

BILL PETROCELLI

A NOVEL

A Defenestration Book | Rare Bird Books
Los Angeles, Calif.

THIS IS A GENUINE DEFENESTRATON BOOK

Defenestration | Rare Bird
453 South Spring Street, Suite 302
Los Angeles, CA 90013
rarebirdbooks.com

FIRST HARDCOVER EDITION

Set in Minion Pro
Printed in the United States

10 9 8 7 6 5 4 3 2 1

Publisher's Cataloging-in-Publication data
Names: Petrocelli, William, author.
Title: Through the bookstore window : a novel of mystery and
suspense / Bill Petrocelli.
Description: First Hardcover Edition | A Genuine Defenestration
Book | New York, NY; Los Angeles, CA: Rare Bird Books, 2018.
Identifiers: ISBN 9781945572906
Subjects: LCSH Yugoslav War, 1991–1995—Fiction. | Bosnian
Americans—Fiction. | Adoption—Fiction. | Sexual abuse—Fiction.
| San Francisco (Calif.)—Fiction. | Transgender people—Fiction. |
Suspense fiction. | Mystery fiction. | BISAC FICTION /
Thrillers / Suspense
Classification: LCC PS3616.E8668 T57 2018 | DDC 813.6—dc23

*To my wife, Elaine, and my colleague, Karen West,
for all of the faith and energy that they put into this book.*

*To my special support team of Petra, Ian, Sammy, Bryn,
Laura, and Dylan—may they all grow up to be writers.*

*To all the dedicated booksellers of America, who are often
overworked and underappreciated.*

Gina—2011

Here's what I think:

*We've all been wounded by war. Some of the wounds come
from big, brutal wars, but others are from smaller bloodlettings
that don't make the front pages. Sometimes the injury arrives in
a personal way—in a one-on-one encounter that invades your
body, your life, and your soul. But it's always there somewhere.
And if you really want to understand a person, you have to find
that wound.*

*That's true of me. And it's true of the person lying next
to me—who, I should note, is a first-time visitor to my bed.
There are sleep noises coming from that other pillow, which are
comforting to hear from someone who has had a close brush
with death. Peace and sleep are what we both need at the
moment. But at some point we'll have to share our experiences
and try to make sense of them. What happens then depends
upon whether our memories—our war-wounds—provide us
any understanding or whether they'll just grate on each other
and move us further apart.*

I have another thought, but this one I'm not as sure about.

*I think reality only exists in our life stories. I'm a character
in your story, and you're a character in mine. And both of
us intrude upon the stories of hundreds, thousands—maybe
millions—of others. Trying to isolate our own story is a
mistake, because everything that makes life worth living occurs*

at the place where our stories intersect. People in my profession just add to the confusion. Downstairs from where I'm lying at the moment are thousands of books on the shelves of the bookstore, waiting for you to walk in and pick one up—and maybe find characters who will invite themselves into your life.

These are some of thoughts running through your head when you wake up at 4:00 in the morning and can't go back to sleep. I've been lying here for a while. The wind has been battering the trees against the front window of the apartment. Now the foghorns are starting their wail, telling me that the morning fog is beginning to roll down the hills of San Francisco and head our way. My worries about the bookstore downstairs have a sharper edge at this time of night. I think about who might be walking by at that moment, wrapped up in darkness, maybe looking in the window and feeling threatened by something he sees. It's a fragile business in a fragile world.

And it's at times like this, when you can't sleep, that you might as well start telling stories.

PART ONE

Bosnia—1996

SHE KEPT WATCHING THE soldier, but his last breath had disappeared. He'd writhed in pain in the middle of the street when he was first shot, but he must have realized he was in even greater danger if he couldn't get out of the intersection and crawl over to the buildings. He pulled himself across the pavement, dragging his wounded leg through the dirt, trying to stop the flow of blood with his free hand. The agony on his face was harrowing. She found herself quietly cheering him on, even though in another part of her brain she knew he was her enemy. He was part of the Militia—a brutal group of killers that showed no mercy. But that didn't stop her from hoping that this soldier—the one outside her window—might survive.

She watched him from the window at the top of the cellar, because that one broken window was her only connection with the outside world. The cellar was the only place where she felt safe. The soldier's last movements were slow and painful, as he kept trying to reach the comparative safety of the alley. He didn't make it. After he'd crawled only a few meters, there was another crack of rifle fire. It came from the roof, where her brother and his friends had set themselves up as snipers. And with that burst of gunfire, there was an eruption of blood from the soldier's chest. After that, he didn't move at all.

When the shooting first started, she tried to sort out the individual sounds, wondering where the bullets were coming from. But as the gunfire became more incessant, she realized it could be coming from anywhere. The Militia troops were shouting in a dialect of Serbo-Croatian that she thought was spoken only in the villages across the canyon. She knew they were patrolling the streets, and she shuddered at the idea that they might be getting ready to burst into the house. The electricity and phone lines had been out for days, so she was by herself in the dark, hovered up against the wall, trying to stay safe and keep warm. She had her favorite books stacked nearby, but in the dark it was impossible to read. The only blankets she had belonged to their family dog, who had fled when the explosions began. She had no idea where he'd gone.

The day before, a shell had ripped through the nearby house where her friend lived, setting it afire. When she saw that, she ran screeching upstairs, trying to force her way through the door and out into the street. But her brother grabbed her. *You can't go out,* he said. *It's too dangerous.* She started screaming that she'd never see her friend again, but his grip got tighter. She tried arguing with him. *You and your friends sneak out every night. Let me go!* But he pushed her back. *Listen to me,* he said, *we're risking our lives to protect you from these animals. We know how to avoid getting killed. There's no place for girls in this fight.* She seethed at his words, but she couldn't force her way past him. She headed back to the cellar, where she began burrowing into the dark.

From the cellar window, she could see the smoking hulk of their local store. By now, they were almost out of food in the house. When she first headed down to the cellar, her mother had grabbed some slices of bread and a hunk of cheese, leaving as much as she could for the others. Her mother's words trailed her down the stairs, as she kept trying to reassure her that her sister would be coming back soon and bringing food with her. But her mother was talking more and more to herself. A day earlier she'd walked in front of the window by the sink and was met by a flurry of bullets that sent a shower of broken pottery down on top of her. But she refused to leave the kitchen. Even now she was upstairs, wandering around, sadly trying to prepare a meal with no food and for no one who would sit down to eat it. She was going mad like everyone else.

♦♦♦

HE FELT A SHOVE in the small of his back that caused him to stumble into the debris from a collapsed wall. He managed only barely to step to the side of the alley, avoiding the sharpest nails.

"Keep moving, you little sissy."

The rifle hit him again between his shoulders. "Are you going to act like a soldier, or are you going to keep being a coward?"

His tormentor let out a high-pitched noise that started deep in his throat and twisted its way into a screech. It was an obnoxious, grating sound, but he didn't dare act like it was funny. No one ever did. The man doing the laughing was far too dangerous. He had a whole series of animal-like sounds that became even more chilling when he was enjoying some sadistic pleasure. Among the Militia troops, it had earned him the name *Hijena*—the Hyena.

The *Hijena* kept pushing him down the street toward their unit's temporary headquarters, slowing down only as they passed the burnt-out remains of some local shops. The *Hijena* stopped, shoving aside the remains of a few books that had burst out of the window of a tiny corner store, and pushed his way toward a bottle of Slivovitz that was sticking out of the rubble. It was somehow still intact. He tore off the top and downed a couple of swallows.

The rest of the men in the unit were sitting on broken boxes or lying against abandoned automobiles, smoking and talking, watching the two-man parade that the *Hijena* was leading in front of them. There was some laughter— but it was uneasy. They all knew the *Hijena* was sending a message that their turn could be next. The *Hijena* and his older brother, the *Komandant*, didn't hesitate to take even the harshest measures whenever they felt the need. Two days earlier, they'd tied a soldier—whom they claimed was a deserter—to a pole in the street and ordered the others to shoot him. When none of the soldiers in the line made any move to open fire, the *Komandant* walked up to the prisoner, put a pistol against the man's temple, and fired. With the gun still in hand, he then walked slowly down the line in front of the reluctant firing squad, staring at each one of them.

◆◆◆

THE BRUTALITY OF IT sickened her. It seemed like the Militia would just keep shooting until there was no one left. Her brother and the others had been warning her for weeks that this would happen. These militiamen were dogs, they said— filthy animals that were capable of anything. Rumors had swept through town about terrible things going on in other parts of the country. There were stories of mass killings—murders in places like Srebrenica and other towns to the north.

And there was more, they warned. There was rape. That thought made her sick to her stomach. She couldn't even grasp the idea that a soldier could stop long enough to assault a woman in the midst of all the killing going on around him. The madness of it was unbearable. Was being raped worse than being killed? That made no sense to her. But the idea that someone attacking her might *think* that it was worse left her gripped in fear. And it was more than just the Militia she was worried about. She was fearful about what was going on in the heads of her brother and his friends. These young, would-be soldiers had decided that the rape of a woman was an attack against them. This was an intolerable offense, they kept saying—an intrusion into their territory. An attack on their women was an attack on their sense of pride. It demanded retaliation.

The things that had held her together were falling apart—her family, her school, and her friends all seemed to be spinning away. This was the time of day when she might be reading a book or be on the phone with her girlfriends, talking about things that had happened in school. They might be planning their next shopping trip or chatting about their upcoming vacation. But it was becoming harder and harder to hold on to any of that. Her clothes, her books, and her other things were upstairs in her room, but when she'd gone up to get them she'd been totally exposed. There was gunfire just outside her window, and bullets had ricocheted off the outside walls. She'd grabbed some underwear and a couple of books, scooping some clothing off of her chair as she raced for the stairs. By the time she got down to the cellar and looked at what she had grabbed, she realized she had only one item of real clothing in her hands. It was her favorite party dress.

Her piano was upstairs, but it was as good as gone. It was buried under rubble from a shell that had struck the other side of the compound, causing a living room wall to collapse. That piano had been in their family for eighty years, and her grandmother had left it to her in her will. She'd thought about her grandmother as she played it every afternoon, trying to learn the Bach Fugue in G minor. Her music teacher had said it might be too difficult for her to master, but she kept working at it. The sheet music was still open to that piece when the artillery shell hit the building. Now the main theme of the Fugue was running through her head as she sat there in the cellar, moving her fingers, trying to remember the sequence of notes.

She picked up the dress and stared at it in the dark, trying to get a sense of its color and design, resisting the temptation to burst into tears. The memories hiding in that soft material seemed to be mocking her, reminding her of times spent celebrating with her friends, flirting with the local boys, dancing at parties—things that she had now lost. But as she ran her fingers around the bows and straps of the dress, it started to come alive to her touch. She allowed herself to be lost in its textures and sensations. Without really thinking about it, she'd slipped out of her other clothes. Now that dress was hovering above her head as she let it slide slowly over her body. The noise of artillery shells was getting louder, but she tuned that out of her mind for the moment. The dress now covered her completely. She felt herself swaying slightly. Was she going mad? she wondered. Was she really dancing in the cellar to the silent music of the Fugue? She caught herself for a second but then gave way to the feeling, letting loose the emotions she had almost lost.

✦✦✦

THE *HIJENA* KEPT PRODDING and shoving him until they got to a small open space at the back of the alley. They were in the middle of a makeshift office, where the *Komandant* was hunched over a temporary desk pieced together from packing crates. He was reading a map and checking it against some other papers. A cigarette dangled from his mouth, holding an ash that looked ready to break loose. He took one ferocious drag and then tossed it away. He reached for the pack on his desk and, finding it empty, squashed it and threw it in the direction of the cigarette.

One hard push by the *Hijena* sent him sprawling against the desk, coming face to face with the *Komandant*. The other man looked down at him with an icy stare. His eyes were uneven, with the right one opened wide and arched while the left one drooped slightly. But the two eyes had one thing in common—they both seemed bottomless.

"What's going on?" Even as the *Komandant* stared in his direction, he kept directing his voice at his brother.

"It's this little coward." The *Hijena* shoved him again. "He's a slacker, and he'll desert us at the first opportunity."

"What do you want me to do about it?"

"It was your idea to put him in our unit in the first place!" the *Hijena* shouted. "He never should have been here."

"Shut up for a minute. You may be my brother, but I'm in charge here."

The *Hijena* didn't back off. "You should take him out and shoot him as an example to the others."

As the back-and-forth continued between the two brothers, spasms of weakness rushed through his knees. He was afraid to move. He tried to think of a way out of that nightmare, but there was nowhere to go. As they debated what to do with him, his life was swinging in the balance.

"You're the one who picked him out of all the other garbage at the orphanage. You should have sold him like the others and made some money for yourself instead of sticking him with me."

He had been dragged out of the orphanage a year earlier. At the time, the man standing in front of him wasn't known as the *Komandant*, and he wasn't wearing any kind of uniform. Whether he had any kind of military authority, no one said. He just appeared one day at the orphanage in Sarajevo, walking slowly behind the director, peering at the children lined up in front of him. He said nothing, but he didn't have to. He had the air of someone you needed to listen to—someone you needed to fear. As he walked down the line, he stared at each of the orphans and strays who were unlucky enough to be there, sometimes grabbing one of the children for a better look, often turning the youngster's head from side to side, as if to assess how much it was worth. The rumor around the orphanage was that he was a child broker. With one flick of the finger he could pack you up and send you off to God-only-knows where.

"What's so important that you had to come bursting in here?"

"Here—look at the books I found in his pack." The *Hijena* grabbed the backpack and dumped the contents on the desk. "Take a look at these."

"Oh, sit down." The *Komandant* flicked his hand at his brother. "You look like you're drunk. What are these books?" The *Komandant* picked one up and turned it over. "You just carry these books around with you? This writing here in the margin—is that poetry? Did you write that?"

"Yes." He could feel his voice breaking.

"When do you find time to write poetry?"

"He doesn't even find time to fire his rifle straight," the *Hijena* broke in. "I've watched him. He always fires into the air."

The *Komandant* gave his brother a gesture to be quiet. He grabbed another cigarette from a pack that he kept in a drawer, holding it between his yellow fingertips as he lit it. His teeth were gritted together as the smoke escaped from the sides of his mouth. He stared straight ahead without blinking.

"What is this, more poetry? It looks like these books are in English."

"They're American... They're American poets."

The *Komandant* poked the pages. "What are these, women poets?"

"Yes, sir, they're...they're mostly women."

"And what's this?" He picked a couple of petals out from the pages and rubbed them between his fingers. "You put flowers between the pages?"

"They're just local... I mean, they're not really flowers. They're wild plants that I found at one of our camps and used as bookmarks."

The *Hijena* leapt out of his chair and poked at him. "What are you doing with all these books? Are you sitting there and reading them and playing with yourself?"

The *Komandant* kept staring at him, ignoring his brother's outburst. "Where did you get these books?"

"At a bookshop. I took them... I mean, I bought them. It was a little shop that was nearby in Sarajevo."

The *Komandant* gave a small laugh that turned into a grunt. "I know that bookshop of yours—or what remains of it. Did you love it so much? The last time I looked, some riflemen had blown all the walls out."

He kept laughing to himself as he thumbed through the other books. But then one of them caught his attention. As he picked it up, his gaze grew more menacing. "What does this mean, *The Laws of War*?"

He flipped it over and looked at the back, and then he opened it and scanned a few more pages. "It says this is the text of the Geneva Conventions."

He looked up sharply, his eyes reaching out like a pair of tentacles. "Did you get this at your bookstore?"

He stammered out a "yes."

"So do you think you are in Geneva?"

It was phrased as a question, but he knew not to answer it.

"Do you look around every day and think, 'I am in Switzerland'? Do you see some laws hanging out there on the trees, saying 'you can do this, but you can't do that'? Do you think there is a set of rules out there that everyone plays by?"

He gave a faint "no." The *Komandant* kept going as if he hadn't heard him.

"Do you think there's some little rule book we look at to see what we can do?" He picked up the book and spat on it. "That's what I think of your book.

"We have one of our soldiers lying out there dead. He's there right now—lying in the middle of the town square with the dogs sniffing at him. There'll be maggots there before long. Do you think that we can send these people a nice little letter and quote them some section of your law book? Do you think we can say, 'May we please go out there to recover the body'? Do you?"

He tried to shake his head, but he was afraid to move.

"Because if you do, let me tell you that it was those same people who shot him from the roof of the house. And then they shot him again as he was trying to get to safety. And it's those same people who will shoot us if we try to get his body back."

He walked around the desk and grabbed him by his shirt. "There's only one law out there. Shoot them before they shoot you. Attack their women before they attack yours. Do you understand that?"

The *Komandant* gave him a shove against the wall. Then he picked up the books one by one, ripping them down the spine and throwing them into the corner.

"What do you want me to do with him?" the *Hijena* asked.

"Get him out of my sight."

The *Hijena* prodded him back toward the alley.

"Just take him somewhere and make a man out of him."

He exhaled a long line of smoke.

"And when you're through with that, get rid of him."

♦♦♦

AN ARTILLERY SHELL HIT somewhere close to her house, sending a shock though the cellar. She squeezed against the wall, but it was shaking. There was more rifle fire, louder than before, coming in short, staccato bursts from somewhere nearby. She heard unfamiliar voices, men screaming commands, as they ran from room to room above her. Suddenly, the door to the cellar smashed open, and a group of armed men poured down the stairs.

♦♦♦

HE'D BEEN RUNNING UP the street with the others, trying to stay invisible in the pack of sweating, panting soldiers.

They reached one of the houses, and the lead man shot at the door until it gave way. The *Hijena* screamed orders as they scrambled through the hallway. Two of the men raced over to the cellar stairs and kicked at the door. The first jolt knocked it off its hinges, and the second one sent it clattering down the stairs. As the two men jumped over the debris, he felt a rifle butt in his back, shoving him down the stairs behind the others. The *Hijena* shouted commands and warned them that it might be an ambush.

Could it be a trap? He looked around quickly, trying to see if there was anyone lying in wait. From the dark corner, he suddenly saw a pair of eyes staring at him. It was a girl—maybe a little younger than him—and she was trying to make herself invisible behind a pile of blankets. He saw fear in her eyes.

He'd been the first one to see her.

The *Hijena* saw her next.

♦♦♦

SHE COULD SEE HIM shaking. She could almost feel his fear, as he seemed to be quietly pleading with her to hide, to dig a little deeper into the corner. He was a soldier of some sort, but she knew he didn't belong there. He was carrying a rifle, but he was pointing it into the air like he didn't know what to do with it.

But there was another man—a very different kind of man. And he had just seen her.

The second man had a high, screeching voice that sent a chill through her. He pushed at the young soldier, forcing him to get closer and closer to her. Then he held up for a second, but only long enough to yell at the other two men to go back upstairs and check the other rooms. She suddenly realized she didn't want the other two soldiers to leave. Every instinct told her she would be in more danger if they left than if they stayed.

Now there were only the three of them. The man with the screeching voice shoved the terrified soldier on top of her. He pushed down hard on him, yelling at him to get even closer.

♦♦♦

"THIS IS HOW WE teach these animals a lesson."

He felt the pressure from above pushing down hard on him, but his body kept refusing to move. The pair of eyes under him were terrified, and he thought he couldn't bring any more pain to those eyes without bringing incalculable pain to himself.

"Rip the dress off of her!" The *Hijena's* hot breath enveloped him. "Do I have to kill you in order to teach you anything?"

He was caught up in the pile of rags with the girl pinned underneath him. His tormentor was on top of both of them, shouting in his ear.

♦♦♦

HE'S GOING TO GET himself killed. That thought spun through her head until it became a certainty: he was about to be shot. The things she had been taught as a child raced through her mind, but none of them had anything to do with what was happening at that moment. There was nothing she knew that made any sense.

The young soldier was pushing down on her, while at the same time he himself was being pushed. The madman hovering over both of them was going to shoot him, and then he would shoot her. They would both be left to die like a pair of pathetic lovers with their bodies entwined in a pool of blood.

♦♦♦

HE TRIED TO GET free, but the *Hijena* was on him, yelling in his ear, and reaching under him to tear at the girl's dress. As her clothes came off in shreds, she seemed to be letting up. Was she giving up, or was she trying to protect him?

♦♦♦

HIS EYES HAD A tearful message: *I'm so sorry.*

♦♦♦

THE EYES BELOW HIM seemed to answer: *I know.*

♦♦♦

THE *HIJENA* FINALLY GRABBED him by the shirt collar and pulled him back up.

"You're through with that. Now, we have to get out of here."

He looked down at the girl and then back at the soldier.

"Now, shoot her."

The *Hijena* waited a second and then yelled at him again.

"Did you hear what I said? I told you to shoot her. You can't leave witnesses around for this kind of thing. Do you want me to shoot her for you?"

He stared at him.

"You have a gun, use it."

PART TWO

San Francisco—2011

Gina

IT WAS A HAPPY crowd. Friday night in a midtown restaurant in San Francisco is usually pretty lively. I was by myself, but there was a guy eyeing me from the other end of the bar. I'd seen him earlier, when he was chatting up the bartender. She hadn't responded to his advances, so he'd turned his attention to me. I could see why she wasn't impressed. He preened every time he moved his body. I'd picked up enough women's intuition along the way to know that was a bad sign.

I did a quick assessment, trying to decide where he fit on my internal scale. Most women develop an alert system as they're growing up—an instinctive gauge that measures the threat or benefit of every man who approaches them. My situation was more complicated. I wasn't born with that skill, but I learned a version of it later on. Right now, the system was working, and I was pretty sure of one thing: This guy wasn't in my green zone.

But where did he fit in? If he wasn't at the top of the scale, was he all the way at the bottom where my fear gets tangled up in paranoia? I tried to visualize him in a warlike setting with hate in his eyes. That's a quick judgment I find myself making with every man I meet. Could I imagine him with a gun in his hand or one bulging under his coat? If I sense anything, my body tenses up, and the old wounds come roaring to the surface. My fears have never really left me. I can be standing in the middle of the bookstore—thousands of miles away on another continent—and suddenly everything might drop out from underneath me. Then I'm back in a dark room staring down the barrel of a rifle.

But this guy hadn't touched that hot wire. As I watched him swirl his drink at the end of that big, brass bar, I decided there wasn't much to worry about. I climbed down from my fears and stuffed them back in their cage. He was still looking at me, but he really wasn't much more than a nuisance. He'd turned his body so that he was facing me, probably trying to decide when he should slide down the bar and make his move. He wanted to be cool about it, but he was failing completely. At that point it was pretty easy to see that he was just some character out by himself on a Friday night, trying to get laid.

I should have been flattered—maybe even gratified— that my feminine charms were working so well, but instead I was just uncomfortable. I'm not that kind of woman. I know that sounds a bit prissy, but I mean it more literally than figuratively. There are things I don't really talk about until I know you pretty well.

When Silvia texted me earlier saying that she'd be late, she said to meet her at the bar. But right then I was wishing I'd told her no and just sat at one of the tables near the door. I had an advance reader's copy of a new novel that I planned to give her, and I would have enjoyed rereading a few pages while I waited. I could have sat with my legs demurely crossed, looking a bit bookish. And those twenty feet or so between me and the bar would have made all the difference.

I would no longer be a pickup waiting to happen. Even in the most sexually sophisticated city in the world, when a man sees a woman standing alone at a bar, he thinks he owns her.

The bartender placed a rye Manhattan in front of me, and I took a slow taste, enjoying the quick, bracing effect of the first sip. I stared ahead, focusing on the array of gourmet wines and liquors that covered the long front window behind the bar. There are times when I've been bothered about the fragility of such a scene, worried that everything could come crashing down. But right then, I was enjoying the moment. The early-evening light from Market Street was filtering through the glass behind the bottles, twinkling through the browns, ambers, and yellows of the liquids, creating a soft, unexpected light show. It was one of the subtle touches that made the Zuni Café my favorite restaurant in the city.

That guy—I didn't even bother to look at him anymore—was going nowhere because I could sense how clueless he was. He wasn't the only one like that. My search for some sort of sensitivity in men had been utterly fruitless, and the selection seemed to be getting worse. I wasn't sure what attracted me anymore. They all seemed to miss the stuff that's important to a woman—important to me, anyway. I'd had my brown hair cut earlier in the day, and it curled softly around the collar of my slate-colored jacket. But ten minutes from now, this guy—and probably all the rest of them—couldn't have told you the color of my hair or my jacket. I was wearing a pair of opal drop-earrings and a handcrafted necklace that I'd picked up at a vintage jewelry store on Hayes Street, and there was a trio of bracelets on my right wrist in a matching color. The skirt was something I'd found in a thrift shop on Fillmore Street, and it went with an old pair of shoes that

I had. My ensemble wouldn't have won any fashion awards, but it reflected who I was at the moment.

The thing I needed in a relationship was proving elusive. I longed for someone who would enjoy the subtleties of my feminine persona, but that kind of man wasn't easy to find. The field, I knew, was very limited. I needed a person I could trust with a long, unpleasant list of things from my past. He had to be someone who wouldn't be shocked by my wartime experiences or freaked out to learn there were people still trying to track me down. If my fears kicked in from time to time, he'd just have to accept them. And he'd have to put up with my dwindling hope of finding a lost child who by now was on her way to becoming a grown-up. And, of course, there was the big thing—the secret about me that wasn't really much of a secret at all. He would have to do more than just accept that part of me—he would have to rejoice in it. My special someone had to be willing to get beyond the outer me and draw on my inner yearning for love.

But the guys I'd been meeting were nothing like that. They were like this one at the bar. I have big brown eyes that draw some attention, and I have long hands that I use to gesture a lot. But that's not where most men stare. When they look at me, they only see a woman in her late thirties with somewhat angular features and a slightly skinny ass. I probably fit some vague idea of what an evening's companion should look like. But guys like this, if they got that far, would be in for a surprise.

◆◆◆

SYLVIA SUDDENLY APPEARED, STRIDING down the aisle toward me. She was dressed in her light gray, take-no-prisoners business suit that I remember her wearing when she had a crucial court appearance. She had one of those that afternoon. Even if she hadn't sent me the text message, I would have known from the way she walked that she'd gotten her client acquitted.

The hostess was a few steps behind her holding a couple of menus. Silvia was all hugs and apologies, and within seconds she gathered me, my purse, my book, and my phone and pointed us toward the back of the restaurant. The hostess had been holding a table along the brick wall at the back of the dining area. Sylvia knew without asking that I wanted the seat with my back to the wall. She'd been around me long enough to know that I liked to see who was coming and going.

"Was that guy trying to pick you up?" Sylvia nodded back at the bar.

"He thought he was. It's probably a good thing that you showed up when you did. You saved him a lot of embarrassment."

Sylvia gave me one of her warm grins. It was a palette full of teeth, dimples, and flashing brown eyes. She used to wrap that smile around me and convince me that all was right in the world.

"Not your type?"

"I don't think so."

"You didn't try to charm him with your Italian accent? That always worked with me."

I guess I got a little exasperated. "Give it a rest, will you? The minute I saw him, I already knew a dozen reasons why I wouldn't be interested."

Sylvia brought her lips together with the hint of a kiss. She was wearing a beige blouse under her suit jacket, and

I asked her where she bought it. But it made me sad that I had to ask. There was a time about a year earlier when I would have known everything about her clothing. If she wasn't wearing one of the blouses I liked, I would have just walked into her closet and slipped it on myself—no questions asked. But those days were over.

She reached across the table, grabbing my hand, rubbing each finger with soft strokes from her own forefinger and thumb.

I tried to break the spell for the moment. "Shall we get the roast chicken from the brick oven? Two orders of that with the bread salad—you know, like we always do?"

She nodded, but she wasn't letting up. "Gina, you worry me sometimes."

I just shrugged. Even though our birthdays were only a few months apart, she'd taken to being maternal with me.

"What is your type?" She was all seriousness. "I don't even know anymore, do you?"

"Maybe, it's still you."

Her smile eased up a bit as she pursed her lips and shook her head. "You know that's not true."

She stretched the thought a little further. "We had to end it. You know that, as well as I do. The only difference was that you didn't want to talk about it. You were too kind—you didn't want to say something that would hurt my feelings. But we had to make the change that we did."

I knew. I even remembered what she said: "We really don't fit together very well." At the time I thought that was a very polite way—even a delicate way—to put it. But I couldn't argue with her.

"I still love you."

"And I still love you." And I knew she meant it.

Sylvia's eyes turned serious and her lips tightened. It was the look she got when she was lining up her facts, ready to make an argument to the jury.

"Gina, we need to talk about this. It's easy for me to live my life the way I want to live it. It's much easier for me than it is for you. I know that, sweetheart, I really do. My life is open. The person I appear to be is what I am. The two fit together—I don't have to explain anything later on at some awkward moment."

I must have acted like I was going to object, but she beat me to it.

"I know you're going to say, 'What about us? How did that happen?' Well, that was just what it was at that time—it doesn't go beyond that.

"My point is that I know how difficult it is for you to find the right relationship. What you are doesn't fit with everything else. I know that guy at the bar didn't appeal to you, but what if he did? What would you say to him? How would you..."

She was searching for the right word, but I interrupted. "Maybe I should just start wearing a name tag. It could say, 'My name is Gina, and I'm...'"

Sylvia stopped me short. There was a flash of anger on her face, and that was mixed with a few hurt feelings. She was trying to be helpful, and I was being sarcastic. And she knew it.

"I'm just trying to help out. Maybe it's a mistake for me to do so. I know you don't thrust yourself in front of people, and I respect that. I think that's one of the things I love about you the most. But at times you seem so lonely and frustrated."

True.

I don't know if I was lonely or frustrated at that moment, but I knew what she was talking about. Sylvia was getting antsy—maybe worried that I might start complicating things with her. But I wasn't going to do that. Our relationship was what it was. It wasn't going to change, and I wasn't going to push it. After we split up, she'd gone back to her old girl-friend—the one she'd lived with before we met. Sylvia knew I didn't think Margo was good enough for her, but she didn't want me reminding her of my opinion.

However, I wasn't thinking about any of that. I was just reflecting on the fact I was Gina Perini—a bookseller who was lucky enough to have a very talented lawyer as a friend. Sylvia was the one person in my life who knew everything about me. When my life got lonely, she could sense it. When things from the past would dog me, she knew what I was facing. She was the only one I trusted, and every now and then I had to grab onto that thought and cling to it.

Sylvia gave up for the moment trying to follow my mood shifts.

"Maybe we should talk about something else."

I nodded in agreement. The waitress came back in time to give us a needed break.

"Let's order some wine and get started on it before the food gets here."

◆ ◆ ◆

HAYES STREET BOOKS WAS only a few blocks away, and my apartment was in a flat above the bookstore. To get there, I walked up Gough Street, took a ninety-degree turn left, and then went a couple of blocks west on Hayes. It was one of the many things that surprised me about San Francisco—all the streets in the main part of town were at a very logical right angle to the other. Where I grew up, nothing was like that. The streets meandered around hills, following the whim of a country path, or they traced the edge of a fortification that some warlord had erected centuries ago to keep out the peasants. But San Francisco was part of the New World— in fact, it was as far west as you could go in the New World without falling into the ocean. Back when it was a fresh-faced American city, some very earnest pioneers, who had just marched all the way across the continent, probably thought they should create a nice, rectangular grid like all the other American cities. My guess is that it never occurred to them that superimposing right-angle streets on a city with steep hills would produce a collection of sheer cliffs and roller-coaster streets. It was something that would drive visitors slightly crazy over the next two centuries.

Sylvia offered to walk with me to my flat, but I told her no. She was probably worried about me. There'd been times in the not-so-distant past when I'd been known to panic without warning. The war that had chased me out of the Balkans had officially ended, but my own personal slice of that bloodletting was far from over. I knew I'd probably be looking over my shoulder for the rest of my life. Still, I'd grown calmer lately. Maybe enough time had gone by to ease things, or maybe it was just the distance—or maybe I was kidding myself. In any event, the streets of Hayes Valley were filled at that moment with a happy Friday night crowd. You had a better chance of being smothered by a restless group of twenty-somethings who were spread out across the sidewalk than being accosted by an attacker or a bad memory. Besides, I knew it was easier for Sylvia just to walk in the opposite direction from the restaurant and grab the BART train. She'd be back at her house in North Oakland in a half hour, and I wouldn't be monopolizing any more of her time. She might even get there soon enough to keep Margo from quizzing her about me.

What was my type? I couldn't get Sylvia's question out of my head. I looked into the shop windows along Hayes Street, walking slowly as I pondered the question. There was a sale going on at Dish. They had some cute jackets on display, but they still looked like they were out of my price range. I loved the vintage skirt that I'd bought a week earlier at Ver Unica, but I didn't see anything like that in the window. What was I looking for in a relationship? I seemed to revel more in discovering clothes than in finding a lover. Maybe I was fated to be a perennial window-shopper.

Absinthe, at the corner of Gough and Hayes, had the usual crowd at the bar. It was another favorite of mine and my go-to restaurant if a publisher's rep offered to take me to lunch or dinner. There didn't seem to be anyone of interest in there at the moment. Sylvia thought I needed a more systematic approach for finding companionship, and she was probably right. The normal kind of minglings and mixers don't work very well for me. She said I should set my sights on someone strong, masculine, and confident. But I knew she had it backward. Men like that scare me. But it wasn't so much that they frightened me physically. It's just that men who are that immersed in their own maleness usually wear me down. I can deal with a man's emotional needs— but if his needs are packed away so deep that he doesn't even know he has them, that blocks off any attempt at intimacy. I was slowing starting to realize something about myself that I wasn't too happy to admit: I seem to do better with men who are on the brink of falling apart.

◆◆◆

THE WINDOW OF HAYES Street Books looked darker than I liked it to be. As I crossed the street and got closer to the store, I tried to think of ways to lighten it up. Maybe I could lighten up some of my apprehensions as well. As with most bookstores, our front window thrusts itself trustingly out toward the street hoping to draw attention. The books in the window are all proper enough–looking, but if you looked closely you could see ideas and provocations behind those covers that might drive some people over the edge. You can never be sure who will be offended by what they see. A few weeks earlier there were two men outside the window, grumbling about a display I had arranged of books portraying the impact of gun violence. They glared at me with a wordless hatred as I stepped past them and into the store.

My mood usually perks up when I'm inside and surrounded by books. Late in the evening, I usually don't do much more than poke around, making sure that the most important books are face-out instead of spine-out. When you manage a bookstore, you can always convince yourself there's something more to do—move some shelves, change the display on the tables—even if you spend the next day unconvincing yourself of the same thing. My apartment is upstairs from the store, and that's both a good thing and a bad thing. The owners of the store also own the building, so when they retired they offered to let me live upstairs as part of the deal for managing the bookstore. There was a promise that they'd sell me the store someday, but it was left pretty vague. Still, the convenience of the deal appealed to me. There was no commute, and I could get downstairs whenever I was needed. I realize now that they probably knew me better than I knew myself. If they wanted someone so obsessed with the bookselling business that she'd be there looking out for things around the clock, then that's what they got—me.

Miriam Brown, my assistant manager, was running the store that evening. She's our unofficial ambassador to the African-American community a few blocks to the west of us—a group that seems to be growing smaller by the day under the pressures of gentrification. She's also my right arm and, I have to admit, knows some of my bad habits. Miriam sometimes does an imitation of me selling books, mimicking me as I try to put a book into someone's hand, letting him or her touch it, as I sing the praises of the author and give a little teaser about the plot. I suppose that's true. I usually count on a book cozying up to the customer and saying, "You need me." Miriam claims that I'm trying to put the idea in the heads of customers that if the book is perched on their bookshelf, people will see it as evidence of their good taste. Am I that bad? I'm not sure, but Miriam is usually right about me.

That evening, Miriam was arranging chairs in the back of the store for our children's story time that was scheduled for the next morning. Morrie, who delighted in his role as storyteller-in-chief, had already placed the books around the wall before he'd gone home earlier. It was beautiful display, but I winced a little whenever I saw an array of children's books like that. It made me think about things—things from the past. There was a little child…but now she's no longer a child, if she's alive at all. When I think about her, it saddens me that she may have missed all this. Did anyone give her a big picture book as she was growing up or watch her face as she traced her fingers around the outlines of the animals? Did anyone sit next to her and read her a story? Did anyone laugh with her as she went through the experience of learning how to read? If she was anywhere at all at that moment, she was now a teenager. I just hoped she was okay. I knew better than to dwell on any of that. Still, I sometimes had a hard time shaking those thoughts, as I trudged up the stairs to my apartment.

♦♦♦

WHY DID I BECOME a bookseller? The idea planted itself in my mind years ago and then bubbled to the surface later on. At the time, I was a scared and desperate teenager. Looking back, I suppose you could glamorize what I went through by calling it some sort of odyssey. But if there was any poetry attached to that experience, it escaped me. I was running for my life—and from my life. The last thing on my mind was my future career.

I was hiding out in Dubrovnik, but for me that city had become a trap. Even though I'd snuck across the boundary from Bosnia and then into Croatia, I had no place else to go. I'd been evading capture for several months, hiding in the back streets, but I feared that my luck had run out. And it wasn't just my own safety I was worried about. I knew that anyone who had been connected with me during those months was in danger. I had to leave Anja and the others, because if I stayed there, I would be putting them in more peril than they already were. Anja had taken Jelena and the others from the place in the mountains where they'd been hiding, and they had moved once again. I was hoping they'd found someplace safe. I didn't want to think about what would happen if they were caught.

I hadn't yet become Gina at that point in my life—that came many months later. For the moment, I was just a kid full of self-doubt. And as dangerous as it was for me to hide out in the back streets of Dubrovnik, I realize now I might have been in even more danger if I had made the change that was awaiting me in the future. As it was, I was just a lost-looking waif who was able to wander around without drawing too much attention. Still, I knew my time was short. If I stayed there much longer, I'd be found.

The Militia had agents up and down the Dalmatian coast, and they had eyes everywhere. At one point I was certain that someone was following me. I caught a glimpse of a man taking my picture, but he darted away before I could find out who he was. I was sure, however, he'd be back soon with his friends. The border with Bosnia was just a few kilometers away, and these people weren't going to let an international boundary stop them. The *Komandant* and his friends were close to tracking me down, and I knew they had revenge on their minds. But in Dubrovnik, I had my back to the sea. If I stayed there, they'd find me. And if they found me, I'd be dead.

And while I was still trying to escape that shooting war, I realized I was fighting a mini-war within myself. During my months in hiding, some basic issues about my own identity were starting to force their way to the surface. These were questions that would dominate my life in future months, but for the time being I couldn't focus on them. I was too confused and terrified. At that moment, there was certainly none of the promise—even joy—that would open up to me in later years. I was just grappling with the deep fear that I was running from something without any idea of where I was going.

Dubrovnik was a strange place to be hiding at that moment. As one of the world's great cultural treasures, it was awash in a sea of tourists. Each day brought a new group of happy, camera-laden people wandering through the streets, soaking up the historic riches. Many of them may have been dimly aware of the war that was going on less than a hundred kilometers away, but it didn't seem to affect their enjoyment of the city. Dubrovnik had been bombarded for three months in 1991 during the early part of the war, but it had recovered to the point where it could present its rich, historic face to visitors once again. But I didn't belong there. It was probably obvious to everyone that there was something about me that was out of place. The city was at peace, but I was still at war. I knew I had to get out of there, and at times it felt like the means of escape were tantalizingly close. When I wandered down near the port, I looked out across the Adriatic Sea and wondered if I could ever to get across the water to safety.

I'd been there a few days when I decided to follow an English-language tour group that was walking around the city, stopping at the various landmarks on Stradun, the main street. As I worked my way around the fringes of the group, I tried to be inconspicuous. Since I was dressed like a universal teenager—hooded sweatshirt, dirty jeans, and sneakers—I suppose I looked like any of the young stragglers from around the world who wandered through the city. But it was all an illusion. If anyone talked to me for a few minutes, they would probably figure out I was on the run from something. The group I had attached myself to was made up mostly of older people, walking at their own pace, focusing on the words of the English-speaking guide. I was listening too, because I was trying to soak up as much English as I could. Somewhere in my mind I knew it would come in handy. I was standing at the edge of that tour group, but suddenly my skin started to bristle. Someone was talking to me.

My fear blocked out everything. I was sure I had been found out, and I started looking around for a way to escape. It took me a few seconds to realize that the man was speaking to me in English. Then I finally realized that he was introducing himself and his wife, who was walking next to him. At that moment, I was so frozen that I didn't hear much of what he said. To this day, I still don't know his name. I must have nodded something in response, because he kept talking pleasantly. After a minute or so, I realized he wasn't any kind of a threat. He was tall with a thick gray beard, and he had on a broad-brimmed khaki hat with a chin strap. He was wearing a gray shirt and khaki pants that had lots of pockets up and down the legs. His wife had on a sundress and a large floppy hat, and there was a camera hanging on a strap around her neck. They both appeared to be in their early sixties, maybe older. They were American tourists, and they just wanted to be friendly.

I finally realized what had caught their attention. There was a book sticking out of the pouch on my sweatshirt, and he recognized the title. It was a dog-eared paperback copy of Salman Rushdie's *The Satanic Verses* that I had picked up earlier that day for next to nothing at a local bookstall.

"Are you enjoying that book?"

I didn't have the heart to tell him that I had just started it and that my English was not good enough to catch the subtleties of Rushdie's writing. I nodded yes, and he nodded back in satisfaction. We continued to talk while the group was moving on to the next stop, and I fell into a comfortable pace walking between the two of them. He asked me about myself, and I answered with only the vaguest generalities. At one point, he wanted to know if I knew about the controversy surrounding that particular book. I told him that I'd heard about it, but the truth is that I knew only the sketchiest details.

"There were death threats made against anyone who sold the book. Some of the big outfits wouldn't touch it, but we decided to carry it."

I must have looked surprised.

"My wife and I are booksellers in Massachusetts."

He told me where the store was located, but I don't remember what he said. I only knew Massachusetts as a blob on a map somewhere across the Atlantic Ocean. At the time, the only thing I could think to ask was whether anyone had attacked them for selling the book.

"We had a couple of threatening phone calls, and one night someone shot a bullet through the plate-glass window at the front of the store."

The alarm must have showed on my face.

"It happened at night, so no one was hurt."

My anxiety was still showing.

"I know. Maybe we should have been more cautious." He nodded toward his wife who was walking slightly ahead of us.

"But we talked about it and decided there are times when you just have to do the right thing. We boarded up the hole in the glass and then put a big stack of *The Satanic Verses* in the window next to it."

I didn't know what to say. I didn't think I could say anything without giving away too much about myself. The two of them just kept walking, and I kept walking with them.

What did they sense about me? Did my hunger show through on my face? Did they see the fear in my eyes and guess what it was? I didn't say anything about how desperate I was to get out of there, but I probably didn't have to. Whatever the two of them may have thought remained unspoken between them. We all just continued to walk, talking only occasionally, as the tour group got closer and closer to the water and their chartered boat. We reached the gangplank, and several of the others in their group started boarding the ship. We were in the middle, and my two companions stood patiently, waiting their turn. I waited with them. I felt something, and when I looked up I realized she had placed her hand on my shoulder.

If I was going to leave, that would have been the moment. And if they expected me to leave, they would have begun their goodbyes and starting giving me their good wishes. I expected at any minute they would start saying, "If you're ever in America…" But they didn't. They just stood there, waiting to get on the boat, not showing the slightest concern that I was still standing there between them. If I'd been in that line alone, I would have been spotted by the dock officials immediately and pulled aside. But standing between them, I looked like a slightly bewildered teenager who was in the middle of a pleasant European vacation with his grandparents.

Once on board, I moved away from them as soon as I could. There was a brief nod between us. They seemed to know that I needed to get out of sight, and they were probably just as happy that I was moving away from them and keeping them out of any trouble. The trip lasted only a couple of hours. At one point, I wanted to walk over and thank them, but I knew that might be a bad idea. The boat's next stop was Bari on the Italian side of the Adriatic Sea, and I slipped off as quietly as I could.

I never saw them again. I've looked for them at book conventions and trade shows but with no success. They may have retired or gotten out of the business. They wouldn't recognize me now, because everything about me has changed. But I'd know them. I just wish I could thank them.

◆ ◆ ◆

THERE ARE DAYS WHEN I hate what I'm doing. This was one of those days.

We received notice that our worker's compensation premium would be increased by 6 percent in the coming year. That news came in a nasty-looking white envelope that was lodged under an even uglier envelope from our credit card processor. That one said that our transaction fee was going up, and we would need to purchase new equipment. Both of those bombs landed on my desk in the same week that San Francisco announced an increased fee for the city health plan. The week before that our bank had raised the interest on our line of credit, and PG&E put another service charge on our utility bill. And that list of horrors didn't even include the new credit manager at a major publisher who said she was "reviewing our payment terms." Where were we going to find the extra money to pay all this? It wouldn't be from our customers. The price of each book is printed on the cover, so there's no wiggle room there. We'd just have to eat it.

We needed more sales. That was the answer to everything— we always needed more sales. There'd been five browsers so far that morning, and only one of them had purchased anything. I wasn't happy with that ratio. One customer in particular was really starting to annoy me. He was thumbing through a biography on the "new arrivals" table, and he'd been standing there long enough to arouse my suspicions. A lifter, maybe? He didn't have a booster bag or a jacket with big pockets, so I decided I was wrong about him. But then he pulled a smartphone out of his pocket and aimed it at the book.

He was showcasing us! I'll be damned if he wasn't photographing the barcode and ordering the book from some online company. And he was standing right in front of me while he was doing it. What the hell? Was he planning to pay for the lights, the rent, the staff, and all the things we provided him, just so he could stand there and buy it from somebody else? Of course not. He was hovering over my carefully arranged display and running the purchase through some soulless computer somewhere off on the cloud. I would have liked him better if he were a thief.

My evil instincts took over. I moved in next to him and dropped a box—quite by accident—that knocked the phone out of his hands. "Oh, I'm so sorry," I told him. "Let me hold that for you up at the counter while you browse..." He tried to object, but I cut him off. "No, no, it's no problem. I'm happy to keep it for you." Fortunately, I'd picked on a guy who was so sheepish about the whole thing that he was willing to wait and retrieve his phone at the counter a few minutes later—along with his book and his change. I was lucky. When I pulled a stunt like that once before, Sylvia pointed out that the customer could just as easily have reported it to the police, claiming that I'd stolen his phone. For a few days, I waited for that guy to come back with a cop.

"How do stores make any money selling books?" Sylvia once asked me.

"I'm not sure any of them do."

Given what I'd been through in my life, you'd think that I would be more detached about these sorts of things. But I love the book business, and it pisses me off when everything seems to be conspiring to make it fail. I walked around the store trying to cool off. I finally settled down and watched Morrie Richards as he sat in the middle of a group of children reading books to them during story time. He'd been coming in on his own for weeks, reading stories to the littlest children, until I finally asked him if he wanted a second career managing our children's events. He'd been bored with his retirement, and the idea of being a kind of troubadour for little kids appealed to him. The look in their eyes as he was reading got to me. I wanted to call Sylvia right then and say, "We're not just selling books. We're spinning dreams."

There were a couple of packages on my desk with advance copies of new books. That always perked me up. One of life's great pleasures is to open a new book and let yourself be mesmerized by the smell and the feel of it. There was also a message from our local booksellers association, wanting to know if I'd be on a marketing panel at the fall trade show. I'd probably say yes, since a couple of my friends from other Bay Area stores would be on the same panel. I was happy to talk at gatherings of booksellers, but that was about as public as I was willing to get. I had good reasons to stay out of view—lots of them. And the next message made me realize I was getting careless. A woman from the Italian Cultural Institute had called. She had heard about Gina Perini and wondered if she would come speak to a business group of Italian American women.

No—she would not. This "Gina Perini" would be doing no such thing.

The Italian American woman that the public saw was something I'd created for myself. Gina Perini came into being at a time when my life had bottomed out and I had to start over again. The original version of me was gone—long vanished, I hoped, from the mind of anyone who used to know me. All of this happened when I was a teenager living in Italy, and it seemed simpler to adopt an Italian name to go with my new personality. The persona I created at that time worked well enough in most places, but I wasn't about to try it on Italians. They'd want to know what part of Italy I was from. Which province? Which *commune*? *"Perini'—what sort of a name is that? Are you related to the Perinis in..."* After an hour or so of that kind of friendly banter, the whole story would come unraveled.

◆◆◆

WHEN I SNUCK OFF the boat in Bari, I had no idea what I would do next. I'd gotten as far as Italy, putting the Adriatic Sea between me and my pursuers, but I hadn't thought beyond that. I had a vague hope that things would get better, and I suppose they eventually did. But before that, they got worse.

A few days after I arrived, I made contact with someone I knew living in Bosnia. But after I did, I almost wished I hadn't. The news he gave me hit me hard. My fears about Anja and the family had come true. They had been taken captive by the Militia, and no one had seen them since. It was all secondhand information, and for a moment or two I tried to deny it as just a rumor. The man I talked to said he hadn't actually seen it himself but had only talked to some people who witnessed it. Maybe they were wrong, I said. But the more he talked, the more I realized that the little details of the story were too accurate for it to be anything but true. A group from the Militia had surrounded the house where the family was hiding. They'd marched them out at gunpoint and manhandled them as they were tossed into the back of the truck. According to the witness, the *Komandant* himself was there, puffing on a cigarette as his soldiers roughed up the prisoners, finally grinding out the butt with a satisfied grunt as the padlock on the truck was snapped into place. No one had seen or heard anything of them after that. What more was there to say? We both knew what that meant. They would probably never be seen again.

"What about the baby? Did they take Jelena, too?"

No one had seen the baby, he said.

"How can that be?" I kept asking. "Are you certain? A child that young doesn't get up and walk off. Maybe she was being carried by someone, and no one noticed her."

"The baby wasn't there."

The people who saw the incident knew there'd been a small child in the house. They would have noticed. No one saw her then or after that.

I hit rock bottom. During the next few days I sensed that the tentacles of war had somehow reached across the Adriatic Sea and were smothering me. I was in a strange country with no papers, no friends, and very little money. The closest thing I'd ever had to a family had now been lost, and what happened to them was partly my fault. My despair had opened up such a big hole that I didn't dare think about who or what I was. There was something going on inside me that I couldn't articulate, but at that point I couldn't do much more than let it rumble around on its own. For several days, all I could do was hold myself and shiver.

I finally headed north for Rome, because it seemed like the easiest thing to do. I had a sense that Rome was a place where you could find yourself—or get completely lost. I still think all of the world's abandoned people must wander through there at one time or another. Later on, I learned to love Rome, but that wasn't true at first. I arrived there on the run and felt totally helpless. I eventually learned how to survive. I hung around the buildings of the *Comunità di Sant'egidio* in the Trastevere area, living off the generosity of that group. They were focused on helping refugees, and they must have realized that the sad-looking kid sitting in their doorway had escaped from something awful. They kept me alive.

After a few months, I found work with a printer who needed an assistant for odd jobs and errands. Paolo worked by himself, but he took me on—no questions asked. There was nothing official about my relationship with him. It was all *lavoro in nero*, as the Italians would put it, "working in the black." Everything about me was off the books. I had no visa or work permit. As far as the authorities were concerned, I wasn't working at all—in fact, they didn't even know I existed. Given the nature of his business, Paolo had a good reason to keep everything *in nero*. Publicity was the last thing he wanted. He called himself a printer, but he was really a forger. Birth certificates, death certificates, marriage licenses, work permits, visas—he could do them all, and he did them well. There's still some paperwork sitting in an office in Rome that was convincing enough to get me an EU passport many months later and a work visa for the United States.

Paolo wasn't the only fraud. I called myself his assistant, but that was just to make me feel better. The exchange rate between us was never spoken, but we both knew what it was. There was sex for food, sex for shelter, sex for medication— sex for whatever I had to have. He had his needs, and I had mine. There wasn't any serious affection between us. When he needed me, he took me—not roughly or without a bit of kindness, but not with any real love either. At that point, love was just a distant abstraction for me—I doubt if I was even capable of it. I wasn't proud of my arrangement with Paolo, but it was better than walking the streets. I knew that firsthand. During my first, desperate days in Rome, I went out one night on a stroll, walking slowly along the Via Salaria, getting set to offer my body to the first taker with a pocketful of lire. But within minutes I got violently sick to my stomach and started to shake. I spent the rest of the night huddled behind a tree.

◆ ◆ ◆

ONE AFTERNOON, I DELIVERED a packet of some of Paolo's specially made documents to a bank manager in the Campo de' Fiori. He looked surprised to see someone like me at the front entrance to the bank. I was wearing jeans and a zippered sweatshirt that hung loosely over my shoulders. I didn't look much like a business courier. It took him a second to realize why I was there, and then he got a stricken look on his face. He motioned sharply for me to go around and meet him at the back entrance, where I slipped him the paperwork. I knew why he was nervous. I'd read the documents as I walked across the Ponte Garibaldi on my way to deliver them. One of them was a woman's birth certificate with a German seal on it. I was certain it was a forgery. There were other dubious but official-looking papers in the envelope along with it. He was probably planning to use the paperwork to keep his mistress in the country. By the look on his face, I seemed to have guessed right.

After he unceremoniously slammed the door in my face, I walked away, feeling as insignificant as I was at that moment. I headed past the cafes on Via dei Baullari, ending up at the Piazza Farnese, plopping myself down against the Vasca—the big bathtub-looking fountain in the middle of the piazza. I found a spot between the bicycles and the Vespas, trying to lose myself among the scruffy, lost kids who liked to hang out there during the day. Scruffy and lost—that's how I felt most of the time, but that afternoon my confusion had built to a crescendo. I was unhappy with my life, with my body, with my soul, and with everything around me. I stared at the Palazzo Farnese. According to Puccini, that was the place where Tosca had shoved a knife in Scarpia's ribs when he tried to rape her. I knew how she felt.

Looking back, it seems clear that the moment in the Piazza Farnese was a turning point. Something inside me had opened a door, and a new revelation was waiting to enter. As my eyes wandered around the piazza, I looked over at a café and saw something that changed my life.

Two young women were sitting at a table, talking animatedly. The one on the left—the one who caught my attention—had mid-length brown hair that curled luxuriously over the back of her neck. As she leaned over her espresso cup to say something, she brushed back her hair—not continually, but often enough to appear that she was following some inner rhythm. I realized at that moment that I was running a hand through my own scraggly hair, trying in some pitiful, subconscious way to imitate her.

The young woman raised her head slightly when she made a point, following the rising timbre of her voice. When her friend spoke, she inclined her head to one side, waiting in that suspended state while the other woman talked. Then she would tilt her head back and break out in laughter. There was nothing forced about her gestures, nothing unnatural. There was an easy fluidity that had me mesmerized. She moved her hand forward until it came to rest on the forearm of her friend. She let it sit there lightly for a few seconds, giving a small, knowing tap or occasionally lifting a finger to wag when she wanted to say something. It was an easy intimacy that plucked at a chord somewhere inside of me.

I moved in closer to hear her speak. She had one leg crossed over the other, and she moved it rhythmically as she talked. It was an unstudied motion that seemed as perfect as all the others. She had a white blouse that was opened down to the third button, and with it was an elegant, understated silk scarf tied around her neck in a kind of casual knot that Italian women seemed to have invented. Her eyes and skin sparkled. She must have taken great care to make everything look so simple. There were probably lotions, hormones, and dozens of other things that she needed to bring herself to that point, but none of that was noticeable in this, her moment of everyday glory. I listened to her voice—a rich contralto that modulated itself into a variety of tones and textures. I tried to imitate the sound in my mind. If I'd gotten close enough to detect the scent of her, I probably would have been overwhelmed.

I was smitten. Later that afternoon, I found some sheer hose in a street market that matched what she had been wearing. I was almost afraid to pick up the package, and by the time I gave the handful of lire to the proprietor, my palms were covered with sweat. She didn't seem to notice how nervous I was as she handed me my change. I went back to my tiny bedroom and made sure the door was closed. I unrolled the stockings slowly up my legs and became immersed in that new sensation, wondering if that was how the stockings felt when they were on her. It was a feeling of enchantment. For a moment I imagined myself back at that table with the two women, becoming part of their world.

You could call it love at first sight, I suppose, but that didn't quite describe the feeling. I didn't want to be with her. I wanted to be her. And from that moment on, I was. Since then, I've often wondered if I had always been like that and just didn't know it. I'm not sure. I only know that on that warm afternoon in the presence of that *signorina*— my unaware mentor—I became Gina.

◆ ◆ ◆

I HAD JUST FINISHED breakfast and was on my way downstairs to the bookstore, when I got a phone call from Rome. It was Paolo. I hadn't talked to him in over a year, and I didn't know what he wanted. It took me a second to get back into the rhythm of speaking Italian. But I wasn't sure that I really wanted to talk to him. I could feel immediately the edge to his voice.

After a bit of friendly conversation, Paolo finally got around to the point of his call. He said he'd had "*dei visitatori.*" It wasn't so much the words but the way he said them.

"What kind of visitors?"

"Well, you know, investigators."

"No, I don't know!" I would have to have to pry it out of him. "What kind of investigators?"

"I don't know, for sure. They wanted to know about you. They had badges that they flashed in front of me."

"Were the badges real?"

"I don't know."

"You don't know?" I was getting exasperated with him. "For God's sake, you've made a whole career out of forging documents, and you don't know a phony badge when you see one?"

"*Cara mia*! What was I supposed to do? Grab the card out of his hand and examine it under a microscope? I just wanted them out of there!"

I wasn't going to get anywhere if I got angry with him.

"Anyway, I don't think they were legitimate—they spoke Italian like you do. In America they probably think you sound like an Italian, but an Italian can tell the difference. These guys were from over there—you know, that place where you came from."

"What did they want?"

"They had a picture of you. They wanted to know if I knew you."

"A picture? When was it taken?" Fear was erupting in my head.

"It was an old one. You looked the way you did when you showed up on my doorstep all those years ago. You were kind of cute, really."

I wasn't going to get into that. "Could you tell where it was taken?"

"They didn't say. But it wasn't Italy—I know that. You could see the waterfront down at the end of the street, and there was some foreign writing on the shop signs."

It was the photo—the one I remembered from Dubrovnik.

"What else did they say?"

"Nothing. After telling them that I'd never seen you before, they just left."

"How long ago was this?"

"About three weeks ago."

"And you're just calling me now?"

I could hear the hesitation in his voice. "I didn't think it was important. The picture was taken so long ago. No one looking at that picture would connect it with who you are now. You've gone through such a big change since then."

The dead air hung between us for a moment. I knew he was waiting for me to talk. He wanted me to ask him why he changed his mind and decided to call me.

"Paolo, what happened?"

He seemed reluctant to answer, and then he switched over to English. I knew what that meant. It would be easier for him to play dumb. "Luca got a call yesterday."

That was not good news. Luca Martinelli was my physician during the time I was in Italy. He knew a lot more about me than someone could glean from an old photo taken in Dubrovnik.

"Was it the same people?"

"I don't know. It was just a phone call. He said he didn't ask them any questions. I don't know—it's probably better that he didn't."

"Did he say what they were calling about?"

"They were asking about someone named 'Bertani.'"

That hit like a thud. "Gina Bertani" was the name I used when I first changed my name. It was the name on my entry papers for the US. The "Perini" part came later. The fear that had been gathering in my head threatened to explode.

"What did Luca tell them?"

"He said he told them nothing at all. He told me that he acted like he didn't even know what they were talking about. He said they hung up after that."

"Were they looking for a man or a woman?"

"I don't know—he didn't say. He didn't say much at all."

"Paolo, that could be important. They weren't just looking for 'someone.' They were talking Italian, for God's sake—it was either *qualcuno,* a man, or *qualcuna,* a woman."

"I don't know." He was squirming to get off the phone.

"Could you find out and let me know?"

I could hear his face drop. "I'll try."

◆ ◆ ◆

SYLVIA HAD CALLED ME the day before to set up an appointment. She offered to buy lunch, but she didn't say what she wanted to talk about. As I headed downtown, I wondered if it had anything to do with what Paolo told me in his phone call. It probably didn't—and even if it did, there wasn't much she could do about it. Sylvia was the person you wanted on your side if someone served you with a subpoena. But if someone wanted your head served on a platter, she wasn't any more help than anyone else.

Her office was in a converted Barbary Coast building just off Montgomery Street. The entrance opened on to a well-manicured alley that sat a comfortable distance between Jackson and Pacific. The whole area oozed a look-at-me Victorian charm that San Franciscans love to display. The bare-brick interior of the waiting room was home to a number of spectacular tinted photos of San Francisco Bay that hovered over the walls with no visible means of support. The nineteenth-century ambiance of the building was interrupted only by a series of modern, crisscrossed metal beams that were firmly anchored to both the ceiling and the floor. Victorian charm was one thing, but everyone in San Francisco knew that the 1906 fire and earthquake had once leveled buildings like this into rubble. The law firm's name was in brass letters on the wall outside their door: "Crichton, Moss, Harris, & Kaplan"—as in "Sylvia Kaplan," my old girlfriend.

Sylvia had come a long way since the days when we shacked up over the bookstore, and she had her files stashed in banker's boxes in our spare bedroom. It was a good spot for her at the time, because she loved books. She'd sometimes sneak downstairs to grab advance reading copies off the receiving desk to get the jump on other readers. For old time's sake, I brought along an ARC of a new book that I knew she'd want to read. It was the least I could do, since she offered to buy me lunch around the corner at Cotogna restaurant, where we both lusted after their *agnolotti*. Still, dining with her made me a little sad. I realized that the passion between us had migrated from the other parts of our bodies and had settled into our digestive tracks.

Sylvia learned her legal skills in the San Francisco District Attorney's office. And after watching her in action, I realized no one was better at getting a defendant acquitted than a former prosecutor. After a couple of her questionable clients walked out of the courtroom as free men—none too deservedly, in my opinion—she caught the eye of Richard Crichton, who was the go-to guy for every white-collar criminal in town. If you hired Crichton, Moss, Harris, & Kaplan, just about everyone assumed you were guilty— everyone, that is, except the juries. He managed to get most of his well-heeled clients acquitted. Crichton was the face of the firm, but someone else had to do the day-to-day courtroom grind. That job had been passed down from Crichton to Moss to Harris and, now, to my best friend.

Life was good for Sylvia, and I was pleased for her. When I was in a generous mood, I had to give credit to Margo. Sylvia had become more focused in her work since the two of them had gotten back together. They were now starting a family. That was a boundary I had to respect. Their plan, apparently, was for Margo to get pregnant first and then Sylvia would do the same the year after. They wanted their two children to be just a year apart. Margo—ever the child psychologist—thought that would be the best age gap. I had a wonderful vision of Sylvia, when it was her turn to conceive, standing in full-bellied pregnancy in front of a jury, spieling out a heartfelt plea. Margo and Sylvia had worked out an arrangement with a couple of gay men they knew so that each man would end up being either a father or an uncle to the two children. The day when Sylvia told me about their plan, Margo hovered in the kitchen, probably thinking I was going to say something insensitive. But that wasn't at all how I felt. I admired them for doing what they were doing. I almost offered to contribute to the process, but I knew that wouldn't have gone over very well.

When I got to her office, Sylvia had a large file sitting on her desk. She seemed anxious to get to it. Normally, we would spend a little time chitchatting with Cristina Brown, Sylvia's legal intern. Cristina was Miriam's niece, and she had spent time working at Hayes Street Books when she was going to college. She usually wanted to know the latest tales from the bookstore. For my part, I often asked her why she wanted to be a famous lawyer and pass up the fabulous wealth she could make as a bookseller, but frankly we'd both gotten tired of my attempts at humor. But there was no time for any of that today. Whatever she had on her mind, Sylvia wanted to get to it immediately.

She pushed the file halfway across the desk, but then she stopped, apparently unsure that she really wanted to give it to me. As I sat there with an empty, outstretched hand, I suddenly realized what it must be—it was something I had asked her to help me with months ago. She hadn't said anything up until now, but she must have found out something important.

"Gina, I'm going to give you this, but you have to promise you won't do anything impulsive once you see what we've found."

I promised—and I think I even believed my promise when I said it. But I would have stood on my head at that point to see what was in that file.

"You've found Jelena?" It came out as a question, but I was already sure of the answer.

"We're pretty sure the information we have is correct."

"Only pretty sure?"

Sylvia frowned. She was starting to realize that she couldn't get by with ambiguous phrasing—not on this subject.

"Okay, we're as sure as we can be without DNA evidence, and there's no practical way to get that."

"Where is she?"

Sylvia gave a little hand motion that meant that I should slow down for a moment.

"Let's get something straight. I know how emotional this for you. In all the months I lived with you, I learned that much, okay?"

I couldn't argue with her.

"We've found her, but that doesn't mean there's anything we can do about it." She looked at me, waiting to see if that would sink in. "We need to decide right now what we can—and cannot—do with this information. Sweetheart, do you understand what I trying to say?"

I didn't, but I said I did.

"We paid an investigative firm a lot of money to put together this report, and I think they did a hell of a job. There's a lot of stuff in here that makes unpleasant reading, and I'm not sure you'll want to read all of it. They didn't have much to work with at first. They took the information you gave us about her disappearance—the date, the place, and everything else—and they worked it from there. They checked the records of every international adoption agency until they had a match. But it wasn't easy. They knew she was only a few months old at the time, and they only had some general idea of her likely features based on her genetics and the description you gave them. That wasn't much to go on.

"And let me say one other thing. They pulled in a lot favors—and *we* pulled in a lot favors—while they were getting this together. We have to be careful not to cause any problems for that firm with their informants or with their other clients. There are some things we can use and other things we have to keep in the background. Also, our firm picked up the tab for this, so I think we need to be cognizant of that fact."

Sylvia could see the look on my face as she went through that explanation, and she knew it wasn't having much impact. Finally, she leaned back in her chair and stared up at the ceiling.

"Why did I even bother with that? I knew it wouldn't make any difference to you."

"Can I just see what's in the file?

Sylvia shrugged and handed it to me.

I thumbed through the pages, skimming a lot of the background information, until a line on page twelve jumped out at me.

"It's says that she was 'found abandoned outside the village.' That's not true. She was kidnapped."

"I knew that phrase would probably upset you. But if you look at the end of the report and read what they say about their sources, you'll see that they weren't trying to investigate the details of what happened. They were focused on finding the right child. They just used the language of what their informants gave them without arguing about it. You'll find that in a few places."

"So what do we know about this..." I flipped back a few pages to make sure I had the right name, "...this 'God's Family Foundation'?"

"That's the organization that handled the adoption and placed her with a US family."

"How do we know they weren't involved in her kidnapping?"

"We can't be absolutely sure of anything, but this is a pretty large organization that handles a lot of international adoptions. In many cases—particularly in a war zone—a lot of things can happen before an agency like that gets involved... Gina, this was Bosnia, for God's sake. You told me over and over again what things were like there at the time."

I thought Sylvia might be trying to convince herself as much as me.

"Look, read the report, you'll see that were several people that apparently had her in their custody for a short time before the foundation stepped in. As far as we can tell, there was nothing improper about the adoption itself."

The skepticism must have still shown on my face. Her voice dropped a couple of notches.

"When I read this, I knew you'd have that concern. So I asked our investigators if they would do a little more checking on the foundation. I'll let you know what they find out, okay?"

I nodded my thanks.

"Where is she now?"

"She was adopted by a married couple who were living in South Carolina at the time. They've since moved to Indianapolis. Her family life looks stable. The investigators haven't done an in-depth examination of her adoptive parents, but there doesn't seem to be any problem. The father's name is Allen Wilder, and he's the pastor at the Church of the Kindly Shepherd. It's a prominent church in the community."

I shrugged, and Sylvia picked up on it.

"I know, it's definitely not what you expected, but there it is. Her mother's name is Susan Wilder. As near as we can tell, she doesn't have a career of her own but does a lot of work within the church organization. There are apparently no brothers or sisters.

"And she has a new name, Gina. It's Alexi—Alexi Wilder."

I ran the name through my mind, fighting the feeling that it was somehow intruding upon my memory of Jelena. But as I silently mouthed it a few times, I started to get used to it.

Neither of us said anything for a few moments, but I could sense Sylvia eyeing me, wondering how I was going to respond to all this.

"Gina, I got this information for you because I know how much it means to you—how important it was for you to find out what happened."

I nodded, quietly mouthing the words, "Thank you."

"But I know you, and I know how impulsive you can be." She waited for me to deny it, but I couldn't. "Please, promise me you won't do anything rash."

I didn't know what to say.

"I'm sitting here, watching the wheels turn in your head, and I don't know what I can say that you don't already know. Alexi is now a teenager—or maybe you still want to call her Jelena, that's fine. But either way, she's living in a stable family that adopted her years ago in a proper court proceeding. Her life up to now can't be undone. We can't go back and reverse anything, and it would be cruel to try.

"And even if you could, there's the problem of you."

Sylvia caught my attention with that.

"Gina, I love you, but that will only carry you so far. You've got some things to think about. I'm not just talking about your lifestyle. That's never been an issue in my mind— not in this case or in anything else. But you know as well as I do that you can never know what a judge somewhere might say about that.

"No, what really worries me is that you're in the country illegally. Not only that, you've told me many times that there are people who would gladly rip you limb from limb if they could find you. Think about that for a minute. I don't know of anything that you can do that wouldn't run the risk of some harm coming to you or to Alexi."

I nodded. I wasn't going to argue. If I told her about my recent phone call from Paolo, I knew that she'd probably be even more worried.

"Just promise me you'll be careful."

Indianapolis—2011

Davey

This time there were lights.

It was just a blink, but there were more of them. His mind was racing, trying to catch up with everything happening in front of him. The lights were spread in a small array just across the river, penetrating the dank night air. He could feel them on his skin.

This time will be different. Things were unfolding in a way that hadn't happened before. The warning last time was just a couple of sounds that came too late to do any good. This time his senses were alive and engaged. The thought that maybe nothing had changed tried to creep into his head, but he shoved it aside.

Jimmy was lying inches away just like before—eyes shut, maybe asleep. That hadn't changed. Jimmy had been reading a love letter from home just minutes earlier. But was that last time or this time? Maybe Jimmy wouldn't have to know what happened all those other times, because everything was coming together differently.

His rifle was over by the trees out of reach, but that was last time. Now it was right here, under the sofa cushion, and he had his hands on it. The squad of enemy troops was just a few feet away, and this time he was ready for them. The gun was out from under the cushion and propped up in position, aimed against the brightest of the lights. The trigger was moving back slowly…

◆◆◆

THE PISTOL HIT THE floor, bouncing on its handle, while the muzzle spun around in the direction of the couch. Then it lay there quietly—maybe pouting over the fact that it hadn't been allowed to fire. Davey struggled to get his heart rate under control. The blanket on Robin's couch was twisted around him, and he was starting to shiver. The remnants of the dream were still tangled up in his mind, and they gave way only slowly as he tried to clear his head. His hand was still shaking. Moments earlier, the weapon had been pointed at the tiny power lights on the toaster oven, coffee maker, and other appliances in Robin's kitchenette. Those devices were still shining through the darkness—warning lights, as of a few minutes ago, of an advancing Viet Cong patrol.

It had happened again, leaving another layer of terror in his mind. By day, his memories and emotions were usually bottled up, as he managed to avoid any deep thoughts about his life and the war that had threatened to consume him. But at night his defenses weakened. And when he was asleep, they broke down entirely. He prayed and pleaded after each such dream that it would be the last, but he had concluded long ago that no one was listening.

Each time the scene was slightly different—just enough to give him a moment of hope until the nightmarish finale. Sometimes it was the light, or maybe the noise, or maybe something else. Some nights the rifle was out of reach; other times it was close at hand, allowing him to rise to a heroic defense. All those versions probably existed somewhere in a parallel universe. But when the reality of this world inevitably broke through, nothing had changed. His subconscious mind might wind its way through as many wormholes as it could, trying every possible outcome, but in the end things were always what they were and what they always would be. Their position that night had been overrun, and they'd been unable to fight back. The medevac teams had flown him out of there and patched up his wounds. But they missed the biggest wounds buried inside him. Those wounds were still there. And Jimmy was still dead.

◆◆◆

IT HAD BEEN A mistake to try to see Robin at work. It was a Saturday night, and she was busy behind the bar at the Hyatt Regency, scooping ice cubes into the glasses and tossing off shots from the bottles in the well. The bar was a little short-handed, but that fact hadn't registered when he walked in. There was an empty stool near her workstation. She gave him a surprised look and in the next breath told him she was busy and couldn't talk. But he needed to talk to someone. If it wasn't her, he didn't know who it would be.

The pressure had built up in him unbearably on the anniversary of that day in Vietnam. It was the same every year: he needed to talk, but no one wanted to listen. Some years he found his eyes moistening, as he embarrassed himself with his tears. There were times when he was dating Robin that she would let him get things off his chest. But even then there was a hint of impatience in her voice. *It's ancient history, Davey. It's time to get over it.* He could see people's eyes glaze over when he mentioned the war. There were many—even those in their fifties—who barely knew what he was talking about. A woman he once met wanted to know if the Vietnam War came before or after World War II. But even people who knew about the war had put it out of their mind. They didn't want to remember it. That didn't surprise him. No one cared about the veterans when they came home after the war, so why should they give a shit now?

Last night was worse—it had been exactly forty-five years since the attack. A round number like that unleashed a scourge of memories. He had to try to put it to rest—if only for a few moments. He thought of Robin, because he couldn't think of anyone else he could talk to.

◆◆◆

"IF YOU WERE GOING to come into the bar where I was working, couldn't you at least have behaved yourself?" Robin shoved at him, trying to get him in the passenger door as they left the hotel.

He tried to tell her he was more sick than drunk, but there was no convincing her.

"Jesus, Davey, try and act your age! You're going to be seventy in a few weeks."

He didn't need to be reminded of that.

"One more scene like that, and I'll probably lose my job. As it is, I might anyway."

Robin was fuming when she demanded that he get into her car after her shift ended. She told him she was taking him to her apartment for the night, because he was too drunk to drive.

"Couldn't you have just sat at the bar and watched the Pacers game like everyone else?"

When he told her he didn't like to watch sports on TV, she jumped at him.

"Davey, did you have to bring the damn gun?"

"I have a permit…"

"That's not the point!" she screamed. "How many times have we had this argument? I don't care what your legal rights are—you're a fanatic! And if you start quoting the Second Amendment at me, I'm going to stop the car right here and throw you into the street."

"I didn't do anything wrong."

"Well, someone thought you did. You were drunker than you think, so you're not a very reliable witness, are you? You got into an argument with the guy sitting next to you—I know he was talking about the war and got you all pissed off—but don't say you didn't get into an argument with that guy, because I saw you. He got agitated. Then you opened your coat, and it looked like you were reaching for your holster. He started to yell—I saw the whole thing."

"Robin, I wasn't going to pull the gun on…"

"What difference does it make what you thought you were going to do? Another guy saw you and dialed nine-one-one on his cell phone—oh, you didn't know that, did you? Well, he did, and the next thing I know the cops are there in the bar. And then the management—my boss—comes over and wants to know what's going on. You tried to charm the cops by telling them that you used to be on the police force. But the more you babbled on about it, the angrier they got. Then you capped off your little performance by slurring out a speech, saying that you were a friend of mine and that you just came in there to see me."

He looked over and saw she was sobbing.

"I'm so sorry."

She sniffed a couple of times and kept driving.

◆ ◆ ◆

A HEADACHE HAD ERUPTED between his ears, and it trailed down in spasms from the base of his skull to his lower back. Any quick movement was painful. He had painkillers—in fact, it was probably the combination of the pain pills and the scotch the night before that sent him off the rails. But the bottle with the pills was back in his own apartment, along with the daily heart medication that he'd been taking since his coronary a couple of years earlier.

Robin's apartment was starting to get brighter, and the clock on the coffee table said it was almost 7:00 a.m. He needed to find his clothes and then circle back to his own apartment before heading off to work. But he didn't know where anything was. He didn't even know where to find Robin, since the apartment seemed to be empty.

The mental energy to get up wasn't there. He couldn't find any reason to move—or to do anything at all. He sifted through his thoughts, trying to find one thing—anything—that he could look forward to. But he came up blank. The feeling of emptiness had started before he left the police force, but it was stronger now. It had carved out a huge hole inside him that was getting harder and harder to fill. He didn't know if he could hold things off much longer. The beast of nothingness was prowling around inside him.

He found his car keys in a small dish on the coffee table. Next to them was a note from Robin.

"I'm spending the night at my boyfriend's apartment. Try not to fuck things up any worse."

◆ ◆ ◆

HE PULLED INTO THE parking lot and found his space. The God's Children Foundation didn't have many cars there on a

Sunday morning. But it shared the parking lot with the Church of the Kindly Shepherd, and within the hour it would be filled up with Sunday churchgoers. The sign on his parking space in front of the foundation read: "David Fallon, Security Director." That lofty title might have impressed someone, but it didn't impress him—not considering the routine crap-work he did from day to day.

He slapped his security card against the electronic pad at the main door, and as he did so he saw John Blaiseck, the director of the foundation, standing on the second-floor balcony outside his office, a cigarette hanging from his lips. He watched as Blaiseck let out a quick puff before tossing the butt down and grinding it out with his foot. He'd been forced outdoors by the anti-smoking ordinance in Indianapolis, and he wasn't happy about it. He figured Blaiseck to be in his late fifties, but he guessed that he'd been acting in that imperious way all his life. He had what seemed to be a Russian accent, but he didn't really talk all that much. Mostly he just glared, which was even more unnerving because of his mismatched eyes. Blaiseck was a bit of an asshole—but so what? He wasn't the first one he'd worked for.

This was nothing like the work he had done with the police force. There, he did real detective work—not the kind of button-pushing he did now. He missed his days as a cop. He could sink his teeth into a case and blot out everything else. It was probably the only thing in life he ever looked forward to doing. But when he was forced into early retirement, someone in the department arranged for him to get this job. So he was in no position to complain about it.

His first stop—like every morning—was a cup of coffee to get him going. From then on, it was just a matter of getting through the day without thinking too much. He had surveillance logs and monitors to check, as he followed the path of the cameras around the church and the foundation offices, hoping to get from point A to point B to point C without stirring up anything unexpected. Sunday mornings were a little different because of the big gathering at the church next door, but after a while even that fit into a pattern.

He wasn't sure what the relationship was between the foundation and the church, but he thought it must be pretty close, since he spent most of his time in one building while keeping tabs on the other one. His paycheck came from the foundation, but he wasn't sure where one organization ended and the other one began. The Church of the Kindly Shepherd appeared to be the moneymaker. The Reverend Allen Wilder was a media star in certain circles, and his sermons were broadcast throughout a network of churches. There were plenty of places on the web where you could buy his podcasts and copies of his books.

The God's Family Foundation was a little harder to pin down. According to the literature, it was doing some important work on behalf of orphaned children worldwide. Blaiseck ran the day-to-day operations of the foundation, but he stayed out of the limelight. The Reverend Wilder seemed to be the face of things, serving as chairman of the board and an occasional spokesman. It was Wilder's media savvy that probably brought in most of the contributions. He'd been featured in an interview on Fox News a week earlier, and the phones started ringing off the hook. Wilder and Blaiseck between them had convinced several national figures, including at least five congressmen, to serve on their International Orphanage Advisory Committee.

He never saw anyone in the foundation offices that really looked like an orphan. Mostly, it was just secretaries and administrative staff who did the paperwork. On Sunday mornings, there was often an odd collection of people hanging around. He knew that Curly and Slim were already there, which seemed a little early in the day for that pair. He hadn't gone three steps past the coffee machine before he ran into Slim. And if Slim was there, Curly was certain to be nearby. Sure enough, he saw him farther down the hallway outside the door to the executive offices, probably waiting for Blaiseck to get back to his desk after his smoke break. He gave a brief hello to both of them as he walked past, and he got a couple of nods in return. Maybe he was just imagining things, but they seemed to be a little more surly than usual.

Curly and Slim weren't their real names. Someone in the secretarial staff had come up with those two nicknames in an inspired moment. It was a bit of a cliché, but the names stuck. By the time he'd been introduced to Jerome—the one with the thin face and shaved head—and Edgar—the short, heavy one with the barrel chest—the nicknames were already lodged in his head. Like a lot of cops, he assigned names to people to match their stereotype. It was a bad habit, because it could cloud his judgment. But in this case the names seemed to fit. Curly and Slim looked like they belonged somewhere in a lineup.

He activated his computer along with the bank of monitors and then began the ritual of looking at the active footage. There were security cameras in both of the buildings and around the perimeter, but he didn't see anything unusual on any of them. A few people were walking through the hallways of the foundation office at the moment, but the meeting areas were empty. There wasn't much going on in the church either, but it would be bursting with activity as they got closer to the Sunday services.

He ran through the log for the previous day and didn't see anything out of the ordinary. There was a video image of Allen Wilder in one of the side-chapels from late in the afternoon. It looked at first like he was speaking to another person, but then it appeared that he was in the room by himself, probably practicing his sermon for the next morning. Wilder's style was way overdone for his taste. But what did he know? He didn't care about sermons one way or another— as long as they weren't directed at him. The reverend's wife, Susan, showed up briefly on the screen, as she walked around the sanctuary, fluffing up the flowers, making sure nothing was amiss. The janitors were following their usual schedule, moving from room to room in predictable fashion. The last screen had a feed from later in the evening. He saw the back of a teenage girl hurrying down the hall, pushing against the crash-bar doors, and running out of the building. He backed up the image until he reached the point a few moments earlier where she had left the reverend's office and had begun running down the hallway. It was Allen and Susan Wilder's daughter, Alexi.

◆ ◆ ◆

THERE WAS A LIGHT knock on the door. He turned and saw Reverend Wilder and his wife, Susan, standing in his office doorway. Allen Wilder didn't wait to be invited but instead strode through the half-open door, moving toward the desk with his hand outstretched. He had a smooth, practiced glide and a smile that spread across his face.

Wilder's blue eyes were topped by a full head of blonde hair and a few softening strands of brown in the combed-back layers. Although he was in his fifties, there was no hint of gray. He appeared to be dressed and ready to stand in front of his congregation, wearing a pair of sharply-creased tan slacks, a deep powder-blue sport coat, and a black silk shirt. Instead of a clerical collar, he wore a gold chain that looped under the shirt collar and came to rest just below the open top button. At the end of the chain was a large gold crucifix that swayed back and forth across his chest as he moved.

"Good morning, Mr. Fallon."

He stood to greet him, running his hand instinctively through his own tousled mixture of grey swirls and bald spots. Then he tried to straighten his jacket. Wilder grabbed at his hand and gripped it between both of his own two hands with a firm shaking motion.

"How are you?" Wilder stared into his eyes, squeezing them with the same intensity as the grip on his hand.

"I think I see a little distress on your face—like you could use a little bit of God's good news this morning. I hope you're coming over to the church for the services."

"I'm afraid I'll have to be right here, watching the services on the monitor."

Wilder's eyes hadn't moved, but a half grin curled up from his mouth. "Of course, we need you up here to keep everyone safe."

"Please, have a seat."

"No, I'm afraid I can't sit down, Mr. Fallon. There's a meeting right now in Mr. Blaiseck's office with some out-of-town people from the foundation, and I told him I would drop in for a few minutes."

He brightened up his smile a bit, showing a few more teeth. "I suppose he feels more comfortable with the chairman of the board in the meeting, perhaps to give things a little spiritual perspective."

"What can I do for you?"

Wilder gave a slight shrug. "Mr. Blaiseck thought you might be able to assist us with a few security issues—nothing too serious, I would think. But it's good to plan these things. Has he mentioned that we're having a meeting with some important folks next month?"

"We've talked about it."

"We're hosting a reception at our home a few blocks from here. There'll be some congressmen there and a few other dignitaries. You know how that can get. They could draw some demonstrators and other troublemakers. I want to make sure that the missus here has nothing to worry about."

He gestured toward his wife. Up to that point, Susan Wilder had said nothing.

"Maybe you two could get together next week and go over the plans."

"I'd be happy to work with you."

Susan Wilder gave him a friendly nod, and he returned the smile.

"Good. I just want to make sure that my wife and daughter have nothing to worry about. You've met my daughter, Alexi, have you not?"

He told Wilder that he had. "Coincidently, I saw her on last night's security video running out of the church. I hope everything is okay."

He knew the minute he said it that it was a mistake. If there had been an altercation in the church the night before, he would have heard about it by now. But what he said appeared to have touched a nerve with Reverend Wilder. He could almost feel a chill in the room.

A few seconds slipped past as Wilder said nothing. His smile was still as rigid as before, but something had changed. What was it—maybe a slight twitch of the lip or some other movement? Wilder's attention seemed to have shifted to a point somewhere behind his own eyes.

"The Lord has blessed us with a beautiful daughter."

His eyes held steady as his focus drifted more and more inward.

"Do any of us really understand the nature of temptation and the continual presence of sin? Do you, Mr. Fallon?"

It was framed as a question, but he didn't seem to be looking for any kind of an answer.

"You used to be a policeman, so you probably know as much as anyone how we all live our days on the edge of perdition. It can destroy us. We're really only sustained by God's willingness to forgive us again and again and welcome us back."

Wilder's words hung out there, seemingly untethered to anything at all.

A few moments elapsed—just long enough to feel a sense of embarrassment for Susan Wilder, who had hardly moved from the doorway.

"I don't understand. Has someone harmed your daughter?"

Wilder's demeanor changed again as he worked his way back to the easy charm of the man who had earlier walked into the room.

"No, no—nothing like that."

He gave a broad smile. He was now miles away from the sense of damnation that seemed to be in the forefront of his mind just moments before.

"I'll leave you two to chat a little bit." He had gathered himself together, making clear that he was ready to leave.

"Maybe you two can set up a meeting in the next day or so. In the meantime, I'll be leading the congregation in prayer this morning on the role of families. They're the most important part of God's plan, Mr. Fallon. You might think that's some sort of an old-fashioned idea, and I couldn't fault you for that. But I believe in it fervently."

Wilder was in an almost playful mood, reaching out with one hand to grab him for a handshake, poking him lightly in the stomach with the other. As he did so, he pulled the open jacket, acting surprised to find a holster and pistol.

"I see you're carrying a gun this morning, Mr. Fallon." He looked up and smiled. "That's good. You never know when we might need you to shoot somebody." He gave a little wink.

"You know I'm a man of faith, so I don't condone violence, but there are times when you need to defend yourself with a weapon.

"Mrs. Wilder and I took target practice at a firing range a few months ago so that we'd know how to use a gun if we had to." He gestured toward his wife. "The missus here is quite a good shot."

His big smile returned. "So if I were you Mr. Fallon, I'd be careful."

Wilder turned and left, seemingly amused at his own comments. The room seemed suddenly lighter.

◆ ◆ ◆

SUSAN WILDER SAT QUIETLY for a few moments, clutching at the small purse in her lap as she stared at the door where her husband had just left. This was a sadder side of Susan Wilder. He'd only seen her in groups of people, mingling with visitors. Around the church, she was thought of as the informal greeter-in-chief, always wearing a big smile and giving a personal welcome to anyone who walked in the door.

She wasn't smiling now. She cried quietly to herself for a few moments until she opened up her purse and took out a tissue, giving her nose a polite blow. She dabbed her face slightly below each eye, looking for any lingering moisture. Finally, she seemed as composed as she could make herself.

"I'm sorry, Mr. Fallon. I don't know why I started crying. Those things he said when you mentioned our daughter… It's just so embarrassing."

"You don't have to apologize… And, please, if you like, call me Davey."

"Thank you."

She had her head turned away slightly, looking inward again. Her hand grasped at her mouth.

"I think my husband's relationship with Alexi is hard on him right now."

She paused a second, stifling a tiny sob.

"I remember right after we adopted her, Allen was so close to her. She was just a little girl, and he used to roll around on the floor with her, laughing and playing as he tickled her and nuzzled her. They were like a couple of kittens. You wouldn't know that side of my husband, if you only saw him carrying around the burdens of our congregation. But it's true.

"I grew up as an orphan. I didn't have that kind of relationship with anyone, so that kind of love within our little family is so very important to me. They are the two people I love the most, and it gave my heart such joy to see them so close."

She looked up, maybe trying to gauge his reaction.

"She's just at that age where she thinks anything Allen does is wrong. I know that, because I have to listen to her complaints. And I do listen—I really do. I love Alexi dearly. But sometimes it's so hard when she goes off in directions where… I don't know, but sometimes I think maybe her fantasies have gotten the best of her. Allen is very strict. He lives—really, we both live—by all of the Biblical injunctions. I think she may be rebelling against that."

She stared away for a moment.

"He seems to think that maybe she's being harassed by someone, but I don't know. Sometimes I think he exaggerates just like she does."

"Well, you're right to be cautious."

Why was she was telling him this? He liked Susan Wilder, but he wasn't comfortable listening to her go back and forth over the same ground. One moment she was talking like her world was falling apart, and the next moment she was belittling the whole thing, apologizing for taking up his time. She finally got around to suggesting that maybe they could meet on Thursday at her house to talk about security. He said that would be fine.

"Thank you for letting me babble on about my daughter."

He told her he didn't mind listening. But as he said it, he knew he couldn't be of much help to her. Of all the people in the world, he was probably the least qualified to deal with a father-daughter problem.

◆◆◆

He called John Blaiseck's office moments later.

"Yeah, what do you need?"

"Reverend Wilder was here a while ago and wants me to set up security for the reception at his house. Is that something you want me to do?"

"Give him whatever he wants."

"Okay, I'll arrange it. But let me ask you something else. I got the impression they're having problems with their daughter. Is that anything I need to know about?"

"There's nothing to concern yourself about."

"But if she's being threatened by someone..."

"Look, if there's anything you need to deal with, I'll let you know."

◆ ◆ ◆

The parking lot cameras were bringing in all kinds of data, as cars crowded into the lot with people heading for the Sunday services. He knew that the videos could be sorted out later on, if necessary, by license-plate number, date, or any other way. Surveillance in the church followed the same pattern. Hidden cameras recorded everything the congregants did while they were in the anteroom and sanctuary. Whenever he thought about it, he realized he hated what he was doing. The heavy surveillance was Blaiseck's idea. He and Wilder had been spooked a few months earlier when some pro-choice demonstrators sprung up out of nowhere right at the doors to the sanctuary. But the whole surveillance thing seemed excessive. The people milling around in the anteroom seemed to be in a happy mood. He couldn't see what they got out of being there— if he had, he might have envied them. But they were there for some sort of spiritual reasons, and he felt funny about spying on them like they were criminals.

The video images from the anteroom didn't show anything out of the ordinary. Mostly, it was just the regular congregants. Susan was in the middle of them, smiling and talking. She had apparently put aside—for the moment, at least—the things that had bothered her a little while earlier. She was talking to a somewhat tall, thin woman he'd never seen before. The woman had an air about her that was different from the people who usually showed up at these services, but he couldn't put his finger on what it was. Susan seemed to be introducing her to some of the other congregants, which was the kind of thing she always did at the Sunday services. Then something caught his eye, as he looked at the corner of the screen, Alexi suddenly emerged from one of the side doors and started walking quickly in the direction of her mother. Was she really as angry as she looked?

◆◆◆

HE KNEW MORE THAN he wanted to know about a daughter's anger—his own daughter, Mandy, hadn't spoken to him in more than eight years. In his battles with her mother, Jennifer, leading up to their divorce, Mandy had a front-row seat. She'd never gotten over it. His role had been shameful, but he'd only realized his mistakes too late to do anyone any good. One fight blended into another. Mostly, it was a lot of yelling and name-calling, but a couple of times he grabbed his wife to make her stop. He didn't think he had really hit her, but the investigator decided that's what it was. Whatever you called it, he wasn't proud of what happened. He knew at the time that it was wrong, even when he was trying to rationalize it.

He was forced to go to a men's counseling group. The judge didn't give him much choice—it was either do that or spend time in jail on a spousal-battery charge. He sat through the meetings, listening to the tales of the other men—all ex-batterers in one stage or another of recovery. After a few meetings, it was time for him to tell his own story in front of the group. He was more nervous than he thought he would be, standing in front of those hardened faces. He began repeating the story he had been telling himself about how he wanted to make everything work in their marriage. He had tried to work things out, but Jennifer had fought him. And then it got to a point...

But at that moment a young man with rolled-up sleeves and tattoos up both arms burst in on his carefully prepared speech. "That's a bunch of shit—tell us what you really felt when you hit her."

He tried to protest, but the other guy was having none of it.

"I don't care if you're a cop or not. You went through the same thing as the rest of us, but you're afraid to admit it. You think you're the only one that's happened to? Everyone tells you that you should be boss in your family. So there you are—trying to be King Shit in your own little world—and something happens to piss you off and the bottom drops out of everything. You suddenly realize you're nothing. You're dead inside. And that's when you hit her. So why don't you just say it?"

Dead inside—the phrase had stuck with him, and it was hard to shake. He tried to come to terms with Jennifer later on, exchanging letters with her a few months before she died of cancer. But Mandy was a different matter. He called her a few times, but she didn't call back. He finally wrote to her after her mother died, but he got only a cool response. He'd learned a few months ago that Mandy was pregnant. He thought he should write again, but he didn't know what to say. Mandy, he realized, could be suffering from the same thing as he was. She'd found herself on the front lines of a war, and it had wormed its way inside her.

◆ ◆ ◆

THE DAY WAS IMPOSSIBLY long. When he finally got home, there was a message on the phone from Robin, apologizing for everything that happened the night before. He called her back and left his own long apology on her answering machine. This was the story of their old relationship—always talking past each other, always trying to make the other feel better, and always failing at it.

He grabbed a few leftovers out of the refrigerator and set them down on a plate next to his computer so that he could munch on them later. He didn't have much of an appetite. He unbuckled his shoulder holster and set it down on the other side of the desk. The wooden butt of his Smith & Wesson stuck out of the leather pouch, inviting him to give it a little squeeze. It was a short-barreled weapon—nothing fancy about it. He knew some guys who spent a lot of time at gun shows, and they were always pushing him to get one of the newer models. He considered most of that just bullshit, and he told them so. His Model 27 had been with him since his days as a cop, and he'd be lost without it. He used it only a couple of times while he was on the force—once as a warning shot and another time to wound a fleeing suspect in the leg. But shooting someone wasn't the point. His pistol was really just an extension of himself. He'd had it with him for years, cradled quietly under his arm, waiting for the moment it might be needed.

He had only one thing planned for the evening. It was something he did every year, but he had to gear himself up emotionally. This was the day when he always wrote to Carolyn to talk about her brother. Jimmy had died forty-five years ago—forty-five years to the day, exactly, in a miserable ditch right next to him. He knew she'd be waiting for the message. Often their string of emails would get so intense that one or the other would pick up the phone to put a voice to their shared memories. The conversations weren't always heavy or sad, but sometimes the emotional context could turn on a dime.

Carolyn sometimes made a point of singing some of the songs that Jimmy had loved to sing and play in his folk-singing days, her voice resonating with an eerie resemblance to that of her brother. Jimmy was a fanatic about folk music. It was strange—and more than a little endearing—that they were so engrossed in that type of music just at the time when other musicians were picking up amplified guitars and plunging into rock and roll. He never did find a guitar in Vietnam. Instead, he'd just sit in the dark, singing his favorite ballads, as he moved his long fingers along an imaginary keyboard, trying to keep his muscle memory alive for the day when he would once again be able to play.

The name of LouAnn, Jimmy's girlfriend, often came up in the conversation. He knew Carolyn had kept in touch with her, so he usually asked how she was and how she was getting along. He'd never met LouAnn, but he felt close to her because of the common bond they had with Jimmy. He always wondered what her life was like after his death.

Carolyn at one point sent him a copy of a picture that Jimmy had sent her from Vietnam. He had written across the front of it, "Me and my best buddy." It was sitting now in a silver frame on his shelf. The day that picture was taken was one that had stuck in his mind. The two of them were standing in front of a run-down building, arms around each other's shoulders and laughing at the camera. They were both flashing peace signs.

It was a happy memory wedged in between a lot of sad ones. They had a couple days' leave in Saigon, and he and Jimmy had peeled themselves away from the others. The two of them seemed to hit it off better than either of them did with the rest of the squad. The building where the picture had been taken was a brothel. They had both been drinking for most of the afternoon before they made the decision to pay the girls a visit. He remembered laughing about it as they worked their way down the street, with him kidding Jimmy about where they were headed.

"What's LouAnn going to say if she finds out?" The cheap beer was making him a little silly.

"Oh, shit…" Jimmy drawled, "Lou wouldn't mind if…" And then he broke out in laughter.

By the time they entered the brothel, they were both in full hysterics. They took a look at the girls, and then they looked at each other. They decided then and there that they didn't really want to spend any time with that sad group of teenagers lined up along the wall. They retreated outside, handed a passerby the camera and a dollar bill, and asked him to take their picture.

His conversations with Carolyn were an odd kind of ritual—even he had to admit that. Was it a symptom of PTSD?

He didn't really know. As far as he could tell, post-traumatic stress disorder wasn't even diagnosed prior to the Vietnam War, so maybe vets like him were moving through life, discovering new pieces of it as they went along. His annual exchange of memories with Carolyn had gone on far longer than he ever thought it would. One time he hinted that maybe they should stop doing it every year, but she broke down crying. Then he started crying with her. He knew what she was thinking: if they ever stopped talking about Jimmy, then he would truly be forever dead.

Gina

I HAD TO DO something.

The day after she showed me the investigator's report, Sylvia sat me down again—she even dragged out the term "tough love" to make her point. She listed the consequences of my doing anything foolhardy, starting with emotional heartache and ending with lawsuits, criminal prosecution, and probable deportation. She made her point. I was vulnerable.

But as much as I loved Sylvia, I don't think she understood the emotional tug that this news had on me. Jelena—now Alexi—was the only link to my past. She might be my best hope for the future. The thought that she was alive and that she was somewhere where I might see her had a strong grip on me. I didn't want to try to get rid of the feeling. I just wanted to get a look at her—if only for one time.

"Alexi"—thanks to Sylvia's investigation, I now had a name for the person she had become. I loved the sound of it. Her original Bosnian name, Jelena, conjured up images of the moon, and I hoped the strength of that name was still running through her. But it was a name she probably didn't even know, and I had no intention of telling her about it. I might never get to meet her to tell her anything—at least, not in the foreseeable future. Still, I couldn't stop thinking about her. I found myself rolling her old name and her new name over my tongue to get the feel of them together.

The couple that adopted Alexi had moved to Indiana. The Reverend Allen Wilder's picture showed up in several places on the website of the Church of the Kindly Shepherd—blonde hair combed straight back, a square jaw, lots of teeth, and a smile that stared off somewhere to the left of the camera. I suppose he looked kindly enough, if you approached things in the right frame of mind. The church had lots of community outreach programs to aid the shut-ins and elderly people in the congregation. The website said that the reverend's wife, Susan, was the head volunteer for those programs, but there was no picture of her. Most of the website was devoted to pages and pages of the reverend's scriptural ideas, which were very heavy on fundamentalism. There were a couple of photos of the children in the congregation, including a group of teenage girls. Most of them were smiling, but one of them was more solemn-faced. It wasn't a clear photo, but it looked like it could be Alexi. I compared it with the grainy picture that had been included with Sylvia's report, and I realized that Alexi was unsmiling in that picture as well. That left me unsettled. I had hoped she was happy, but I wondered what would cause the sadness in her eyes. The more I looked at the photos, the more I realized I had to see her—even if it only at a distance.

I'd never been to Indianapolis, but the opportunity to go there was staring me in the face. There was a flyer on my desk from the American Booksellers Association, announcing a two-day meeting about Internet book sales in Chicago near the O'Hare Airport. Indianapolis was only about a five-hour drive from there. So I signed up for the meeting and arranged to pick up a car at the airport that I could drive to Indiana on Saturday afternoon. I thought if I stayed there Saturday night, I could be at the church the next morning.

The drive from Chicago was long and flat. I was spoiled, I suppose, by living in San Francisco and Rome—and, before that, the Balkans. I was looking for a hill, a bay, a tower, a cathedral—any kind of landmark to tell me where I was. It started to sink in just how different Alexi's life was from mine. The trip droned on, interrupted only by a few freeway exit signs. Interstate 65 eventually merged with Interstate 465, which circled the Indianapolis. I got off at a shopping center called Keystone Crossing and checked into a Marriott Hotel just behind the main part of the mall. After throwing my suitcase in the room, I walked over to the shops and browsed awhile before heading back to the hotel. The restaurant looked pretty quiet, but that was okay with me. I wasn't in the mood for anything too exciting.

My plan was to attend the morning service at the church and then catch an afternoon flight out of the Indianapolis International for San Francisco. What do you wear to a fundamentalist church in the Midwest? I stared into the full-length mirror in the hotel room and tried to assess the woman staring back at me. She looked presentable—maybe, just barely. She was thin in places where she might be a bit fuller, a little long where she could have been short. But I thought she would be okay, if I could get the clothes right. I put on a light touch of lip gloss, some eyeliner, and then completed the look with low-heeled pumps. The result was nothing out of the ordinary by San Francisco standards, but would she blend into the congregation here? I hoped so. I wasn't looking to win any fashion awards. I just wanted to be passable.

The parking lot around the church was huge—larger than anything I was used to. But it was surprisingly full. Apparently, Reverend Wilder knew how to draw a crowd. The sign outside the church announced the sermon for the morning service: "Living in God's Family." I walked in and slipped through the foyer without talking to anyone. There was a display against the wall with a few announcements and handouts about the church. I thumbed my way through them, and I found a brochure about the church's club for teenagers, listing the names and emails of some of the leaders. Alexi's email address was on the list. On an impulse, I grabbed the brochure and stuffed it in my purse.

There was a large crowd. I was probably younger and thinner than most of the people in the congregation, but that didn't stop a few of them from looking at me as if they knew me. I didn't really want to talk to anyone. I'd learned to tone down my Italian accent when I needed to, but there was no way that I was going pass as a Midwesterner. I thought I might remain invisible, until I was stopped by a pleasant-looking woman who seemed to have taken upon herself to greet visitors to the congregation. She grabbed my hand and gave it a friendly shake. She was probably in her fifties and had a full head of hair that was styled nicely. She was wearing a prim tailored suit that immediately made me feel dowdy. There was a grin spread across her face, but it didn't convey as much happiness as she probably hoped it would. Her eyes looked a bit red, as if she may have been crying at some point.

She had an embossed gold name tag with her name in black: *Mrs. Reverend Allen Wilder.*

It was Alexi's adoptive mother—I wasn't ready for that.

Questions had been piling up inside my brain for more than a decade, and now they threatened to come tumbling out all at once. Where is Alexi? What's she like? Is she smart? Is she happy? Fortunately, my mouth was frozen shut. I found myself just mumbling, but that was probably for the best.

"Welcome to the Church of the Kindly Shepherd."

I answered as politely as I could without really saying anything.

"My name's Susan. We're always getting new people at these services, and I like to talk to them and make them feel welcome. The reverend—that's my husband—is usually too busy to do any of that."

I made some sort of response, and she picked up on it immediately. I got the feeling that Susan Wilder found any dead air space in a conversation to be a challenge. If no one else was going to talk, she'd step in and carry on by herself.

"Oh, I love your accent."

I told her it was Italian. She seemed to like that, but I wanted to drop the whole subject.

"Sometimes people get self-conscious about their accents. I know I do. When the reverend and I moved here from South Carolina, everyone thought I talked funny."

◆ ◆ ◆

WHILE SUSAN AND THE others chatted, I looked out of the corner of my eye for Alexi, hoping not to be too obvious about it. I hadn't seen her anywhere in the crowd, and I was beginning to think that she might be missing from this Sunday service. But then a door opened on the other side of the anteroom, and a young woman stood in the doorway for a second, scanning the room. She seemed to be looking for someone. But from the look on her face, she was none too happy about it. It was Alexi.

She apparently saw her mother, because she started walking quickly in our direction. She was wearing a pair of sneakers, some faded jeans, and a gray sweatshirt that hung loosely over her waist. I remembered a time when I dressed like that myself. Maybe I was reading too much into it, but she seemed to have dressed way down for the occasion. There was a lot of anger in her stride. As much as I had longed to see her over the years, it pained me to see her like that. She got close to where we were standing and then stopped. If Susan Wilder had turned around at that moment, she would have seen her daughter's eyes glaring at her back.

I must have been staring at her, because Alexi looked up suddenly and caught my eye. I fantasized a glimmer of recognition but quickly dismissed the idea. She dropped her gaze and looked back toward her mother. Susan Wilder saw her at that point. But before Alexi could say anything, her mother grabbed her by the arm, escorting her into the group and introducing her to the others. Alexi looked like she'd been through that sort of thing before—her mother talking hurriedly about something else, pushing aside any conversation that might have been unpleasant. She stood there with a barely subdued anger, her body almost rigid.

I must have said something—I don't remember what— to let Susan know that her daughter needed to talk to her. Whatever it was, it slowed Susan down for a moment and earned me a brief nod from Alexi. Susan's face turned more serious. It took only one angry sentence out of Alexi's mouth to convince her that she needed to usher her daughter away from the crowd, hoping to avoid a scene. She grabbed Alexi by the arm, making conciliatory gestures to her as they walked, promising to listen to her when they were somewhere alone. I caught only a couple of sentences from Alexi as she and her mother headed toward the other side of the room.

"I'm not going to do it—I'm not! He's just trying to humiliate me."

◆ ◆ ◆

THE CONGREGATION STARTED TO make its way into the sanctuary. I headed off to the aisle on the left side, where I found a seat as near to the back as I could. The organist caught everyone's attention with a few loud, trembling chords. That seemed to be the signal for everyone to reach for the hymnals. The couple in the pew next to me pulled a well-worn book from the rack in front of them and started to follow along. The man seemed to have internalized the music, singing with great intensity even though his eyes were closed. I picked up a copy of the hymnal and stared at the pages so I wouldn't look out of place.

The singing went on for several minutes without any sign of the reverend. In the interlude, Susan Wilder walked in from a side door of the sanctuary and headed toward the front, stopping frequently at several of the rows of pews, reaching in to greet the people who were seated there. One couple stopped her a little longer, and she leaned in to them, seeming to listen as attentively as she could to what they had to say over the loud volume of singing. She finally nodded in sympathetic agreement. An older woman reached out to her, and Susan took the woman's outstretched hand in one of her own, patting it lightly on the top with her other hand as they talked. Everyone who wanted her attention seemed to get it.

If there was any carryover from her confrontation with Alexi, it wasn't apparent.

As Susan made her way to a seat near the pulpit, Alexi slipped through the door behind her, keeping close to the wall as she moved toward the front. She walked with her head down, not making eye contact with anyone. As she got to the pulpit, she tried to take a chair off to the side. But Susan saw her sitting apart, and she motioned for her to move in closer. Alexi responded with what looked like a flash of anger but then seemed to settle into a smoldering sadness.

My own feelings were hitting me from all directions. I had to scold myself for a second for being almost happy that she seemed so miserable with the life she was in. It wasn't a life I would have chosen for her, so maybe deep inside her soul she was really like me. But that thought brought with it a sense of shame. Did I really want her to be unhappy? This was the life she was in, and that wasn't likely to change. Wouldn't it be better if she could make the best of this world? As I pondered those thoughts, I knew that the next intruder in my head would be a sense of guilt for my part in getting her into this predicament in the first place. But before I could wallow any further in those useless arguments, the lights in the sanctuary suddenly went dim.

The people in the pews around me stopped talking, as the church settled into a dark, evening-like dusk. Within moments, the lights over the center aisle got brighter, illuminating a pathway from the rear of the sanctuary to the pulpit. Suddenly there was a booming voice from the back of the congregation as a figure began walking up the center aisle. The Reverend Wilder moved slowly with a Bible in one hand and his eyes in a gaze that seem to have no real point of focus.

His free arm was stretched out in front of him like he was trying to seize something that only he could see, some invisible presence that was drawing him forward. He wore a lavaliere microphone, but he probably didn't need it. As he approached the pulpit, his voice boomed out over the congregation:

I feel the presence of the Lord with us. He is right here in this room, calling upon us to do his bidding. Hear us, oh Lord, as we raise our voices in song.

Accept us, oh Lord, as we happily submit ourselves to your will.

The lights came up slowly, signaling the start of one last round of singing. As the voices echoed around the sanctuary, Reverend Wilder was now at the front of the church, walking slowly back and forth in front of the pulpit. He was well-tanned, and his smile was in full bloom. He'd loosened his suit coat, and the crucifix around his neck swayed back and forth as he reached out toward the parishioners in the front rows, exhorting them to stand with the Lord. He began with a quotation from the psalms, and after a few moments of scriptural recitation he urged the rest of the congregation to join with him. While the drone of the psalms filled the room, I saw Alexi sitting in the front row, looking defeated.

Wilder paused for a second, as if reaching back in his thoughts. After he had his audience poised to listen, he launched into his sermon. *Just as we are all part of our own families, so we are part of God's family. It is he who draws us together and shows us how to live.* He did a recitation from scripture, drawing together quotes and thoughts that sounded strained to me, but the people around me were hanging on his every word. He moved back and forth in front of the congregation as he talked, exhorting, quoting, charming—using his considerable rhetorical gifts to get his audience to go where he wanted them to go.

I sensed he was finally nearing the end of the sermon. He suddenly stopped and walked over to where Susan and Alexi were sitting. He grabbed them both by the hand, urging them to stand and join him in front of the congregation. Susan looked embarrassed at first but then yielded to his urgings. She melded her body into his and cradled herself in his outstretched arm, smiling as she looked up to into his eyes. The reverend had his other arm around Alexi, but unlike Susan, she hadn't yielded to the idea. Her face had a look of resignation as she stared down at the ground. The more he drew her in, the more she seemed coiled and ready to escape if he ever loosened his grip.

"Let us pray," Wilder intoned. "Just as God the Father draws us together in his heavenly family, let us draw our families together. Let us ask God's help to do everything in his awesome power to keep our families intact."

The congregation murmured its approval.

"Let us ask Almighty God to defeat the enemies of his family. And let us pray that he smites down those who would destroy our families and would rip out the gift of life that he so lovingly places inside a woman's womb."

The approval grew louder, with several people shouting, "Amen." I was starting to squirm.

"And let us pray that those who would pollute God's family—those who would violate his ordained plan of one man and one woman—will be cast down and given the punishment that God has decreed."

I couldn't take it anymore.

I got up and headed for the door. A few people gave me dirty looks, but I didn't care. I wasn't going to see them again, and I didn't care what they thought. My mind was frozen at that moment, unable to think through what I had just seen. I hurried through the anteroom and out the front door, moving quickly across the parking lot to my car. I got into the driver's seat and took a few minutes to compose myself.

There was nothing I could do about Alexi's situation. I simply had to swallow my bile and move on. Whatever I might attempt to do would make it worse. If I tried to do anything, I'd be putting both of us in jeopardy. Alexi had her life to lead, and I hoped she would find herself.

◆ ◆ ◆

I CAME CLOSE TO doing nothing. But as I was getting ready to drive away, I looked up and saw the sign on the building next to the church. The large letters etched into the wall said: "God's Family Foundation." That sign changed everything—I suddenly realized I had been deluding myself.

Ever since Sylvia told me what she'd discovered about Alexi, I had gotten used to the idea that a modern miracle had occurred. The good-hearted people of two countries, I told myself, had come together to rescue a child from the horrors of war and dislocation and had given her another chance. A little child from the Balkans named Jelena had somehow been transformed into a healthy American teenager named Alexi. In the back of my mind, I visualized the God's Family Foundation as an organization of staid but dedicated social workers and lawyers, probably affiliated with a large hospital or university. I assumed that the foundation tried to unite families whenever they could. But if that proved impossible, they would look around to find the child a good, new home.

But I'd been assuming too much. As I sat there staring at the two buildings, looking at the people who were walking back and forth on the covered pathway between the foundation and the church, I knew that something else was going on. The church and the foundation were just one incestuous organization. Someone had manipulated the adoption process right from the beginning. Alexi had probably been destined to end up right here from the minute the foundation got its hands on her years ago. Her plight suddenly seemed a lot worse.

I had to leave if I was going to catch my plane, but my mind was so immersed in what I'd seen that I missed the turn-off for the Indianapolis Airport and had to double back at the next exit. I finally dropped off the car, putting my thoughts on hold for a few minutes as I worked my way through the ticket line and security. There's nothing like a modern airport to cut you down to size and make you feel insignificant. I was trying to grapple with what I had seen, but it wasn't getting any easier to solve. Although my sense of urgency about Alexi had grown dramatically, there was still nothing I could do about it. I could never convince anyone to investigate her situation. What could I tell them—that my instincts told me something was wrong? Sylvia would tell me to save my breath.

By the time my plane reached Dallas for the three-hour layover, I'd made a decision. It was risky, but I knew I had to do it. I found a Wi-Fi spot in the airport, and I pulled the laptop out of my flight bag and logged on. I stared for a moment at the church brochure that had Alexi's email address. Writing to her under my own name was too risky, because it might be intercepted. But I had an email account that I had opened under an assumed name several months earlier with the vague idea that I might need to use it someday. I needed it now.

I wasn't sure what kind of reaction I'd get. Maybe I was reading the situation all wrong. Maybe Alexi would be offended—or even scared—to receive an email from someone she didn't know. I sat there for a second, trying to decide what to say. I couldn't tell her everything in just one message, so I had to tone things down a bit. I told her I was the woman she'd met briefly before the church services, and I tried to give her some idea of why I was writing. I had to tiptoe around that gingerly, finally saying that I remembered her from years ago when she was a baby and had been thinking about her ever since. The message ended up being vaguer than I would have liked, but I couldn't figure out a better way to word it.

The ending, at least, was clear: "I'm here, if you ever need me."

Was that enough? I didn't know. But I could hear Sylvia's voice in my ear.

"Sure it's enough—enough to get you in a lot of trouble."

◆◆◆

Two days later, I got a response. I was apprehensive about opening it, and I couldn't understand what was making me so nervous. Maybe I had a premonition of what was about to happen. The email text was short and disturbing, and it ended with this phrase: "Please help me."

There was a video file attached. The first minutes were dark and indistinct, and then suddenly it became clear. I felt like someone had just kicked me in the stomach.

I called Sylvia on her cell phone and told her we had to talk immediately. She had left her office early and was already at her house in North Oakland. I said I would be there within the hour. She was surprised by my vehemence, asking me if it could wait until the next morning when she could squeeze me in for an appointment at her office. I told her no—it had to be right now.

I raced down to Market Street and jumped on a BART train heading to the East Bay, squeezing myself in with the last wave of commuters heading home. At the Rockridge Station, I headed south down College Avenue a couple of blocks, then up Lawton Avenue to the craftsman house that Sylvia and Margo were restoring. Normally, I'd spend a few moments chatting about the latest renovations they'd made, but I couldn't bring myself to talk about that at the moment. Margo met me at the door and was only slightly frosty about the fact that I was delaying their dinner. Sylvia ushered me into the small study that she'd been fixing up for herself. Even before I sat down, she wanted to know what this was all about.

"Look at this video," I said, "and then we can talk."

Sylvia was shocked by what she saw—I knew she would be. After she stopped the video, I could see the wheels clicking in her head, as she began thinking of ways we could act. She told me she'd contact the US attorney first thing in the morning and try to find the right agency to take action. She rattled off a list of alternatives, weighing them and comparing them, trying to settle on a course of action. I wanted her to take all of the legal steps she could, and I knew she would do everything possible. But that wasn't enough.

"I'll move as fast as I can on this," she said. "But it's going to take time."

I knew she'd say that.

"Please try to step back from this and let me handle it."

I knew she'd say that, too.

But I already had my boarding pass printed, and it was sitting right there in my purse.

Alexi

IT WAS HARD TO breathe.

The room felt thick and heavy. It was always like that when he forced her to sit and listen to him. Something got inside her senses and curled them into a knot. The only window in the room was closed and covered with a blackout curtain. The ceiling fixture was on, but that light was so dim that it made the room seem more eerie than it already was. The walls had closed in, and even the chair—the one he insisted she sit in—felt cramped. The ceiling seemed lower each time she looked up. There was a door behind her, but she feared that if she turned around she might find that it was blocked—or gone entirely.

"When I think of the power to God's mercy, I am humbled."

The Reverend Wilder paused for a second before going on any further. He'd begun by talking to her, but he must have known she wasn't listening. Still, he kept talking. He was in some sort of conversation with himself, maybe trying to rehear his own words.

"You have to think about that awesome power, Alexi. Remember that God could destroy us—both of us, all of us—in an instant. He could consign us to eternal damnation just like that." He snapped his fingers, and the sound hovered in the air.

The only real light in the room came from a small desk lamp, which was aimed at the pages of the Bible on his desk.

He'd read from it minutes earlier, and his voice was heavy in the gloominess of the room. He said he wanted her to know what he would be saying in his Sunday sermon the next morning. But she'd given up trying to make sense of anything he said. Months ago—before he had browbeaten her into submission—she'd argued with him and called him a hypocrite. She yelled at him for the nerve of talking about God or sin or salvation. She kept protesting that night, only to let up when she saw the violence in his eyes. Right now she was just as angry, but she knew it was useless to argue. Her fury had been reduced to a lump in the pit of her stomach.

He kept talking, telling about the times in his life he'd sinned and how the Lord had taken him back. She'd heard that story over and over, but he made her sit in the darkness and listen to it again. She didn't know how much of it he really believed. It was a conversation without listeners—something he might have recited even if he had been sitting there alone. He talked about his transgressions and his blasphemous acts, and he'd go on about his lustfulness and the sins of Sodom. He spoke in a twisted Biblical language that made it hard follow what he was saying. At times he'd turn and look at her with moisture in his eyes, choking slightly on his words. *These are my sins, Alexi. I've had to ask God's forgiveness for all of them.* At that moment it was hard not to be moved by the tears streaming down his face.

And then the illusion would be shattered. It might be an offhand remark. Or maybe he would change the tone of his voice to prettify his sins and make them ready for the Lord's forgiveness. At that point she'd feel a growing disgust. He was trying to draw her in with the shock of his revelations, making her feel part of everything he had done. He said that no one knew about these things but her. He hadn't told anyone—least of all her mother. The message was clear: *You're in on this with me. Now that you know all this, you're no better than I am.*

He got out of his chair and walked over to where she was seated.

"Alexi, it's a wonderful thing, God's mercy. You have to keep that thought close to your heart, because the Lord always allows us to cleanse ourselves. We can be restored to his grace."

He put his hand on her shoulder.

"Get your hands off of me!" She leapt from her chair and screamed.

She shuddered at his words. It was the same every time. No matter where he started, he eventually got down to that one word: "we." He'd start talking about his own sinfulness, and within moments he had dragged her into it. It wasn't "him," it was "we." It was we who have sinned, and it was we who need to ask for God's forgiveness.

She yelled at him to let loose of her as she pushed her way past him to the door, busting out of the room and racing down the long hallway to the exit. She leaned on the crash doors, forcing her way out, and started running across the parking lot.

What was she going to do? Every direction she might have turned seemed blocked. A few weeks earlier, when she'd sat in that same dark room having that same dismal conversation with him, she decided she had to do something. She'd leaned across the desk, poking her finger in his direction.

"I've had enough of this. I'm going to tell Mother everything that's been going on."

His blue eyes were icy cold as he stared back at her. "What makes you think she'll believe you?"

That caught her for a second. The stare continued.

"And if she does believe you, who do you think she'll blame?"

◆◆◆

"ALEXI, WHAT WOULD YOU like for dinner?"

Her mother was rustling in the kitchen, using her most soothing voice.

"Your father's meeting with the foundation people, so it's just the two of us. Think of something you'd like. Afterward, we can make some cookies."

Those words deepened her sadness. She hated the meanness of the thought, but she wondered if there was there was anything her mother didn't think could be solved by a plate of cookies. The thing she was doing right now was so well-meaning—and so clueless—that it almost made her cry.

Things hadn't gone well between them since the Sunday services that morning. But it wasn't much worse than it had been for a long time. Her mother tried to do everything right, but it was still all wrong. Their chances to talk would stretch out for hours, but the gap was never bridged. Why was it like that? Her mother had a teacher's degree from Purdue, and her former students loved her. When she worked with young school kids around the church going over their lessons, she got the same happy response. She led groups of volunteers to retirement homes, bringing snacks and gifts, and she would sit there and listen to the bedridden patients. They'd grab her hand and refuse to let go. Many of them said she was the only one who had listened to them in years.

But where was that woman around here? Her mother blamed all their problems on the decision to tell her she was adopted. She was angry at herself afterward for doing so, saying she should have followed her husband's advice. Her mother was right about one thing: that information had burst open a well of anger that had been building up for years. From then on he became just her mother's husband, and she would only call him "the reverend"—never her father. Her mother was upset with her for doing that, but would it open her eyes? It hadn't so far. Maybe she was secretly worried that Alexi would do the same thing to her—start calling her by a different name. But as angry as she was, she could never do that.

When she thought about the ugly thing that had taken over her life, she couldn't even put it into words. Giving it a name would make it worse. She couldn't tell anyone—not even her friends. When she got close to saying anything, she would shy away, hinting only that she was unhappy. She had a friend, Laura, who knew she was miserable, but she only knew that she was having a problem with her parents. The secret was too scummy and dirty to talk about. She was sure she'd be ostracized if anyone knew.

Maybe we can make some cookies.

Her mother always wanted to calm things down at home and push aside anything unpleasant. Keeping the family together was her biggest goal, but why couldn't she see the terrible things going on in her own house—things happening right in front of her? Did it have to be forced upon her? Did someone have to sit her down and tell her all the things that had been happening until the ugliness of it finally got through to her? She knew she couldn't do it. She hoped and prayed that her mother would find out about it some other way and put a stop to it, but she couldn't tell her. The horror on her mother's face if she tried to describe the sordid story would have been more than she could bear.

But her mother lived in the same house. She had eyes. Some hint of it had to be somewhere in a part of her brain. On those nights when her mother was lying there by herself, didn't the thought ever spring loose and race around the room?

◆◆◆

SHE HALF-SAT, HALF-SPRAWLED ON the living room couch, where she'd been sitting most of the afternoon, surrounded by a comforter that she'd dragged from her bedroom. She tucked the blanket around her legs, as she felt suddenly chilled. Her phone was in the folds of the blanket, and she picked it up and fiddled with it, experimenting with the video camera just to take her mind off of things. Her journal was next to her. There were things she needed to write, but that could wait until her mother had gone to bed. She'd already filled a couple journals and stuffed them into the side pocket of the guitar case in her closet. She had to do something with them eventually, but right now she just needed to keep writing.

She'd slept on the couch the night before, but she didn't know if her mother knew that. She'd snuck out of her bedroom just after her mother had turned out the lights and found a place to curl up. The couch, which was a gift from one of their congregants, wasn't very comfortable, but she decided to sleep on it again because it felt safer. The middle of their wide-open living room seemed more secure to her than her own corner of the house. She'd hinted about that, but her mother hadn't picked up on the fact that she'd become terrified of her own bedroom.

The living room was quiet after her mother went to bed. The only light was a low glow from the lamp behind the couch. Around midnight, she heard the door open from the garage into the kitchen, and that was followed by someone opening and closing the refrigerator. The reverend was home. He paced around the kitchen for a few minutes, and then she heard him walking down the hall toward the bedrooms. She heard the door to the master bedroom being opened and then gently closed again. After that, she heard him walking farther to the back of the house where she had her own bedroom. There was another faint sound of a door being opened and then closed. A few seconds later, she heard him doubling back down the darkened hallway. Then the footsteps stopped. He must have been standing in the dark at the end of the hall, hidden in the shadows, looking into the living room where she was huddled on the couch. She didn't dare look up. It stayed that way for several moments as the room started to feel smaller and smaller.

She finally sensed that he was gone. She wrapped the comforter around herself tightly, reaching around for whatever she could find. She was scared to be alone at the moment. She found her phone and started scrolling through it aimlessly. There was an email message she'd missed earlier. It was from a woman she didn't know—or, at least, she didn't think she knew. She read it quickly, but her nerves were so frazzled she found it hard to focus. The woman said she'd seen her at the morning church services. That set off alarm bells in her head. She remembered how angry she had been at the moment the woman described. This woman had apparently seen her in all her anguish, and everyone else had probably seen her, too.

She put down the phone and stared into the darkness. She wanted her nightmare to be over, but it seemed now like it could be getting worse. What if the whole world found out? She had screamed out in anger whenever the reverend said that she—like him—needed to ask forgiveness for her sins, implying that the stain of everything had rubbed off on her. He'd even put himself on a higher plane by saying he had asked forgiveness for his sins while she was still wallowing in the evil of hers. He warned her of that. He said people would say she was the sinful one because she hadn't confessed. She knew he had to be wrong, but would people believe her? Or would they just point their fingers at her and say she brought this all on herself? Was this email just the first step in an endless trail of humiliation?

She sat there for a few minutes, trying to fight her depression. She picked up her cell phone and read the message again, but this time she saw some things that she'd missed when she raced through it the first time. What was this woman really saying? She mentioned something about knowing her in the past. When was that? She had assumed the worst when she first read the message, but now she realized the woman was being much more sympathetic. She stared at the words at the end of the message: "I'm here, if you ever need my help."

She felt a whisper of hope. "Help"—she hadn't dared think of that word.

The words had come from a complete stranger, but still she could feel the power of them flowing through her. She had a dizzy, momentary feeling that things might get better. She didn't know if this woman could really do anything to help her, but for the moment her doubts were pushed aside, as the thought of being done with all this raced through her mind. Suddenly, she could visualize herself on the other side of her pain, looking back as her shame and degradation receded into the background.

She hit the reply menu, but she found herself just staring at the screen, too scared to go any further. What would she say? How could she explain what was going on without making herself sound terrible or pathetic? And maybe none of this was real—maybe this woman didn't mean what she said. Her reply could go nowhere, bringing her newfound hope to an end. She typed a few words, but her hands were shaking too much. She finally cancelled the reply page and sat back to think about what she should do.

And then suddenly it was morning, and the light was coming through the living room window. She'd fallen asleep on the couch with her cell phone still in her hand. Last night she had thought about staying home on Monday and skipping school, but that was before she got the email message. Now, she was energized. She read the message one more time, hoping that it wasn't just a dream. It was still there. She thought all day about how to reply to the woman's email. She had to do it right. The safest way was to move slowly, starting with an exchange between them that she could build on when she was sure she trusted her. Between classes, she hinted about the message to her friend, Laura, but she knew it had to be her secret.

When she got home from school, her mother was in the kitchen, cooking something for dinner. She took a step into the living room but then stopped in her tracks. The pit of her stomach started to drop, and she was afraid she'd fall down. She must have let out a gasp.

"What's the matter, honey?"

Her mother hurried in from the kitchen.

"Oh, I'm sorry. I should have warned you that the couch is gone. Your father called the people at the furniture store this morning, and he talked to that nice Mr. Lewis—you know, the man from the congregation that sent us the couch in the first place? Well, he's arranged for an even better one to be delivered to us from the factory early next week."

She just stared.

Her mother seemed surprised.

"I didn't think you even liked that old couch. I've seen pictures of the new one. It's so much nicer. It's a beautiful, soft gold—you're going to love it. Your father said they needed to pick up the old one this morning, but I said that's okay. This way we'll have a few days to clean the room and get everything ready.

"Are you okay?" her mother asked.

She wasn't okay—she didn't know if she ever would be okay. The reverend was everywhere in that empty room. He was sending her a message, displaying his power in a way she wouldn't be able to miss. He'd hollowed out that room in the same way he had hollowed out her soul. He'd keep doing that, she knew, because no one could stop him. The plan she'd worked on all day now seemed hopelessly inadequate. It was replaced in her head by a sense of desperation.

◆◆◆

WHEN DID IT BEGIN?

She tried to remember the first time she knew something was wrong. She couldn't pinpoint it exactly. She was around twelve when she finally realized it was something bad, but the things that led up to it started earlier. Nothing happened quickly—one thing just led to the next thing. At first, it was just the tickling—a small thing. *Please stop!* She remembered laughing about it when she was younger, telling him to stop even while she was thinking that it was enjoyable. *Please stop!* In those early days she didn't really want him to stop even when she told him so.

Please stop!

But at some point things changed. He was doing something different. Even something as simple as a backrub left gave her a queasy feeling. *Please stop!* As she got older, she was becoming more sensitive to her body. *Please stop!* She wanted him to stop, because he was hurting her—not in the way a skinned knee would hurt, but somewhere deeper inside her. *Please stop! Daddy, don't do that.*

But he didn't stop, and he acted like he didn't believe a word she said. He laughed at her protests, and he continued laughing even over her tears, making light of whatever she said. At some point he no longer bothered to laugh or even acknowledge what she was saying. Each new thing he was doing seemed to justify in his mind the next new thing, until finally they ended up with the biggest thing of all.

She stared at the door to her bedroom, bringing herself back into the present moment. It always started with a slow turn of the handle, letting her know that he was on the other side ready to ease the door open and tiptoe his way into her room. She always thought that her mother must be in their bedroom asleep, somehow unaware that her husband wasn't lying at her side. But she didn't know that for sure. Her mother's name was never mentioned.

She waited now for that door handle to turn, as she knew it would. After the couch—her nightly refuge—had disappeared from the living room, it was inevitable that he would be making the walk down the hallway toward her room and turning that door handle. She once tried locking that door when she went to bed, but when she came home from school the next day she found that the locking mechanism had been dismantled. There was no way to keep him out. Once he was inside, he had something that he managed to stick between the door and the frame that apparently kept the door from being opened by anyone else from the other side. He'd figured it all out. There was no way to stop him from coming into the room, and once he was inside no one could follow him.

She was in bed with the lights off except for one small lamp on the nightstand between her bed and the wall. She needed to keep that light on at a soft, subdued level no matter what he said. At the base of the lamp sat her cell phone, propped up on its side, facing in a direction she had worked out earlier. She checked it again to make sure it was in the right position, feeling around the back once again for the little red button. That button gave a telltale ping whenever you pushed it, so she knew she'd have to do it the minute she saw the door handle moving and before he was inside the room. Then she would have to lie down and wait, but she wouldn't have to wait long.

The door handle turned, and he quickly moved inside the room, shutting the door behind him. He walked over and sat down on the bed, reaching through the covers to massage her back. She heard him muttering something to himself.

"Baby, I've looked forward to this all day, do you know that? Do you know how much I need you? You must know that."

He was talking fast, speaking in a breathy, anxious whisper. She tried to get away from the hand that was massaging her, but he leaned over even farther. "Don't try to hold back."

Suddenly, he was back on his feet, unbuttoning his shirt and ripping off his clothes. Within seconds he was in her bed, pushing himself up against her, urging her to turn over.

"Daddy, don't do that!"

Calling him "Daddy" just added to the misery of the moment. But she had to do it. She had to say it no matter how sick it made her feel. Anyone seeing the video would have to know.

"Please get out of my bed."

"Just be quiet."

"You shouldn't be here."

She refused to turn over, as he kept forcing himself against her. She kept looking at the wall, toward the lamp, and toward the little white spot on the cell phone.

"Please don't."

PART THREE

Gina

IT WAS THE SAME trip I'd taken a few days earlier, but my mood was much darker.

The idea that Alexi might be suffering abuse at that moment made every small delay intolerable. I fumed at the security lines, the baggage checks, the departure delays, and everything else until I finally convinced myself that I wasn't going to make things go any faster. I just had to get there the best way I could. That video had torn me apart—I couldn't even imagine how miserable Alexi felt.

When I got her message, I was online immediately buying a ticket to fly back to the Midwest. I didn't think twice about it—I'm not sure I even thought once. My fingers propelled themselves across the keyboard, while my brain was still trying to catch up and develop a plan. The flight left at 5:00 a.m. That was fine—the earlier the better. I wasn't sure what I would do when I got there. I just knew I had to see her. What happened then would be decided when we had a chance to talk face-to-face.

We connected by email as I was getting ready to go and then later at the airport, but I knew she felt uneasy communicating that way. I had burst in upon her life out of nowhere. But though she didn't know me at all, she was at a point where she needed to trust me with her darkest secrets. It was the kind of pressure situation that would generate enormous tension for anyone—particularly a teenager. I could sense the conflict going on inside her with every sentence she wrote.

I was almost as uncomfortable as she was. I had no idea how secure her email was, and I was worried that others might have access to it. If our communications had gotten into the hands of others, it could have been disastrous. I worried about phone calls and text messages as well. I found an anonymous cell phone that I had purchased months earlier, but even with that device I felt skittish. I knew I would have to phone her or text her as I got to close to confirming when and where we would meet, but I didn't know what kind of privacy she had on her end. I was leery about trying to talk to her for any length of time. But I decided I had to phone her at least once. Everything seemed better after I heard her voice, and I was able to reassure her that it was going to be okay. I think she felt relieved talking to me.

There were all kinds of things we needed to say to each other—a lifetime of them, in fact. But most would have to wait. There were things I couldn't tell her until we were face-to-face. But despite the fact that she knew almost nothing about me, she seemed willing to trust me. At that point, it seemed clear that she didn't want to talk about what had happened with the reverend. She just wanted to get away from him.

Rather than fly directly to Indianapolis, I decided to fly again to O'Hare Airport in Chicago and follow the route I'd taken earlier. Although that meant I had to drive from Chicago to Indianapolis, I thought it might take less time overall because I wouldn't have to wait around to change planes. But there was another reason. I wanted to be as invisible as I could. Until I was sure of my plan and what

I was going to do, I didn't want to wave any red flags. I didn't know what would happen. But if someone started searching for a mysterious out-of-town stranger who was there to help Alexi, the first place they would look was for someone who'd flown in and out of the Indianapolis Airport.

Despite all the back and forth in my mind, there was still a possibility that I might not do much of anything at all. Certainly, Sylvia would be happier if it worked out that way. She'd been following me with text messages, trying to talk some sense into me ever since I left home. Maybe I would get to Indianapolis, find Alexi some help, and then head back to San Francisco. But it didn't feel that way. When I said to Alexi that I might be able to work out something with her mother that would get the reverend out of her life, she didn't respond. When I repeated it, she answered with an anguished "no." It was the first sign of anger I'd seen from her. That made me realize I was probably kidding myself about the extent of what I had offered to do. I had promised to help, and she was clinging to that promise like a life raft.

◆ ◆ ◆

THE FUTURE WAS GOING to be painful for Alexi no matter what happened. Getting her away from the reverend and his sexual abuse was the overwhelming priority, but what happens after that? Would her family split up? Would she go live somewhere else? Would it be handled quietly, or would the reverend be prosecuted? And what would happen to Alexi if the scandal became a TV spectacle? It could go viral and career around the Internet. Alexi's psychological health might teeter on the edge, but would anyone pay attention to that? Would she just be trampled in the rush of an ongoing news story? The thought made me shudder. No matter what—Alexi's life was about to change drastically. And it wasn't just her life. As the miles rolled by, the life I'd been living was rolling away with them. I'd offered to help Alexi, and she'd grabbed it. I couldn't go back now even if I wanted to. But the life I'd led as a bookseller for the past decade was about to be altered—maybe radically. I could feel myself changing as I began sensing what it was like to have someone else in your life that you needed to think about. She was a part of my past, and I was beginning to realize she was also a big part of my future.

My memories wandered back to the time when she was still baby Jelena. The family was in hiding, and I was hiding with them. It was a tense time for everyone. My being there put the others at even greater risk, but still they welcomed me. The only one who wasn't living in fear at that moment was the precious infant in our midst. It was her unbounded joy that kept all of us going. For me, it was like a budding love affair. Each afternoon I'd tiptoe quietly into the room in the tiny back building where she slept. I'd wait until I could hear her stirring and see her movements through the sides of the crib. Then, it became a game. I would sneak over to the tiny bed and stop just at the point where she could see me. Then, I'd wait for her to recognize me. She'd begin to smile and wiggle, getting more and more excited as I made silly faces. She'd be lying on her back with all four limbs moving in different directions, looking wildly into the air as she waited for me to pick her up. Once she was in my arms, she would make some baby noises, sometimes a small burp, and then nestle her head against my shoulder.

Those were memories to be cherished, but would they survive any of this? I wondered what my relationship with

Alexi would be. Would it be anything like the love there was in that tiny house in Bosnia fifteen years earlier? There was so much to tell her. There were years of overlapping stories that branched in every direction, and each facet of that history demanded to be told first. They were the kinds of stories that should be unfolded gradually over a friendly meal, with the patience and care that come after a long period of trust. But we didn't have time for any of that. I would have to unload the whole story on her in one surprising, confusing, and— probably—shocking narrative.

◆◆◆

I GOT TO THE mall at Keystone Crossing several minutes before Alexi and I were scheduled to meet. It was the only place I could think of to tell her, since I'd stayed there less than a week earlier. I told her to stand in front of the Cheesecake Factory, thinking she'd blend in like any teenager who'd been shopping at the mall and waiting for a parent to come by and pick her up. But I didn't want her standing at the curb very long. I had no idea how many security guards or cameras there were in the shopping center or what they might be looking for. It was better that I circle the parking lot a few times instead of her standing there drawing attention. But after I did that a few times, I decided maybe my constant circling of the parking area might also be drawing attention. I decided to pull into an empty parking place and just wait.

As soon as I turned off the engine, my cell phone rang. I thought it might be Alexi. If not her, it was probably Sylvia with one more warning. But I was wrong. It was Paolo.

He must have heard how flustered I was when I heard his voice on the phone. He started to protest that it had been my idea that he should call me if he found out any more news.

If I wanted to hang up and call him back later, he said that was all right with him.

"I'm sorry, Paolo. I didn't mean to bite at you. We can talk now."

The truth is I did want to hang up. I didn't want to think about what he had to say. Alexi's problem had shoved everything else out of my mind, and I hadn't even thought about those who might be pursuing me. Paolo's call was a rude jolt, telling me I had more than one thing to worry about.

"I talked to Luca."

I didn't like the sound of his voice. "What did he say?"

Paolo hesitated for a second, probably worried that he was about to make me upset. "The people who contacted him were looking for you. They knew the name you used—'Gina Bertani.'"

As he said it, I could see the name in bold type on all of the paperwork we filed to get me into the United States. The top document said "Gina Bertani is a resident of…" right under that was another one that read "Gina Bertani was born in…" Those documents and all the others in that stack were false. Paolo knew that as well as I did—he's the one who made them up. But false or not, they would lead to me.

"What else did they say? Did Luca tell them where I was?"

"No," Paolo said quickly. "He hasn't thought about you in years. He didn't tell them anything—he didn't even know where you were."

There was a word there I didn't like. "He 'didn't' know, but he definitely knows now?"

There was silence on the other end of the line. Finally, Paolo knew he had to say something.

"The people talking to him acted like they already knew you were in America."

That news curdled in my stomach and threatened to force its way up my throat. I finally regained my bearings and began hammering him with questions. At the same time, I kept checking my watch to make sure I wasn't late in picking up Alexi. Her problems and my problems were starting to whirl around in overlapping waves.

Paolo kept trying to reassure me. He swore he didn't know anything more than what he had just told me. As far as he could tell, my pursuers probably didn't know anything more than the fact that I'd left Italy over a decade ago. Since I only began using the name "Gina Perini" after I landed in the United States, Paolo was sure they had no hint about that name or anything else. He kept telling me that I had nothing to worry about. As long as I was Gina Perini, living in San Francisco as a bookseller, I would be safe. All of that might be true, I suppose, as long as Paolo could believe Luca, and I could believe Paolo—and I could get over the fear that the ground had just shifted underneath me.

My pursuers had breached an important barrier—I had to face it. They now knew what they were looking for, and it was something different than what they had originally thought. When I made the transition to the life I have now, I did so for my own emotional well-being. When I became Gina, I became myself. I didn't do it to escape anyone—that kind of reasoning would never have entered into such an important, personal decision. But later on I realized that the change I had gone through might end up being a form of protection. My looks, my mannerisms, my attitudes— everything about me had changed to the point where anyone who knew me earlier would be unlikely to recognize me as

I am now. At the time, that included my enemies. But all of that was over. I knew I was Gina, and so did they.

◆ ◆ ◆

I FINALLY FOUND ALEXI standing at the curb, but I was few minutes late. My call with Paolo had thrown everything off. She had her backpack over her shoulder, looking a little scared, maybe wondering if I was going to show up at all. She was peering at each of the passing cars, probably trying to guess if any of them were mine. I pulled up to the curb and reached over to open the passenger-side door. I'd been rehearsing what to say when I actually met her for the first time—something about our relationship and about all that had happened. But with all of the delays and worries floating around my head, I forgot all of it. I mumbled something clumsy about putting her backpack in the back seat.

I drove out of the parking lot, turning onto North Keystone Avenue. The next entrance put me on Interstate 465, the ring-road around Indianapolis. I wanted to get out of that area as quickly as I could and get to some place where we could talk. I took a quick glance at the rearview mirror, but I wasn't sure what I was looking for. I was hoping that nobody was following Alexi. And after talking to Paolo, I was hoping no one was following me.

As I turned back, I saw Alexi looking up at me.

Suddenly, I felt a pounding in my heart. I was looking at the anguished eyes of a teenage girl, but it was something more than just that. I'd seen a pair of eyes just like those many years before. And at the time, they were looking up at me in a moment of panic for both of us.

Davey

HE WANTED TO SLEEP, but he couldn't. The clock said 4:15 a.m., and he swore to himself as he trudged off to the bathroom to pee. After he'd been back in bed a few minutes, there was a more ominous sign—a feeling of pain in his chest, along with a deep steady pull that had him almost anchored him to the mattress.

He tried to stifle his fright. He had nitroglycerin pills in his night stand that his cardiologist had prescribed in case this happened. He fumbled in the dark for the tiny bottle and finally managed to get one of the pills under his tongue. He was supposed to hold it there for five minutes. If the pain didn't go away, he was to take a second pill and repeat the process. If the pain continued after that, he's have to take a third pill and dial 911—he would need help from the EMTs. They'd probably put him on a stretcher for a ride to the emergency room.

As the seconds clicked by on the clock, his worries started to grow. If he had to call the EMTs, he'd somehow have to get downstairs to open the apartment door to let them in. But if there was a heart attack lurking in his chest, that kind of movement would make it worse. It was either that or lie there, listening to them batter their way through the door and the security locks to get to him. Being alone made everything worse. But no one wanted to share that tiny townhouse with him—let alone share a bed. He dreaded the idea of going to the hospital alone, but he couldn't think of anyone to call.

Robin had been with him last year when he had the heart attack, but he couldn't call her again. That was all over. At the time, they'd been lying in her bed in the early stages of trying to make love when he recognized the symptoms—excessive sweating, abnormal breathing, pains in his chest. He didn't want to admit what was going on. But Robin finally saw the symptoms herself, and she called 911. She'd probably saved his life.

They'd been drinking and playing around all evening before that, nuzzling a little while she was cooking, making suggestive comments about how the evening would go later on. But the times before that hadn't worked out so well. When they'd gotten into bed on their last few dates, nothing much had happened. He worried that it had become a pattern. He didn't know if it was him, or her…or whether it was him reacting to her, or what the hell was going on. She didn't say she was unhappy, but he figured she must have been. He wasn't getting hard and staying hard, so on the way over he grabbed something out of the back of his medicine cabinet that he hadn't used in months.

When the EMTs rolled him into the ambulance, Robin talked her way into the back with him. As the ambulance moved out of the parking lot, the medic wrapped a blood pressure cuff around one arm and placed an IV in the other. He ran through a list of questions, trying to get what information he could on the way into the emergency room. When the question got to medications—he knew he had to tell him. After he named the drug, the medic reacted in surprise.

"That's a pretty strong ED drug to use in a dosage like that, given your medical history. Does your doctor know you were taking it?"

He didn't—and neither did Robin. Robin didn't want him to use it, so he'd taken it without telling her. He could see the look on her face. If he survived that night, he knew he'd hear about it later.

Five minutes had gone by. Was this another attack or just a false alarm? The pain and the pressure in his chest hadn't gone away, so he slipped a second nitro pill under his tongue and waited.

After he was released from the hospital, he went by Robin's apartment to pick up the things that had been left there. His shirt, jacket, and trousers had been folded and placed in a shopping bag, along with his underwear, which Robin had washed for him. She hadn't touched the shoulder holster and the gun, which were still lying where he'd left them a week earlier. She made it clear that he couldn't get his stuff out of her apartment fast enough to suit her.

He'd expected her to yell at him, but what she did was worse: she calmly took the empty space inside him and dissected it in front of him. It wasn't the pills, she said. It wasn't a question of whether he was hard or soft, fast or slow, orgasmic or flaccid—it was him. He had no sense of how to reach out and be warm and loving with another person. With him, it was all mechanical—just get the fluid pumping through the pipe and be done with it. Life wasn't that way, she said, her calm voice starting to crack a little. She didn't know why he wanted to be with her at all, since he showed so little feeling of true intimacy.

He wanted to object. He wanted to say that he was really a loving person who kept tripping over himself—that he just needed to work harder to understand what she wanted. But it was useless. Their relationship was over. ED pills or no ED pills, he would never be sleeping with her again. In fact, he hadn't slept with anyone since then. Sometimes he wondered if he ever would.

At the three-minute mark on the second pill, the pain and the pressure started to subside. It was gone a few seconds later, and he wouldn't need take the next pill or call the EMTs. But the pills had left him exhausted. He closed his eyes for a second.

The phone rang a little after 8:00 a.m. He'd fallen into a deep sleep after his bout with the nitroglycerin pills, and he tried to clear his head to find out who was on the phone. It was Susan Wilder.

"Mr. Fallon, I hate to disturb you this early, but I don't know where else to turn."

"What's the matter?" He could hear the tears in her voice.

"It's Alexi. She's gone missing. I've been worried about it all night. I know you used to be an investigator, and… I just thought maybe you could help."

"When did it happen?"

"Yesterday evening. I got a text message from her cell phone."

Gina

I KNEW IN THE back of my mind that Alexi would be coming with me, but still we needed to talk.

Once we were far enough away from the pickup point, I planned to stop, pull the car over, and discuss what would come next. It was important to explain to her all of the options she had and to talk them through. She had to be clear on whatever we decided to do. I knew that was the right thing to do, but I was fighting myself on it at every step. My instinct was just to take her and run.

One thing was pretty clear: Alexi had no desire to talk about the sexual abuse she endured from the reverend. I'm sure it was occupying a big part of her mind—I knew I couldn't get it out of *my* head—but every time I got close to discussing it, she steered the conversation in another direction. I decided that was probably healthy. There would be time enough later for the lawyers and the psychologists to find out what had happened. Maybe by then it would be a less painful for her to discuss it. The reverend's name did come up, however, but mostly because she was worried about his power to control things. As we drove, she started to loosen up a bit, but her fear of him wasn't far beneath the surface.

There were some practical questions we had to deal with. Did she get away from the house without anyone knowing where she was going? Alexi nodded yes. How about clothes—was she able to stick a few extra things in her backpack? She did. I glanced over at her a couple of times as I was driving, and I could see her stealing quick looks back at me, not knowing if she should do much more than that. She might not have been exactly sure what she was seeing. A lot of people have that reaction when they look at me the first time, so I'm used to it. She was nervous—who *wouldn't* be nervous in that situation? I was a little shaky myself, but everything depended on my keeping my wits about me.

We reached Interstate 70 near the southwest part of the city, and I turned west and took the exit that led to the parking lot for the Indianapolis International Airport. I wasn't planning to fly anywhere, but if someone was tracking our movements, it might not be a bad idea for them to think that we were getting on a plane. I pulled into a small turnout about a hundred feet or so before the parking lot entrance and turned off the ignition. Then I twisted around in the driver's seat to get a better look at her.

She was beautiful. It was more than just the eyes—although I was still startled by them. Before this, my only memory of her was as an infant, beaming like a ray of hope in a tiny village. She was a gorgeous baby with a big smile. I could sense that the same smile was still there, but it was below the surface, looking for a reason to emerge. There was a sense of wariness on her face. I knew she wanted to ask me a lot of things, but she didn't quite know how to go about it. I'd been putting off telling her the whole story until we could sit down and really talk, because I wasn't quite ready for that at the moment. She was calm about how things had gone so far, but I could tell she was still sitting on a lot of uncertainty.

We had to talk about what we were going to do next. I assured her that I would *not* leave her there in the control of the man who was abusing her—that was out of the question. But what were the alternatives? She sat there looking at me like I had all the answers. I wasn't sure I did.

"Alexi, we have to decide what to do. I could contact your mother and tell her you're with me. We should think seriously about that. I would do the talking and try to explain to her everything that's happened."

Alexi got a stricken look on her face, and I could see tears in her eyes. "Please don't do that."

"I'm only saying that because it might be the right thing to do. It could be the easiest for everyone."

"Don't," she implored. "She'll never stand up to him."

"Okay," I said, trying to reassure her. "Don't worry. I won't do that unless you want me to."

She wiped away the tears, nodding that she understood. We talked a little bit about her mother, but she wasn't comfortable with the conversation.

"Another thing I could do is drive you right now to the Indiana Child Protective Services, and we could file a report with them. They have an office just south of where I picked you up."

"What would happen? Would you be able to tell them what to do?"

"Probably, not. They have their own staff for that, but I could help you fill out the complaint and tell them what I know."

"Would I have to go back to…to that house?"

"I'm not sure. They might want you to do that. I don't know what their procedure is in this kind of situation.

I'm sure they would do an investigation, but I don't know what happens while that's going on."

"I can't do that." She shook her head and kept repeating the same thing. "I can't do that."

"We have to do what's best for you."

It was just a phrase that came out of my mouth. Of course it was the truth, but in this situation it didn't mean anything at all. It was just a bunch of words that hung out there in midair, ready to fall of their own weight. I knew what was coming next.

"Can't I just stay with you?" Her eyes were pleading with me now. "Maybe, for a little while at least?"

"Alexi, I'm not going to let you down."

She was staring at me, her eyes watery.

"But you don't even know me."

She just kept staring.

As I was getting on the airplane in San Francisco, I knew in my heart it would probably work out this way. Over the last few days, Alexi had gathered together all the energy she had to contact me and then to meet me. It was a huge step that took an enormous amount of courage. Now she was spent. She wasn't ready for any more risks or difficult decisions. She was leaving it up to me. I wished there were an alternative, but I couldn't see it.

Sylvia knew me well enough to know what I would probably end up doing. There was a text from her when I got off the plane. "*Gina, it's not going to work. Don't try it.*" There was another, longer text a few minutes later in which she talked about the FBI and taking minors across state lines. I couldn't bear to think about it. The only thing I could see now was Alexi pleading with me to help.

"Alexi, I live in California. That's a long way from here."

That may have fazed her a little but not for long. She seemed determined to stay with me no matter where I lived. I looked at her for several long seconds.

"Okay. If you're coming with me, then we need to get going."

She gave a slight smile when I said that.

"But you have to remember this is only temporary. At some point, after we've talked to the lawyers and the counselors, we will have to be back in touch with your family—at least your mother. This has to be resolved in the right way."

She nodded okay. She may or may not have understood what I was talking about when I elaborated on what I knew about the legal procedures and all the things that had to be resolved. None of that had much impact on her. As long as I wasn't going to abandon her, she seemed willing to do whatever I asked.

"First, I need to see your phone." As she handed it to me, I asked her for her mother's cell phone number. As she gave it to me, I could see the questions on her face.

"I know you don't want to hurt your mother..." The alarmed look in her eyes told me I was right. "So we need to let her know that you haven't been kidnapped, or, in an accident, or something like that. Is that all right?"

She nodded yes. She waited as I typed in a message:

Mom

I have to go away for a few days, and I don't want you to be worried. I'm safe, and I will contact you as soon as I feel that

*I can. Please don't try to reach me. If you want to know why
I left, you should talk to Dad.*

Love, Alexi

"You want to write it just like that?" she asked.

"Is there something you want to change?"

Alexi nodded. "The last line—I never call him Dad, and
she knows it." She stared out the window, maybe staring into
her own thoughts. "If I were to write it that way, she wouldn't
think it was from me."

"How about if I change the wording to 'your husband?'"

She thought about that for a second and nodded yes.
I modified the wording of the message and looked at it again
to make sure I hadn't left anything out. Then I pushed the send
button. There was a slight whoosh, and the message jumped
up to the sent portion of the screen. I saw the serious look on
her face. We both knew then that there was no going back.

If Alexi hadn't already known the seriousness of what we
doing, she would have realized it after seeing what I did next.
We needed to cut off communication—at least temporarily.
I opened the cover of her phone and removed the batteries.
I stuffed them in my pocket. I'm no expert on cell phones,
but I know they give off a signal that can be traced whether
the phone is on or not. I didn't know how soon anyone would
try to find us, but probably the first thing they'd do is look
for the cell phone's signal. I didn't want her phone leaving
behind a little trail of electronic breadcrumbs.

◆ ◆ ◆

I STARTED THE ENGINE and pulled back on to the freeway,
heading west on Interstate 70, hoping that we could get as

close to Kansas City as possible before we'd have to find a place to stay for the night. The drive was long and tedious. After we left Indiana, we headed west across southern Illinois in the direction of St. Louis and the Mississippi River. We crossed the river without any fanfare and stayed on the freeway that skirted St. Louis; from then on it was just a straight line west across the width of Missouri. The rolling farmlands didn't change very much. But with the sun in my eyes and a lifetime of thoughts that were about to spill out of my head, I didn't pay much attention to the scenery.

I'd gone over what I wanted to say to Alexi and how I wanted to say it. I needed to tell her about me, about her, and about everything that had thrown us together. But it wasn't going to be easy. There was no logical starting point— no way to get from here to there along a nice straight path. Nothing I said would make sense without me explaining something else first, and the likelihood was that it would all come out in one big, incomprehensible rush. I talked a little bit as we drove, not saying much, probably frustrating her by focusing on little things.

We had just passed Columbia, Missouri. I was hungry and tired, and I guessed Alexi was too. I began looking for places to stay, eyeing a few of the chain motels that started appearing along the side of the highway. I wasn't sure which one to pick. I sensed that Alexi was getting anxious.

"Gina, can I ask you a question?"

"Of course." I glanced at her and saw that she was all seriousness.

"Are you my real mother?"

I was glad I had a good grip on the wheel because otherwise we might have had an accident.

We were near an exit with a hotel a few hundred feet up the frontage road, so I moved quickly into the right lane and turned off the freeway. I pulled into the parking lot without paying much attention to the name on the sign. It was just a place to stop. We would check into the room and then go to the little restaurant next door. We needed to get a booth—hopefully somewhere away from the other patrons.

"Alexi, after we sit down, we can talk."

Davey

"I'M JUST SO WORRIED."

Those were the first words out of her mouth as he walked through the door. It was about an hour after she called, but she hadn't calmed down at all.

"Does your husband know about this?"

"Yes. I think he's down there talking to Mr. Blaiseck right now—at least, that's what he says he's doing. He told me not to worry, because they would handle it. But I'm scared—I don't know what's going on. I asked if they'd called the police, and he just sort of brushed me aside. Davey, I don't know what to do!"

"You did the right thing to call me."

Her eyes were red from crying. He hoped she'd had a chance to think things through—maybe even figure out why it had happened. She was still as upset as she was earlier, but a touch of wariness had crept into her voice. She welcomed him into kitchen and poured him a cup of coffee. He asked her to tell him everything, starting at the beginning.

Susan stopped for a second to focus her thoughts.

"I got a text message last evening from Alexi, saying that she wasn't coming home and asking me not to try and find her. I was shocked when I saw it—I still am."

He nodded. He could see how hard it must have hit her.

"I was so upset, that I didn't notice the time on the message until later. It looks like it was sent at eleven forty a.m., but I didn't check my phone until around seven when I was fixing dinner. The only reason I looked then was because Alexi wasn't home."

"Do you know where she was supposed to be at the time she sent it?"

"No, I'm not sure."

"Did you try to reply to the message?"

"I did, but the message didn't go through. After a few moments, I got an error message back saying that the phone was 'not in service at this time.'"

Susan looked at him, scared. "Do you think it was really Alexi using the phone? I mean, someone could have grabbed her and forced her to write that."

He tried to reassure her. "I doubt that's what happened."

Was she overreacting to Alexi's disappearance? Probably. Most likely it was the case of a runaway child, and it would probably end—like most such cases do—with the child returning home. But Susan seemed to be caught up in the feeling that it was something worse. She could be right. And there wasn't much he could do at the moment to shake her out of that mood.

"Did you check her room? Was anything missing— maybe her clothes, her suitcase or anything like that?"

"As far as I could see, everything's still there. I can't say for sure. Most of her clothes are still in her closet and dresser, but there might be a couple of things gone. I wouldn't know unless I went through all the hampers and yesterday's wash."

"How about her toothbrush or anything personal?"

"There was a toothbrush there, but I think she may have more than one. Oh, I don't know…"

She suddenly blurted out in anger.

"I'm so mad at them! I wanted him to call the police. But the minute we realized what happened, Allen had Mr. Blaiseck on the phone, and they were talking among themselves, making all the decisions about what they were going to do. When Blaseck came over here, they couldn't get me out of the room fast enough. I probably should have called you right then."

But as quickly as it started, her anger calmed down.

"Oh, don't pay any attention to any of that. I'm just upset. I know we're all trying to do what we can to get her back. I just feel so helpless."

There was still some bitterness in her mood. But there was something else—a sense that life might be slipping out of her grasp and she had no way to get it back. When she wasn't flashing her anger, she gave the appearance of being on the edge of defeat.

"Can I look at the message?"

She handed him a piece of paper. "It's still on the phone, if you want to see it. But I copied it down word for word."

Mom

I have to go away for a few days, and I don't want you to be worried. I'm safe, and I will contact you as soon as I feel that I can. Please don't try to reach me. If you want to know why I left, you should talk to your husband.

Love, Alexi

"Do you have any thought about where she might have been headed? She seems to be saying that she knows someplace safe. Do you know what she means?"

"I have no idea. I can't think of any place she might be talking about."

"How about the last sentence—the phrase where she says, 'You should talk to your husband.' That's an odd way to put it. Do you know what she was trying to say?"

"Allen says she is just rebelling against him because he's been so strict."

"Do you think that's it?"

"Oh, I guess."

There was some hesitancy in her answer.

"Would it be all right if I took a quick look around the house?"

There had to be more information about what had happened than just that note—anything at all might be helpful. They walked into the living room, and Susan stopped short for a second, staring at an empty space where it appeared that a couch had been.

"What is it?"

"The couch," she said.

"Is it missing?"

"No, it's not that. It's just that…Alexi was so upset a few days ago, when the furniture movers took the couch away and we had to wait for a new one."

"Why do you think that bothered her?"

Susan hesitated for a few seconds. "I'm not sure."

There was probably something more to it than that. Susan seemed to be rerunning the whole scene through her mind.

"Did Alexi spend a lot of time on the couch?"

"I suppose so."

They walked slowly through the rest of the house, while he asked her questions. Susan offered only brief replies. They got to Alexi's room at the end of the hall.

"Can we go in?"

Susan nodded yes.

There was nothing in the room that looked helpful. There were no pictures on the wall, no stuffed animals, no rock star posters—not much decoration of any sort. If Alexi had spent much time there, she must have squirreled away the things that mattered to her somewhere else. There was a guitar in a soft plastic case sitting in her closet. From the dust on it, it didn't look like it had been used in a while.

"Does Alexi play the guitar?"

"She used to, but I don't think she's touched it in quite a while."

"Do you know why she stopped?"

Susan hesitated for a second. "I don't know. It was like everything else..." She let the thought hang there.

She walked over to a dresser drawer and moved a few things, finding a picture she wanted. It showed Alexi holding the guitar, getting ready to play it.

"I think this is the most recent picture I have of her."

"Can I take it? It might help if I have it to show it around. I'll make sure you get it back."

Susan nodded yes.

He scanned everything again, but there was nothing that caught his eye. The room left him with a strange sensation. What was missing was Alexi—not just the girl herself but any feeling she'd ever been there. It was an unnerving sensation. He remembered having the same thought when he looked into the room of his daughter, Mandy, after she and her mother had packed up and moved out.

He took a look at the handle on the door to the room and gave it a couple of twists. Then he bent down farther to examine it.

"Is there something wrong with the door?" Susan asked.

"It looks like the lock has been disabled."

"I know the door locks." She had a concerned look on her face. "There've been a couple of times when I've walked down the hall just to see if she was okay. I've tried the door, and I wasn't able to open it."

Her statement struck him as a little odd.

"Were you worried about something in particular—maybe, that there was an intruder? Or were you thinking she might have left?"

Susan shook her head, deflecting whatever thought she might have had.

"No, no real reason. I guess I was just being your typical worried mother."

◆ ◆ ◆

HE PROPPED UP THE picture of Alexi next to his dinner plate that evening and stared at it for a few seconds, finally setting it aside with the stack of notes. He tried to figure out how the image of her squared with what else he knew. There were still a few bites left on his plate, but the leftovers from the takeout chicken weren't too appealing. He shoved them aside.

The photo had his attention, but he wasn't sure why. There was nothing in the picture or anything else that suggested why she might have run away. There was even less to hint that she might have been abducted. What had really happened?

He'd gone by the foundation building late in the afternoon after he talked to Susan. When he walked by Blaiseck's office, he saw Wilder in the room with several men. Curly and Slim were there—they gave him blank stares. The others were men he had never seen before. When Blaiseck saw him in the doorway, he came out and shut the door behind him.

"Where have you been?"

"Talking to Susan Wilder, trying to help with her missing daughter."

"Who told you to do that?"

"Nobody *told* me. She asked me if I could help, and I decided to do it. You can understand why she would be upset, can't you?"

"We're handling that, so I don't see why you've gotten yourself involved."

"Everyone else has left her out of the loop, and she's worried sick about Alexi. I just thought someone ought to have some respect for her feelings."

Blaiseck stared at him for a few seconds.

"Okay, do what you have to do to keep her happy, but try not to interfere." Then he seemed to have another thought. "And I want you to keep us informed of what you're up to, okay? If you find out anything, you tell us. You still work here, you know."

"How come you haven't told the police that she's missing?"

Blasieck glared him.

"I don't need you second-guessing everything we do. But in case you've forgotten, there are some important reasons why Reverend Wilder doesn't want this to get out to the public. We have a big conference coming up with a congressional delegation in a few weeks, and we don't need any bad publicity about a child running away." He paused for a second to let his words sink in. "And by the way, when you're not wasting time like you did today, you're supposed to be working on security for that conference."

As he got back to the door to his office, he turned once more.

"And don't worry about the kid. We'll find her."

◆◆◆

WHERE WERE HIS LOYALTIES in this thing? He thought about that as he scraped the remains of his dinner into the garbage disposal. When he'd worked for the police, he never had to ask those kinds of questions. It was someone else's job to decide whether a person had been pushed into a life of crime or had managed to get there on their own. The same was true of the people he worked with—it didn't make any difference what he thought of them. The moral decisions were made somewhere up the chain of command. If you were assigned a case, you chased after the suspects—no questions asked. Your boss could be an idiot, a sleaze, or a total prick—he'd had all of them—but that was irrelevant. You did your assignment and let the others deal with the peripheral issues.

But what he was doing now was different. When you're working with a private client, personal feelings can complicate things. Supposedly, he was employed by Blaiseck and the foundation. That's fine. As long as they were paying him, he'd have to report to them and give them what they wanted. But he wasn't going to be their robot, just following orders no matter what. If he had any loyalties, it was to Susan Wilder. As the day wore on, he became more and more sympathetic with what she was going through.

As they continued to talk that afternoon, Susan apparently decided she could open up to him. It was an odd situation in some ways. There was no personal attraction between them. He just seemed to be there when she needed to talk. The conversation wandered around for over an hour as Susan strung together her reminiscences, talking about Alexi and their life together. He started to get a clearer picture of her daughter, but there was nothing Susan said that shed any light on why Alexi had decided to leave—if, in fact, that decision was hers. According to Susan, she was a serious, intelligent child with no drug problems, no bouts with alcohol, and nothing else to suggest she might have gone off the rails. Allen Wilder's name crept into the conversation, but it was mentioned almost tangentially in a story that was mostly about Alexi. Missing from her narrative was any sense of Susan's usual deference to her husband. Her role as the reverend's happy help-mate seemed to have disappeared along with their daughter.

The whole thing was a puzzle. When teenagers do a runner, you can usually chart a path of troubling behavior leading up to it. And, more often than not, their destination is clear—some drug underground or other wild bunch of kids that they're trying to hook up with. And they're rarely considerate of their parents' feelings. He pulled out the text of her note and looked at. *"I have to go away for a few days, and I don't want you to be worried."* What was going through her head when she wrote that? She apparently pulled the batteries out of her phone and stopped calling or texting her friends. How many teenagers do that kind of planning? And what were her words? *"I'm safe, and I will contact you as soon as I feel that I can."* That didn't sound at all like a fifteen-year-old.

Alexi never told her mother why she stopped playing the guitar, just saying something vague about not feeling good about it anymore. But as he looked at the picture of her smiling and cradling that instrument on her lap, she seemed totally happy at the moment that picture was taken. On a whim, he went into his bedroom and pulled out a guitar that had been sitting in the back of his closet for several years. He opened the case and compared it with the one in the picture. As he guessed, the guitar in the photo was a knockoff. The one he had was a Martin D-28, while the other one was a much newer instrument that was trying to copy that classic design. He held the guitar for a few minutes longer. He knew he was just distracting himself from what he was doing, but his investigation seemed to be going nowhere. He didn't mind his thoughts wandering off in a different direction.

It wasn't his guitar—it was Jimmy's. He'd gotten a call from Jimmy's sister several years back to say that she was giving away some of his stuff. But she couldn't part with the guitar—it was his favorite possession. Out of the blue, she asked him if he would take it. He was too surprised to say anything but yes. When it arrived a few weeks later, there was another package with a note from Carolyn, saying she'd sent some of Jimmy's folk music books along with it. He remembered opening the box and seeing something out of another world. There were dozens of dog-eared copies of *Sing Out* magazine and a five-volume set of something called *The English and Scottish Popular Ballads*. As he thumbed through the first book, he realized that it would take him months to read the entire set.

At the bottom of the box was Alan Lomax's *Folk Songs of North America*. Jimmy had talked to him so often about those songs that he became intrigued by them. He thumbed the pages and saw many of Jimmy's favorites. And in the margins were his long, handwritten notes. Whenever he read those words, he had the sensation that Jimmy was talking to him.

♦♦♦

THIS WAS THE TIME of night when memories about Jimmy often popped into his head. They were usually an odd collection of bits and pieces that came and went with a will of their own. But there was one memory that stood out—one that he never talked about to anyone. He never told Carolyn about it, and he didn't even mention it to Jimmy when he was alive. It was something that would have been too embarrassing. Maybe he was being too secretive. After all these years, someone hearing the story might find it more endearing than scandalous, but he kept it to himself nevertheless.

One afternoon, the two of them found themselves in a ramshackle building where their squad had been stopped for over an hour. Jimmy had received a letter and a photo that morning from LouAnn, and he was anxious to find a place to read it. He located a spot behind the building, knowing his buddy would cover for him. But the spot he chose turned out to be not all that private. Through the broken walls at the back of the building, Jimmy could be seen holding the letter with the photo propped up in front of him.

He couldn't help but look at him. There was a different kind of expression on Jimmy's face. And after a few moments he realized why: Jimmy's pants were open and he was stroking himself. That vision froze him for a second. He had never seen another man do that. He looked way, trying to sort out his emotions. But the shock of it gave away to an instinctual feeling that he wanted to be protective of Jimmy, making sure that no one else saw it and that it remained their secret—really, only his secret. And over the years, that scene had mellowed in his mind, becoming another very personal memory to add to all the others. When he thought of it now, he remembered it only as a lonely act of love.

◆ ◆ ◆

HE HAD DOZED OFF, caught in a sea of strange images. But he awoke when his phone pinged with a text message from Susan. She'd received another message from Alexi.

Alexi

SHE STUMBLED INTO THE motel bathroom and threw up. It was still dark in the room as she raced toward the toilet. Gina was sleeping in the bed closer to the door, and she tried not to wake her. But the noises she made as she cradled her arm around the toilet were so loud that Gina woke up anyway. *Are you all right?* she wanted to know. She mumbled something in response. The next thing she heard was Gina getting out of bed and plodding toward the bathroom.

She'd never known anyone like Gina. She was angry at first when Gina talked about herself and told her who she was and what she was like. She couldn't believe it. She probably said things to Gina that she shouldn't have said. She couldn't really remember what she had done. But after a few minutes, she realized she wasn't so much mad at Gina as she was angry at the world for creating so much confusion in her life. The more they talked, the more she calmed down about everything.

The thing was, she liked Gina. She felt good about her from the moment she got into the car, because she realized that Gina was on her side. But she was confused and still angry that things had to be so complicated. After they talked awhile, she started feeling a little embarrassed about how she had reacted. She didn't want to hurt Gina's feelings, but it just took a little while to get used to her. She wondered what she might do if Gina got up real close to her at some point. She didn't know if she was ready for that. But ready or not, it was happening at that moment. The door to the bathroom opened behind her, and within seconds Gina was squatting down next to her.

"Is there anything I can do?"

She just wanted the vomiting to stop. But when she tried to say something about it, she felt another foul surge in her throat. A week earlier, her mother had been hunched down next to her in the same position at another toilet. It seemed like she had asked the same question.

"No, I'll be all right."

"Okay, take your time. Don't try to talk."

Gina's hand was resting lightly on her shoulder. She flinched for a second at the feel of it, but then she relaxed. Gina eased up a bit, but seconds later the hand was still there. Her touch at that point was so light she could barely sense it. It felt good.

She shuffled back to her bed and put her head on the pillow, trying not to disturb her stomach. If the room didn't start spinning around again, she thought she could get some more sleep. Gina was blaming herself for making her sick, even though it wasn't really her fault. She kept saying that the whole day had been too stressful and that she never should have gone into that long discussion during dinner. Maybe that was part of it, but more likely it was just the foul-tasting hamburger she'd ordered. She wished she had scraped the sauce off of it.

But Gina wasn't letting up on herself.

"It was my mistake. It was too much all at once, and I feel terrible about it."

When she awoke again a couple of hours later, Gina was already showered and dressed. She probably wanted to get back on the road, but she wasn't pressing her about it.

"If you're okay," Gina said, "maybe I'll take the car out and get some gas. You can stay here and rest a little longer."

◆ ◆ ◆

SHE WAS GLAD JUST to lie there for a few moments while she tried to sort things out. She needed time to think. She'd gotten a little light-headed when she found out that they were headed for California. It had never occurred to her that Gina lived so far away. Was it just yesterday that they had left Indiana? So much had happened.

Everything they talked about at dinner had just added to the pile of unexpected news. She knew almost nothing about Gina at the time she got into the car. But then after listening to her for a while, she realized she didn't know anything about her own early life either. She wasn't angry with Gina for explaining everything the way she did, even though at times she felt a little dizzy about it.

She found out she was born in Bosnia, and that was a surprise. She always assumed that she had been born somewhere in the United States. She had only heard the name Bosnia mentioned once in class, and she didn't know if she could find it on a map. Gina described it as a beautiful place, and she wanted her to see it someday. But it sounded like Bosnia had just gone through something terrible. At the time she was born, there was apparently a war going on all around her. That news confused her. Why couldn't she remember anything about that? She never thought about her early childhood memories, but she wondered how, even as a baby, she could have forgotten about all of those things as they were happening.

She had to catch herself every so often as she was listening. She couldn't believe she was sitting somewhere in the middle of America, with someone she hardly knew, listening to an entirely new story about herself. It was a wonder that all the food didn't catch in her throat. Gina told her a lot about her family and about her early years, and each new bit of information seemed to carry her further and further away from the life she'd grown up with. A couple of times she thought about her mother and how worried she must be. She didn't want to hurt her, but she didn't regret taking off like she did—not with him around.

Every bit of news had its own little jolt. She found out she had another name: Jelena. As Jelena's story started to become more and more real, she worried that her own story might be starting to fade. For a moment, she feared that Gina would begin calling her by that name. Would she have to start using that name herself? Gina seemed to sense that this was bothering her, and she tried to reassure her. Jelena was a pretty name, she said, but it was now just part of her personal history—like something in a museum. The way Gina put it made her feel good. "I now know a wonderful young woman named Alexi, and I don't intend to change her a bit."

She learned about her birth mother. When she first got into the car, she had fantasized that Gina was her real mother. But Gina said no. Her mother was a beautiful young woman named Anja. She was very musically talented. She had gorgeous black hair. "And she had beautiful eyes, just like your own."

"Alexi, she would have been very proud of you."

The way Gina said it made her ask, "Isn't she still alive somewhere?"

"I don't think so," Gina said, "but I don't really know for sure. From everything I've heard, she may have died in the war or in the killings that followed afterward."

Her heart sunk. That wasn't fair. As she listened to Gina describe what happened to Anja, the food on her plate suddenly became more indigestible than it already was. She had just found her real mother, and now she was suddenly jerked away from her.

◆◆◆

GINA HAD ONE OTHER thing to tell her. But from the way she was fidgeting around, it was clear that she wasn't looking forward to saying it.

"I hate to spring this on you without warning. But it's something you need to know, and I can't think of any other way to tell you."

She told her it was okay. Whatever it was, she wanted Gina to say it, because she hated seeing her so uncomfortable. But she didn't realize that the thing that Gina had to say would spark her sudden burst of despair.

"Alexi, I'm your father."

Gina

Alexi, I'm your father.

Alexi, I used to be your father.

Alexi, before I started living as a woman, I was your father.

I DIDN'T KNOW HOW to tell her, so I ended up stumbling over it. I wanted to say I felt very close to her. I wanted to tell her I loved her and let her know the whole story behind that love. I wanted to say I was still her father even though I didn't appear to be anyone's father. But I didn't say any of those things very well. You'd think after years of selling stories—and *telling* stories—I'd be better at that sort of thing. But I wasn't.

Alexi was shocked—how could she not be? There was a look of bewilderment on her face at first, and that was replaced by a flash of anger. Then came a lot of the sobs and tears. I tried to reassure her as best I could about me—about the real me—about the real me that would always really be me. Most of all, I wanted her to know that I was there for her. She let me wander through my story. After a while, I think she started to get used to me as I was. It was a lot to ask of her; she had never known anyone like me. But I sensed she was starting to figure out how I fit into her world. That was more a tribute to her understanding than to my eloquence. I reached across the table and gave her hand a squeeze. She squeezed back.

As a transgender woman, I've had to deal with all kinds of reactions from others. How do you reveal your gender history? Do you do just blurt it out at some point in the conversation? If the people you're talking to haven't already figured it out on their own, it can get awkward. Some transgender women are right up front, mentioning it as soon as they meet someone. There's something to be said for that, but that's not how I am. I almost never say anything about myself unless I'm asked, and—surprisingly, I guess—I'm rarely asked. Many of my bookseller colleagues certainly know, and I'm fine with that. The rumors about me have probably wended their way around the business more than I know.

Others might disagree, but I think that's the right way for me. I would never deny that I'm a transgender woman, but I don't really define myself in gender terms. When you look at the way I live my life from day to day, you could just as easily categorize me in some other way—like, a bookworm. What I really fear is that if people learn that one big thing about me first, they'll never take the time to learn anything else. It's the kind of information about a person that can blot out the sun, if you're not careful.

But I didn't have that luxury with Alexi. In telling her the history of her own life, I had to tell her about mine as well. The two stories were hopelessly intertwined. I told her about a forgotten war in a distant land. It was a tale in which she was conceived and born under a different name to people she'd never heard of. And if that weren't enough, the only link she had to those events was someone who had begun the story as her father but had been living as a woman ever since.

◆◆◆

I TOLD HER THE whole story, but that doesn't mean I told her everything.

I couldn't tell her that I'd been forced to rape her mother. If I was going to tell her the details about what happened that day, I knew that conversation would only be many months later—if ever.

It took me a long time to come to peace with what had happened in the basement of that house. Even though there was a war raging upstairs—one that I had been dragged into against my will—I was still anguished by the role I played. I was on the run for many months after that day. But no matter where I was forced to hide, I was obsessed with trying to locate Anja again. I wasn't even sure of her name, but I had to find her and make things right. I didn't know what kind of a reception I would get. I was technically part of the Militia that had tried to kill her family, and they would have every right to hate me when they saw me. When I finally learned that the family was hiding up in the mountains, I found out Anja had a baby daughter. That just added to my anxiety. Until then, I hadn't realized that she had become pregnant.

I'm not sure why the family was so kind to me, but they took me in. They were just fundamentally good and decent people. I was there less than three months, but I became very close to them. In truth, they were the only family I've ever had. Somehow, I wanted to make it up to them for what they had gone through, but there wasn't much I could do. Finally, they got word that their enemies—and mine, as well—were closing in on them. They knew they had to flee. But in that short time, I became enchanted with that beautiful baby. I could still not bring myself to call her *my* child, but that seemed far less important than having her there in my life.

What I felt more than anything else was the simple joy of being around her. It was during those brief months that I finally got up the nerve to talk to Anja about what had happened that day in the basement. She listened to me spill out my apologies, and then she came over and sat next to me, holding my hand.

"We were both raped," she said calmly. I could tell by the look on her face that she had thought through the whole sordid incident and had come to peace with her feelings. "I knew by the look on your face that day that you had no intention of attacking me."

When I tried to interject something, she calmly shut me up.

"I could feel the terror in your body. A brutal force had been let loose in that room, and it was attacking both of us. There's no doubt in my mind that if you hadn't been there— if you hadn't been sandwiched between us—he would have raped me himself. That would have been far worse."

"So what happened between us was in some sense up to me. It happened because I let it happen. If I hadn't, he would have killed us both." She leaned against me, trying to control her tears.

◆◆◆

"And then you did what you had to do."

The thing that Anja said I "had to do" was kill him. I couldn't tell that to Alexi either.

The scene is still fresh in my memory. The *Hijena* goaded me, practically inviting me to do what I did. I knew that if I didn't do it, he would kill Anja and probably kill me as well. So I picked up the rifle, like they taught me to do, and I shot him.

It was brutal. The *Hijena* grabbed at his chest in surprise, his mouth moving through a range of sounds, as if he were trying to say something. Finally, he just coughed up blood and sank to the floor. Within seconds, he stopped moving. I was shaking all over. If I'd thought about it, I never would have been able to pull the trigger. And even with my aversion to guns and war—and with all my hatred toward the man who had been tormenting me—I still had no idea how ugly it would feel to kill another human being. I was gripped with revulsion. Within seconds, I dropped the weapon to the floor and ran up the stairs as fast as I could. I somehow made it out of the building and into safety. It wasn't until hours later—after I had hidden myself in the woods surrounding the town—that I was able to think about what had happened. Once the *Komandant* and the others figured out what had happened, they would be screaming for revenge against me and anyone connected with me.

◆ ◆ ◆

AS WE DROVE THE next day, I could see Alexi glancing at me a little differently than she had before. She was still trying to fit me into her universe. There were probably some male pronouns in her head, struggling to get loose. I knew she would be embarrassed if she slipped up and used one.

The truth is, I've always found it easy to pass as a woman. I've been blessed with narrow shoulders and a relatively small waist. My body was practically hairless when I was a boy. The modest levels of hormones that I've taken over the last decade have stopped most of the growth of facial hair and kept the hair on my head intact. My voice isn't very high—

sort of a contralto—but I've learned that the light touch of an Italian accent somehow creates a feminine mood.

I'm never sure what comes into a person's mind when they hear the word "transgender." Alexi knew a few things, but there were some big omissions in her understanding. I spent a good part of the next morning—driving across Kansas, of all places—trying as gently as I could to fill in the gaps. The thing to know is this: men who leap into the world of women can end up in all kinds of places. Transgender women can be quite different from each over. The images that people conjure up can be as broad as the prairie—ranging from men who have been surgically altered to the guy who just puts on his wife's lingerie out of curiosity. The images are so different because the transgender women are so different.

I've tried my best to resist categorization. But don't get me wrong: I have a soft spot in my heart for every person who has the courage to take on a woman's identity—no matter how permanent or fleeting. But I worry when people latch on to a generalization and use that like a pair of blinders to block out everything else about a person. I didn't want that to happen to me. And I certainly didn't want that to happen between Alexi and me.

At one point, Alexi wanted to know if I was "seeing anyone." I was so proud of my child for the delicate way she framed that question, I almost let go of the steering wheel and hugged her.

No, I was not, I told her.

I was actually happy to be able to report to her that I was living quite alone, because that made things easier. She was already on overload from everything else that I'd told her.

Bringing one more "significant other" into the mix would have probably broken the scale altogether.

I didn't bother to report the details of my love life, and Alexi had the good sense not to ask any more questions about it. But the fact is, my romantic life was in shambles. People who think that all transgender women lead exotic sex lives would probably find my social life pretty pathetic. I'd dated a couple of men who were attracted to me as a woman—*only* as a woman. When it became clear that they were not likely to be pleased with the body parts that Mother Nature had given me, I tried as gently as possible to ease my way out of the relationship before embarrassing everyone. One guy, however, figured it out and was mortified anyway.

There have also been men who've approached me from the other direction, presenting me with the opposite problem. One man who shall remain nameless—I'm not into outing anybody—reveled in my male attributes and seemed to use my feminine persona as a cover for that. I saw nothing wrong with his desires, and I think I understood what was driving him. The problem was he acted like he had trouble even remembering my name. If he'd shown a little more affection for the female side of me, I might have put up with the rest of it.

I could have added Sylvia to my list of romantic attachments, but I had no intention of saying anything to Alexi about my relationship with her. The minute we reached the West Coast, I'd be counting on Sylvia to begin the legal process for protecting her, and I wanted to keep that relationship as professional as possible. I didn't want to complicate things any more than they already were. In truth, my affair with Sylvia was an aberration—really, an aberration for both of us. She prefers women, and I prefer men. But somehow we ended up with each other and fell madly in love—for a while. I've never quite figured that out. The only thing I can think is that our friendship is so right because our romance was so wrong.

◆◆◆

WE STOPPED AT A place in Colorado for lunch. After we finished our sandwiches, the waitress reappeared at the table with the dessert menu. I watched Alexi's eyes move from the waitress to me and then back again. It was a quick movement, but it was one I rather expected.

"Would you ladies like anything for dessert?'

"Nothing for me," I said.

Alexi hesitated for a second, and then said she didn't want anything either.

The waitress turned to me. "Okay, honey. Can I bring you the check?"

I nodded yes.

After she left, Alexi looked at me with a bit of a smile. She didn't have to say anything, but I knew what she was thinking. I had passed some sort of test.

◆◆◆

WE WERE DRIVING ONCE more into the late-afternoon sun. Alexi had been quiet, and I knew she was thinking about something. Finally, she told me what she wanted.

"Gina, will you do something for me?"

"Of course. What would you like?"

"Can you take a picture of me and send it to my mother?"

I didn't have the heart to say no. Alexi was getting a little homesick—for her mother, if not for the home itself. I knew exactly what she was thinking. If her mother got a picture of her, she'd probably know she was all right. Alexi would then feel a lot better about what we were doing.

But that meant putting the batteries back in Alexi's phone, shooting the picture, and sending a phone transmission back to Indiana. We could have done it with my phone, but that would have been even more problematic. As it was, it was risky enough. One more barrier would be dropping between us and those who were probably trying to find us.

But I couldn't tell her no.

Davey

THEY FINALLY HAD A break.

The email with the photo of Alexi was like a godsend to Susan. When she saw the picture—one that even showed a bit of a smile—she seemed to know that Alexi was safe. She started talking like they were going to find her and get her back.

They would. It was just instinctual, but now that he had something solid to deal with he thought they would find her. It was starting to feel like a case with a shape and a pattern— something he could sink his teeth into. And the more he applied himself to that case, the further away he got from the self-doubts and the sense of uselessness that had settled into his bones.

Susan forwarded the picture to him, and he was at his office by 7:30 a.m. looking at it on his computer screen. The picture said a lot. The most important thing was the smile— seemingly genuine and unforced. He couldn't be sure, but it appeared that Alexi wasn't being mistreated. According to Susan, the clothes she was wearing were different. She recognized them as Alexi's clothes, but it wasn't the same outfit that she were wearing when she left home on the day she disappeared. That was important news—and, almost certainly, good news. What it said was that she hadn't been snatched up off the street in some sort of kidnapping. Instead, her disappearance had been planned enough in advance for her to take a change of clothes. Alexi seemed somehow to have been involved in the planning of it.

What other information was the photo giving him? One thing seemed sure: Alexi was not in this alone. The photo was no selfie. She was anywhere from eight to ten feet from the camera. Although she could have set it somewhere with an automatic timer, it looked far too posed. It was also possible that she asked a stranger to take the picture, but he couldn't imagine a fifteen-year-old on the run being comfortable enough to do that. No, there was someone with her who had taken the picture, and that person was probably the one who had arranged her disappearance.

Susan said the photo had appeared on her phone in the early evening. Although the sun had set by the time she received the message, the photo was taken while there was still natural light. There was no time stamp on the photo, but it was definitely taken during daylight. Could Alexi and her mysterious companion have taken the photo several hours earlier before sending it to her mother? Why would she do that? The note with the photo said simply, "Mom, I'm okay." If she wanted to give her mother reassurance about her safety, it made no sense for her to wait and do it later.

She hadn't waited at all—he was sure of that. Alexi was standing in full daylight, with the sun off to her left and her long shadow stretched out to her right. Judging by the length of that shadow, the photo was taken sometime between 3:30 and 4:30 p.m. The question, then, was not *when* it was taken but *where* it was taken. It seemed clear that she was no longer in Indianapolis or the immediate vicinity. When the photo was taken, Alexi was probably about two time zones to the west.

Where was she exactly? The photo seemed ready to give up that information as well. The background behind Alexi was hazy, but if you looked at it carefully you could see the outline of a large mountain range that appeared to be rising up from the broad plain. There was nothing like that in Indiana or anywhere near there. After studying the photo and comparing it with a few stock travel photos on the Internet, he thought he had it pinned down. The timing was right as well. If someone had been driving west from Indianapolis ever since Alexi disappeared, that's just where they would be when the photo was taken. Alexi and her traveling companion were somewhere just east of Denver.

He sat back in his chair and rubbed his eyes, trying to decide what to do next. At some point he had to tell Susan, but he didn't want to do that just yet. If he thought she had information about why Alexi was heading west, he would have asked for her help immediately. But their conversation the day before had been pretty exhaustive, and he doubted if she knew anything. He knew he'd have to tell her what he had discovered before the morning was out, but he didn't want to alarm her any more than he had to. It was one thing for her to think that her daughter was away from home, just hiding out somewhere. But it was something else for her to find out that Alexi was on the road, heading west, and probably getting farther and farther away by the hour.

There must be something in his notes that would help. He'd spent yesterday afternoon walking a tightrope with Alexi's friends, trying to get as much information as he could without telling them that she had gone missing. He hated working under those kinds of restrictions. Nevertheless, he got the impression from her friends that she didn't hang around with anyone suspicious—no one who might have enticed her to run away. If there had been someone in the shadows, worming their way into Alexi's life over a period of time, they would have left some sort of pattern or trail. No one was that careful.

But perhaps that's the clue—or the non-clue. Maybe he should be looking for something that had happened just recently—someone who had just come into Alexi's life and caused her to get up and run. What had her friend Laura said? He found the page with his notes: "Alexi said she had just met someone who might be able to help her." Apparently, that was all she said. There was no hint of what she meant.

"Met someone"—how do you narrow down the possibilities? Theoretically, Alexi could have met someone anywhere. It might have been in a place or in a context that no one would ever imagine. But the starting place was the everyday things she did. She led a rather orderly life— predictable days in a very structured environment. There was a lot of footage of her movements in the video files from the cameras around the church complex. That was a good place to start.

He looked at the videos for the last few weeks, skimming through them, using all the shortcuts. But the work was still tedious. If he found a snippet in which Alexi appeared, he hit the pause button and scrolled back to look at that section more closely. But it was pretty dull stuff—mostly, Alexi in a youth group meeting, Alexi walking through the sanctuary with her mother, and things like that. If he hadn't already invested so much time, he might have given up the whole idea as useless. But after searching through nearly two weeks' worth of video files, he decided to go all the way to the end.

Then the video from the last Sunday service caught his attention. There was something that could be important. He ran back the portion that began with Susan talking to the other congregants in the waiting room just before the services. He remembered that sequence, because it occurred just before Alexi emerged from the side door into the waiting room with an angry look on her face. He went through the video again, following Alexi as she worked her way through the crowd until she was face-to-face with her mother. But it wasn't the confrontation with her mother that caught his attention. What jumped out at him was the other woman in the picture.

He remembered that woman as she entered into the church. She was tall, quite attractive, and seemingly out of place. She had a brief conversation with Susan, but after a few moments, Susan turned away to talk to some other people who seemed to need her attention. The important part came next, as he watched the other woman's eyes over the next several minutes. He took the video that was focused on the woman and ran it on another monitor side by side with the feed from the camera that had been pointed at Alexi. Looking at the two monitors in sync, he saw something that he otherwise might have missed. As Alexi crossed the room and changed directions to get around groups of people, the woman's eyes changed direction as well. By the time he was through playing through the videos again, he was more convinced than ever. The woman was ignoring everything else and following Alexi's every movement.

The excitement surged through him as he realized that he may have found the person he was looking for. He froze the screen for a minute and tried to enlarge the picture of the woman, but he couldn't see anything else that was really helpful. But what happened next on the video reinforced his theory. When Alexi finally reached the area where Susan was standing, her mother was talking to someone else. Alexi's anger and frustration was apparent from her body language, but the mysterious stranger seemed eager to help her. She had a few brief words with Alexi and then reached over toward Susan, letting her know that her daughter needed her. It was a brief encounter, but it was a contact nonetheless. He'd have to check with Susan to see if she had ever met this woman before, but he felt certain she had no idea who she was.

And then he remembered something else. He fast-forwarded the video until it reached the point several minutes later after the waiting room had emptied and the last of the congregants had filed into the Sanctuary. The video monitor showed only an empty room for several minutes while the services were going on. But suddenly, it happened as he remembered. The door to the sanctuary opened, and the same woman came walking out alone well before the end of the services. She headed across the waiting room, walking in long, hurried strides, until she reached the outside door and continued out into the parking lot.

He quickly checked his library of video files, searching for the batch that had the videos from the parking lot cameras. He found himself hurrying at this point, as if his quarry might somehow get away. He found the parking lot video with the same time stamp as the last scene from the interior of the church. As if on cue, the door to the church opened up, and the woman emerged and began walking across the parking lot until she reached her car. She opened the driver's door and got in and sat down. She remained there for a few minutes and didn't move. That struck him as a bit odd, but he kept watching the screen waiting for her to leave. She finally pulled what looked like a smartphone out of her purse and aimed it straight ahead through the windshield, apparently taking a picture.

That last gesture had him puzzled. He checked the files from the other cameras monitoring the parking lot, looking for some movement in that direction. If there had been anyone there, the cameras would have recorded it. But then it hit him. She wasn't taking a picture of a person but of the sign that appeared in large letters on the outside wall of the building: the God's Children Foundation.

◆ ◆ ◆

IF THERE WAS ONE thing the foundation's video cameras were calibrated to do, it was to focus in on the license plates of cars in the parking lot. Davey wrote down her license number, noting that they were Illinois plates. Then he saw something next to the license plate that he quickly seized on: the sticker from the rental car agency. Luckily, it wasn't just any agency but rather one that he knew exactly how to deal with. He found the phone number he needed in an old pocket calendar from his days on the police force. After a few rings, there was a voice he recognized.

"Denby."

"Jim, it's Davey Fallon."

"Davey! How are you? I haven't heard from you in a while. I understand you're not on the police force anymore."

He exchanged pleasantries with Jim Denby until he was ready to ask what he wanted.

"Jim, I need a favor."

"Davey—anything you want. You want me to set you up with a good deal on a rental car?"

"I don't need a car. What I need is information."

Denby's voice lost a little of its joviality. He was looking for information about a customer who had rented a car, and he wanted her name and address. More than that, he wanted to know if she had rented any other cars since then.

"I don't know if I can do that. We have a pretty strict company policy about giving out that kind of information without a warrant or a subpoena—or something."

He feigned a bit of commiseration for the plight that Denby was in, but he pressed on. This involves a missing teenage girl, he told him. She may have been kidnapped. She could be in danger. He kept pushing buttons.

"The people holding her might be abusing her right now, so every minute counts. We need that information right away."

That button opened the door. Seven years earlier, he'd worked on a case in which Denby's own teenage daughter had been abused by a school counselor. When the case was over, Denby kept telling him how grateful he was for his help. He said if he ever needed anything, just ask.

Now, he was asking.

"Okay, give me the license number. Do you want me to call you back?

"If you don't mind, I'll just hang on the line."

Five minutes later, Denby was back with the information. He had the name, address, and phone number of the woman who rented the car.

"She rented it last Saturday at O'Hare Airport and left it off the next day at the Indianapolis Airport."

He thanked him, and then he waited.

"And like you guessed, she rented another car at the same place three days ago, and this one is scheduled to be returned in San Francisco."

◆ ◆ ◆

HE GOT HOME AT about 8:00 p.m., wondering if his sense of exhilaration would last. He'd accomplished something. He hadn't been able to say that to himself in a long time. But there was still something tentative about it. It could be that he was starting to get control over the direction of his life… but, maybe not.

There was a letter in the mail from Jimmy's sister, Carolyn. Just looking at the envelope gave him a sudden sinking feeling. He didn't know why he was alarmed, but it was probably because Carolyn always contacted him by email and never by letter. But why should that be a problem? Had the world reached the point where a simple written letter had become ominous?

He walked upstairs and checked the phone for messages, and then he looked to see what was in the refrigerator. But these were time-wasters. He was just putting off Carolyn's letter. For reasons he couldn't quite fathom, he had a feeling it was going to be unpleasant. He opened the envelope and pulled out the letter. As he did so, a picture fell out.

Dear Davey

I've put off telling you this for far too long, and now I feel terrible about it. It would have been a lot easier for me to come right out with it many years ago, because I could have avoided so many lies. Now I feel ashamed.

Jimmy only hid the truth from you for the few months that you knew him, but I've been holding back things for the last forty-five years. I feel awful about that. There were times when I wanted to say something. And there were other times when I was afraid I would slip up and use the wrong name and be mortified about the whole thing. But all of that is now in the past. I only hope that you won't think badly of me for deceiving you for as long as I did.

My only excuse is that I thought I was doing what Jimmy would have wanted. He had a reason for hiding the truth, because things were so different then. He didn't feel he could trust anyone connected with the army. He knew the consequences would have been far too harsh if it had gotten out. I know he loved you, and I'm sure he wanted to tell you. But he was afraid. But as I think about things now, I know he would approve of what I'm doing. He probably would have wished I'd done it sooner.

Davey, I've received word from New York that Lou has died. I heard about it just before I talked to you the other night, but I just couldn't bring myself to say anything. I had to do it in writing. When Lou was alive, I could rationalize that I had a reason for keeping the whole story from you. But with Lou dead, that's over with. There's no reason to hide the truth.

Davey, it was just Lou. "LouAnn" was a name that he and Jimmy agreed to use when they were around others and felt that a male name would give too much away. Lou was a sweet boy with whom Jimmy had a very tender affair. He grew up to become a wonderful man—a successful art dealer in New York. A few years ago, Lou went to Canada and got married to the man he had been living with for twenty-five years. They were *very happy together. It was his husband who called me to tell me that Lou had died.*

Davey, I know this will come as a shock to you, but I hope you won't think badly of Jimmy. The affection that he had for you was very real, and he was very lucky to have had you as a friend.

I don't know if what I'm sending you is something you'd like to have or not. However, I just thought you might like a copy of a picture that I took of the two of them together before Jimmy was sent to Vietnam.

Please forgive me for all of this. Your friendship means so much to me. I just hope that I haven't done anything to destroy it.

Love,

Carolyn

He stared at the photo. It showed Jimmy sitting on a bench with a guitar resting on his right thigh. It was the same guitar that was now sitting in the closet. Jimmy's left arm was draped over the shoulder of a young man who was sitting just to his left. They were both smiling into the camera.

His hand started to shake. But before the photo fell out of his grasp, he found a place to put it on the shelf next to his own picture with Jimmy—the photo that had been taken so many years ago in Saigon.

He stood there for a second, gripping the side of the table, as he looked at the photos. Then he realized he had to sit down.

Alexi

SHE WROTE IN HER journal as they drove, but she stopped doing it when she began to get carsick. Gina asked her if everything was okay, and she said she was fine. She decided to just lean back against the headrest and focus on the music.

Gina had what she called her "road pack"—a little battered case of CDs to play when there was time to kill on a long trip. Alexi had never heard of any of the singers before, but she liked the music and the acoustic guitar that accompanied the words. The songs all seemed to have a story to tell, and she got caught up in several of the more poignant ones.

"I have a guitar at home," Gina said. "I get it out every so often and try to play some of those songs—especially the ones from the Indigo Girls. There are also some Chris Williamson and Ferron tunes that I like to work on. Do you play any musical instruments?"

"I used to."

The memory wasn't a happy one. But she finally told Gina about the guitar that she had sitting in her closet. She hadn't played it for almost a year.

"I had no idea you knew how to play the guitar. If I get out my guitar when we get home, will you play something for me?"

She hesitated for a moment and then said she would.

"Why did you stop playing?"

"I don't know. I guess I just didn't feel like it anymore."

There was a longer explanation, but she didn't have energy to go into it at the moment. It was the reverend—he cheapened everything. She used to practice the guitar and sing to herself in the evenings just before dinner. Her mother would usually say something nice about her playing, but he wouldn't say a word when all of them were together. It was only later on when he snuck into her room that he would start swooning to her in his oily voice and telling her how much her music turned him on—telling her she was a sexy little temptress with the voice of one of God's angels. After the last time he did that, she shoved the guitar into the back of her closet and never played it again.

◆ ◆ ◆

SHE LIKED GINA. SHE had already admitted that to herself when she wrote it in her journal. She was forming some sort of relationship with her, but she didn't know what to call it. She couldn't get used to the idea that Gina was her father. But she was happy that her real father wasn't some abusive character—she'd had enough of that.

As she looked at the woman sitting next to her behind the steering wheel, there was no way in the world she could think of her as "Daddy" or any other name that she might associate with a man. Her tongue and her brain just didn't work that way. She tripped over that problem as she wrote in her diary, starting a sentence that said, "She is my father," and then deciding that it didn't look right. She finally decided to get around the problem by just thinking of Gina as her new friend—a special kind of friend, maybe, but a friend nevertheless.

"Gina, it looks like we're getting close."

"We are, sweetheart."

"Is this the Golden Gate Bridge?"

"No, we're on the Bay Bridge. The Golden Gate is the prettier one over there on your right. That's San Francisco ahead of us. We're almost home."

PART FOUR

Gina

I HAD A BUSINESS to run, and I'd been letting it go to hell.

Miriam pointed that out to me—in much more polite terms—when I got back to the store. I'd cancelled three sales rep appointments while driving across the country. And when I got back, there was a larger-than-usual stack of invoices awaiting my approval for payment. I'd also missed a couple of big author events, including a "Community Book Forum" that I had cooked up a few months earlier. I was supposed to be the lead person for the whole event, but when it happened I was driving somewhere across Utah.

The staff did a great job, but I always worried about missed opportunities. In the book business, you can't afford to miss a thing if you're going to stay afloat. Part of my job is to convince the newer staff members that we don't just sell books—we sell the book experience. People walk into bookstores because they like the feel and the majesty of books, and they want to be surrounded by them. If we had to rely on people coming in just looking for something with lots of words, we wouldn't survive for a minute. They want knowledge, they want passion—but, most of all, they want someone who will get out of their chair and meet them at the bookshelves.

So imagine my delight when I discovered I'd just added another passionate book person to the team. Alexi and I arrived late in the afternoon, and I suggested we go straight upstairs to my flat and just rest awhile. But as soon as she saw the bookstore, she insisted on going in and finding a few things to read. She glanced at our young adult section with a critical eye, pulling out one, then two, and finally three books that she wanted. She didn't stop at that. She talked to a woman who was browsing in the section and pulled a book off the shelf that she was sure that the woman's daughter would like. She gave her a nice little talk that resulted in the woman walking to the counter with the book in hand. How much do I believe in genetics? I believe in it a lot more, after watching her in action.

Miriam asked somewhat guardedly where I had found this talented young woman. I decided, for the moment, to tell her she was my niece. Miriam was getting an enthusiastic bookseller to help with customers, so that answer was fine with her. Morrie was also pleased to have a teenage assistant to help with the young adult books, and the same was true with rest of the staff. I knew that I would have to tell them the real story sooner or later, because I had no intention of keeping Alexi's identity or whereabouts a secret for very long. Once I'd gotten her out of that awful situation, I wanted to do what was right for her.

While this was going on, Alexi was figuring out her relationship with me. She said in rather touching fashion that she considered me her friend—a special one at that. I loved her, and that was good enough for me. She was my daughter, of course, but I didn't feel very paternal. I managed just once to tell her I was her "father," but I couldn't bring myself to utter the phrase after that. Maybe I was feeling maternal, but Alexi already had a mother—two of them, in fact. I know how Anja would have felt toward her, and I was guessing Susan probably felt the same way. Alexi wanted me to send her another picture, and of course I said yes. Alexi's disappearance must have been causing that woman a great deal of pain, and that made me realize all the more why we had to resolve things quickly.

◆◆◆

BUT THE TRUTH IS, I was a nervous wreck about the whole thing. We'd gotten across the country without incident, but I knew that was just the beginning. There were sure to be people looking for Alexi, and I kept waiting for them to show their faces. And then there were the ones looking for me. Despite Paolo's assurances, I'd been looking over my shoulder ever since I talked to him, thinking they might appear at any minute. After a while, I started wondering if I could tell one group chasing me from another.

Miriam seemed to pick up on my mood. A day to so after we arrived, she said that she'd seen a guy outside the window, spending a little more time than normal looking into the store. Something about him made her uneasy. "I don't know for sure, but it looked to me like he might have been packing."

The minute she said that, I jerked my head around expecting to see something—I don't know what, maybe a hit squad—staring at me through the glass. But there was nothing there. Miriam must have sensed how much she had alarmed me, so she made a point of assuring me that the whole thing was probably nothing at all. I tried really hard to believe her.

No matter how jumpy I was, there were still things we had to do. We paid a quick visit to a couple of the women's clothing shops on Hayes Street to get something more for Alexi to wear. She couldn't keep wearing the same things she'd stuffed in her backpack when we left Indiana. I also set up an appointment with my doctor to get her a checkup. She still wasn't feeling great, so I wanted to take every precaution. My meeting with Sylvia was the last thing on the list but maybe the most important. When she said she was cancelling a couple of appointments to fit me in, I knew she understood we needed to move fast.

I settled down into the chair in front of Sylvia's desk and went through the usual ritual of telling her secretary that I didn't want a cup of coffee or anything else. Sylvia surprised me a bit by just letting me talk. She wanted to hear the whole story from the minute I set foot on the airplane to the moment we got home. She asked a couple of questions, but for the most part she said very little. When I was done, she rubbed her eyes for a few moments before saying anything.

"I know you're expecting to be scolded."

I was.

"Did any of my warnings sink in?"

I shrugged but didn't answer.

"You're like a lot of my clients who never ask my advice before getting into trouble. They think I'm a janitorial service that can clean up their mess later on."

She looked up at the ceiling for a second and then back at me. Then she said something that surprised me.

"I have to say I admire you for doing what you did."

She shook her head slightly, probably wishing that I hadn't put her in a position where she had to admit such a thing.

"I wouldn't love you as much as I do if you weren't the kind of person who would risk everything to save someone else."

I came close to breaking down in tears.

"What shall we do?" I asked. "Do you want me to bring Alexi in right now so you can meet her?"

For the first time since I walked in the door, I saw Sylvia get agitated. "Is she right here in the office?"

"She's sitting out in the waiting room. When I walked in here, she was talking to Cristina."

Sylvia stared at the ceiling again, tapping her fingers on her desk.

"Did I do something wrong by bringing her here?"

She let out a sigh.

"Look. You know you could be in big trouble for all this, okay? I've been checking the filings and police reports out of Indiana every day since I found out what you were doing. For some reason, nothing's been reported. I don't know why. Apparently, her family hasn't decided whether to report her as kidnapped or missing or anything, but we have to assume that they will sooner or later. And when they do, there could be both state and federal charges hanging over your head for abducting a minor."

She held up her hand as if to stop anything I might say in protest. But I kept my mouth shut.

"I know you did what you did for the best of reasons. That gives us something to work with, if and when an indictment comes down."

I didn't like the sound of the word "indictment," but I didn't argue.

"What I'm trying to assess right now is my own involvement in all this. The minute Alexi walks through that door, I run the risk of some prosecutor arguing that I stopped being your attorney and became a coconspirator in a kidnapping plot. They'll say I should have turned her over to the authorities immediately as soon as she was in my presence."

"Do you want her to leave?"

Sylvia fumed.

"No, of course not. You might as well bring her in so I can meet her."

Alexi walked in, and Cristina came in with her. Apparently, Alexi had hit it off pretty well with Sylvia's legal intern. Sylvia walked around from behind her desk and pulled up a chair next to the two younger women.

"I'm happy to meet you," Alexi said. "Gina's told me a lot about you."

I was beaming about her good manners. Her mother had raised her right in that department, at least.

Sylvia's smile broadened. "And Gina's told me a lot about you, as well."

And I decided at that point to keep my mouth shut.

◆ ◆ ◆

A COUPLE OF DAYS went by, and nothing happened. I was waiting for the world to come down on my head, but so far there hadn't been a sound.

Sylvia had made a slight change to our arrangement—I called it a technical change, but she seemed to think it was important. Alexi was now Sylvia's client as well. Sylvia decided she could continue being the attorney for both me and Alexi until someone told her she had to give up one or the other because of a conflict of interest. That all sounded very lawyer-like—and very Sylvia-like.

As she promised she would, she had her law firm's investigators taking another, closer look at the God's

Children Foundation. The lead investigator had called her that morning and said they might be on to something. He didn't say what it was, but he did make an appointment to come in and talk with her. I begged her not to hold out on me, but she just threw her hands in the air.

"I don't know any more than what I just told you."

Sylvia had a contingency plan worked out if we got any hint of a criminal investigation. She'd made copies of the original, heartbreaking video that Alexi had sent to me and picked out some particularly damning passages from the diary that Alexi had carried with her. She'd tied all this together in a group of affidavits that would be ready whenever we needed them. Once we got word of any law enforcement action, Sylvia planned to contact the prosecutors involved and offer to assist them in finding Alexi in exchange for their commitment to investigate the child abuse charges. No names would be mentioned at first. I would be identified only as her unnamed client until a deal was struck. She also saw no reason to give up Allen Wilder's name until it became necessary. I questioned her on that, but she persuaded me that it was better to get the DA's commitment to go after a child-abuser-to-be-named-later than scare them off with the name of a prominent member of the community. She'd be asking them to grant me immunity in exchange for my testimony. That was an unusual approach, but she thought that the law firm name of Crichton, Moss, Harris, & Kaplan might carry a bit of weight even in Indiana.

I wasn't sure how this was all going to work. "Have you ever handled a case like this before?"

Sylvia looked at me with astonishment. Then she started to laugh.

"Of course not! *No one* has ever handled a case like this. No one's ever had a client like *you*."

◆ ◆ ◆

SYLVIA CONTINUED TO MONITOR the law enforcement bulletins out of Indianapolis, but there was no word of anything. She was starting to get the idea that the Reverend Wilder was too scared to call the police. If that's what he was thinking, the whole thing might drag on for a while. But something in me knew that it wouldn't happen that way.

I left Sylvia's office and headed for the Ferry Building. I'd made a commitment a month earlier to appear there at a noon panel about "Mysteries set in San Francisco." The city looked beautiful—in full picture-postcard mode—as I walked down to Jackson Street and then turned down the Embarcadero. I tried to enjoy the surroundings, but I was in a nervous mood, getting skittish at every corner. The events director from the bookstore at the Ferry Building was chairing the event along with a couple of local mystery writers. The topic was "noir mysteries set in San Francisco." I couldn't help thinking that I was about to play a part in one of them.

◆ ◆ ◆

I LEFT THE COMMISSION Board room when the panel was over, heading across the rotunda for the big staircase that would take me downstairs. Then I felt a hand on my arm.

"Ms. Perini, do you mind if I talk to you for a minute?"

I turned and saw a man I'd noticed earlier. He'd been sitting in the audience during the panel about mystery books. He'd caught my eye because he seemed totally out of place. Most of the people in the audience were young office workers from the nearby buildings, some of them brown-bagging it while others had takeout plates from some of the vendors downstairs in the big food hall. It was a pretty jovial group that picked up quickly on all the arcane references to San Francisco mystery writers that the panelists threw out. There were lots of questions and lively, hand-waving comments. Names like Dashiell Hammett and Joe Gores were tossed around, and everyone had favorite books to discuss.

But not this guy—he looked more like a refugee from a mystery rather than someone who spent any time reading them. He stared straight ahead during the presentation and never cracked a smile. He was gray-haired and partially bald, and I guessed him to be in his late sixties or maybe seventies. His rumpled sport coat bulged out in several places. At the time, I didn't focus on what was behind those bulges, but now that he wanted to talk to me, that was all I could think about. Was he carrying a pistol in a shoulder holster under his coat? His most dominant feature was his eyes—some of the saddest I'd seen anywhere. And right now I could feel those eyes on my neck, as I realized that he'd been watching me throughout the entire panel discussion. My instincts told me to get out of there.

I sped up a bit, but he kept pace with me even as I hurried down the stairs.

"I'm sorry," I said over my shoulder. "I'm in a hurry to get back to work, so I don't have time to talk."

"It'll just take a few seconds," he insisted. "I have a couple of questions to ask you, and after that I won't bother you."

He didn't say what he wanted, but I had a bad feeling.

I turned and went into the main floor of the Ferry Building, heading north down the big food aisle, hoping that the crowds would distract him or—if I was lucky—swallow him up. But he was still tagging closely behind. I finally headed out to the walkway along the pier, using that time to sort things out in my head. I pointed to an empty bench.

"Okay," I said. "We can talk here for a minute, and then I really do have to go." I grabbed a seat, sitting on the edge of it to make the point that I planned to get up shortly. He sat down next to me.

"What is that you want?"

I conjured up my most bland voice, trying to stifle a sense of panic.

"I'm trying to get some information about a young girl who's gone missing, and I'm hoping you can help me." He pulled out a picture and showed it to me. "This is the girl."

I looked at the picture, and my heart jumped. It was Alexi, and she was holding a guitar—probably the same guitar that housed a lot of her bad memories. I tried to turn down the voltage on my feelings, hoping they wouldn't show. I had to keep everything under control until I could get away from him.

I handed the picture back to him. "I'm afraid I can't help you."

He kept looking at me. I thought I saw a touch of sadness in his eyes.

"Her name is Alexi, does that mean anything to you?"

"I'm sorry, there's nothing I can do for you. I wish there were."

"We've had information that Alexi might be in this area, and we have reason to think that you might be able to help us."

My mind was racing around the inside of my skull, while I tried to maintain a bland exterior. Had my cover been blown that quickly? How did I screw up? My instincts told me the best thing to do was to say nothing, but I was dying to find out what he knew. So, I snuck in a question.

"Are you with the police?"

He shook his head no. "I used to be on the police force in Indianapolis, but now I'm just working on behalf of the family to find out what information I can about her."

His manner was disarming. He didn't talk like any cop I could remember dealing with. What seemed like aloofness minutes earlier now appeared to be restraint— even gentleness. In another context I might have found him to be charming, but not when there were alarm bells going off in my head. I wanted to find out what he was planning to do about Alexi's disappearance, but I knew it would be mistake to go into anything like that with him. The minute I showed the slightest interest in what he was saying, I would confirm everything he suspected about my involvement. He was smart enough not to tell me anything unless I asked, and I wasn't going to tip my hand by asking him. So for a few seconds, we just sat there, watching the Larkspur Ferry pull into the dock and not saying much of anything.

"I really wish you could help, because her mother is frantic to find her."

He almost got me with that. I knew I had to get up and walk away from that bench before I broke down in front of him.

As I left, he offered me a business card and insisted that I take it. I was certain I hadn't seen the last of him. I knew I had to tell Sylvia about this encounter immediately, but I didn't think she would have any better idea of what this guy was up to than I did. She was gearing up for a legal struggle, and this guy seemed to be working an entirely different approach.

I looked at the name on his card: David Fallon.

Davey

WHY WAS SHE LYING?

Every word out of her mouth was some sort of evasion. *I'm afraid I can't help you. There's nothing I can do for you*—did she think she could get away with that?

He'd been watching her for days as she and Alexi wandered around town. She probably thought she would put him off by weaseling around everything. But none of that was going to do her any good. She was lying—but why?

He sat on the bench overlooking the water for a few moments after Gina Perini walked off, trying to figure out what to do next. For the past couple of days, he'd gone back and forth in his mind about how to approach her. When he saw the flyer announcing the mystery panel at the Ferry Building, he thought that was a good opportunity to hear her speak and learn a little more about her. But after listening to her bantering back and forth with the others, he realized she wasn't at all what he expected.

One surprise was the accent. Given her name, it wouldn't seem odd that she had an Italian accent. But he'd already discovered that the "Perini" name was fictitious. She'd entered the United States under the name "Gina Bertani," but that didn't explain the Italian accent either. The "Bertani" name—and maybe even the "Gina"—could be phony as well. He'd learned as much as he as he could by slogging through the Internet, and he'd confirmed some of what he had found with sources in Homeland Security. But her identity was still a mystery. If he kept digging he might find the real story, but it wasn't clear what his next step should be. Until he learned more, he had to deal with "Gina" in the latest of her manifestations.

But the accent wasn't the biggest surprise. The real puzzle was how normal she seemed. There was usually some character flaw in a child molester or kidnapper that marked them as a little strange, but there was nothing like that here. She joked around with her fellow panelists for over an hour and gave no hint of any deep-seated trouble. He couldn't figure it out. He knew she had just grabbed a minor child and transported her across the country, but she didn't act like anything had happened.

She defied his expectations in other ways as well. Her stride was a bit ungainly—not that it bothered him, but he'd never seen a woman walk quite like that. The other panelists seem to think she was funny. He probably would have laughed at some of the things she said, if he hadn't been so focused on trying to figure out what made her tick. Her hands seemed different. They were long, and she used them to gesticulate in midair whenever she talked, but they really seemed to have a life of their own. Her hands and her voice wrapped themselves around words in a way that he'd never seen before. There might yet be an arrest in this case. But given Reverend Wilder's apparent reluctance to report Alexi's disappearance to the police, he wasn't so sure. Even so, the thought of this woman in handcuffs was disturbing.

Her seeming normality was making his job harder. He'd found Alexi—that part of his work was done. She seemed to be in no danger. Maybe he should have been satisfied with that, but he wasn't. He needed to know why she had been taken. It wasn't in his nature just to let that part of the investigation go by the boards. There was no obvious motive. Why had this Gina person traveled halfway across the country to pick up a teenage girl and take her to San Francisco? What the hell was she up to?

◆ ◆ ◆

HE KEPT SUSAN APPRISED of everything from the moment he got there, emailing her often and talking to her by phone. When he called her the first day to tell her he found Alexi, he could hear the relief in her voice. This was the first real assurance she'd had. Even though she'd received another message and picture from Alexi—this one two days after the one from Colorado—she was still relieved to find out that he had actually seen her. It was the high point in a case that didn't seem to have very many high points.

He asked Susan the question he'd been having so much trouble answering: "Do you have any idea who this woman is and why she may have taken Alexi?"

Susan said she didn't. Nothing jogged her memory. They'd gone over everything before he left Indiana, and since then he'd sent her a whole series of pictures and videos of Gina from San Francisco. Along with that, he gave her a report of the research he had gathered on her—including her former name, her shaky immigration status, and all the other questions about her background. He hoped something would ring a bell, but nothing did.

Susan's next question was the one he'd expected. "Can you just pick her up and bring her home?"

"I can't do this my own. If I tried, I wouldn't be in any better legal position than this Perini woman. I know you gave me a letter of authority, but it still wouldn't be a good idea. Gina—or even Alexi—might resist, and the situation could get out of hand."

"So, do we just do nothing?"

It came back to an issue that had bothered him from the beginning.

"Why hasn't a missing-person report been filed? If that had been done, it would be a relatively simple matter of contacting the San Francisco police and letting them handle it on your behalf. Have you talked to your husband about it?"

"No." But before he could ask anything more, she finished the thought. "I haven't talked to him about that or anything else."

The bitterness in Susan's voice had deepened in the last few days.

"You don't have to wait for him. If you want to report it to the police, I'll help you do it."

She hesitated for a second. "I'm not quite ready to talk to the police."

That was a strange way to put it. He couldn't decipher what she meant.

The best thing was for her to fly to San Francisco. She needed to talk to her daughter herself. Susan was unsure about doing that, but he convinced her that it was a good idea. Maybe a simple mother-daughter conversation could end the whole thing.

As far as Blaiseck and the Reverend Wilder were concerned, he had decided to stop talking to them altogether. He had sent them the pictures about Alexi's whereabouts, along with all the background information he had on Gina Perini. He had agreed earlier to do that. And even if he hadn't, it was probably best to keep them informed so they wouldn't suddenly change their minds and send the Indianapolis police on a wild goose chase. Neither of them had responded to his last email, but that didn't make any difference. Either way, he wasn't talking to them anymore.

◆ ◆ ◆

HE'D FOUND A CAFÉ across the street from Hayes Street Books the first day he was in San Francisco, and he'd been more or less camped out there ever since. There was a miscommunication at first between him and the young woman behind the counter about what type of coffee he wanted from the long menu on the wall, but he finally decided on a café Americano, adding his own milk and sugar, whenever he sat down to watch the bookstore. He thought Alexi might recognize him, so he stayed in the cafe when she was around. A few times when he knew she wasn't there, he walked across the street and spent some time looking in the window trying to get a feel for the place. He hoped he wasn't too obvious about it.

He was puzzled by it. Was it really a bookstore, or was it a front for something else? He'd taken several pictures, some with a long-distance lens. There were photos of Alexi reading, Gina standing in the doorway, and Alexi pulling books out of a box. He had a video of Gina and Alexi leaving the store and walking the fifteen feet or so to the doorway of the upstairs flat where Gina lived. It would have been a stretch to say that Alexi was "being held" there. The video showed Gina unlocking the door, as Alexi bounded up the stairway to Gina's flat without any prodding.

One time, when he was sure Alexi wasn't around, he crossed the street and went into the store. He stayed in the corner browsing through the bookshelves, but he was really watching Gina out of the corner of his eye as she unpacked boxes. He thought about confronting her right there, but then he saw the flyer about the mystery panel down at the Ferry Building the following day. He decided to wait until after that. He wanted to hear her talk—there had to be something in her voice or mannerisms that would give her away.

But he couldn't get away from the bookshelves before someone approached him.

"I wrote that."

He looked up and saw a man a little younger than himself. He was thrown off-kilter for a second, until he realized that the man thought he was looking at the book on the shelf in front of him. He wasn't doing that at all. He was just staring blankly at the shelf while he eavesdropped.

"You wrote that book?"

"No," the man laughed. "I wrote the shelf-talker right underneath it, you know, where it says, "Morrie recommends." He pointed to the little tag pasted on the shelf. "That's me, Morrie."

He apologized for his mistake.

"No," Morrie said. "I wish I had written the book. It's one you'd enjoy."

He fumbled an excuse, saying that he was just browsing. He made his way to the door as quickly as he could without arousing suspicion. He'd come closer to blowing his cover than he had anticipated.

Following Gina and Alexi was more strenuous than he had bargained for. The two of them left the store and headed in the direction of downtown. He followed them at a discreet distance, while they window-shopped and visited a couple of dress shops. They reached Market Street and headed down the escalator to the underground train. He picked up his pace a bit, so he could purchase a ticket and follow them though the turnstile. They got off at Powell and headed up toward Union Square, and he followed along behind them, watching as Gina talked and gestured toward the sights around them. The scene started to nag at him. She was looking less and less like a kidnapper and more and more like someone who was showing a visiting guest around town. What was going on?

They turned left on Post Street and went into the Medical-Dental Building. He spent an hour across from the building, cooling his heels until they reemerged, reminding himself of how much he hated doing stakeouts when he was with the police. Then Gina and Alexi stopped at the Café de la Presse on Grant and Bush for lunch, and there was another long wait. The long walk and the standing around were starting to take their toll on him. After they ate, they headed farther across town to the old Barbary Coast area where they walked into an older, expensive-looking brick building. He was dog-tired at that point, but all he could do was sit outside and wait. The brass plaque on the wall of the entrance read "Crichton, Moss, Harris, & Kaplan, attorneys at law." Lawyers—they must be up to something.

He wasn't sure what he was looking for anymore. After two days following these two women, he'd come up with a big nothing. There was no evidence of foul play or coercion. He kept looking for signs of restraint, but there were none. When Alexi wasn't with Gina, she'd head off on her own down Hayes Street and window-shopped. No one was tracking her movements—except him.

◆ ◆ ◆

AFTER HIS CONFRONTATION WITH Gina at the Ferry Building, he called Susan again to give her an update. But the minute she came on the line, he knew something had changed. There was a long gap between the time he said hello and when she responded.

"Susan, are you there?"

Another pause. "I'm here."

"What's the matter? Has something happened?"

When she finally spoke, she said something that took him by surprise.

"I think you should come home now and just leave things be."

"I don't understand."

"Alexi should probably just stay right there. There's no life for her here."

He felt a slight twinge of guilt. Had he gone too far in reassuring her that Alexi was okay? For the past few days he had been telling her that there were no signs of her being held against her will, but had he painted too glowing a picture of her life in San Francisco?

"Susan, I know I told you that Alexi seemed to be okay, but I didn't mean to suggest that you should just leave her here. She loves you and needs to have you back in her life."

"No, it's nothing you said."

"Then what is it? Something must have changed."

There was another pause. Susan seemed to be in deep pain.

"I found something, that's all. It's just…it's just that we've failed her miserably."

"What is it? What did you find?"

"I don't know if I can talk about it." He heard her taking a deep breath. "I was cleaning her room this morning. I moved the guitar case. There was something in the inside pocket, and..."

He had to draw out the rest of the sentence. "What was it?"

"There were pages from a journal. I didn't know she'd been writing one."

"What was in the pages?"

There was another long pause. He had to prompt her again to see if she was still on the phone. Finally, she spoke almost in a whisper.

"I don't think I can tell you."

She was crawling deeper and deeper inside her shell. He knew the warning signs of depression, and he thought he was seeing all of them in Susan Wilder. It took all he could do to convince her not to cancel her flight. She agreed reluctantly to keep the ticket she'd bought for San Francisco, as they had planned. When they met face-to-face, he thought, maybe he could find out what was going on.

"We've just failed her so much."

◆ ◆ ◆

THAT NIGHT, EVERYTHING FELL apart.

He spent the day across from the bookstore like he'd been doing for the past few days, but now he was doing it by rote. Surveillance was just a way of filling the day and preventing his mind from wandering where it shouldn't go. But at night, that mental discipline disappeared, and he was left alone with himself.

He watched as the bookstore reached its closing hour. The overhead lights were turned off in sequence until the store was in darkness. The employees left in a small group, heading up to the corner where they all went their separate ways. Gina and Alexi were the last to leave, shutting out the last light near the front of the store and then moving a few steps down the street to the doorway of Gina's flat. He saw the light go on in the stairway and watched it go off again a few minutes later, giving way to the lights in the apartment. He stared at the upstairs windows until the lamps in those rooms were turned off one by one, leaving just one light, which appeared to be a small lamp in the rear bedroom. Finally, that light went out as well, and Gina and Alexi were locked up for the night in their world. He was locked up in his.

He couldn't stand the thought of spending another night in the dreary hotel room he had a couple of blocks from the bookstore. The room had a cheap, flimsy feel to it. For the last two nights, he'd sat there with most of the lights off, staring at the oversized television screen on the wall. He never turned it on. It remained a glistening presence with a sleek blackness that seemed to taunt him. *Turn me on,* it seemed to be saying. *Turn me on even though you know there will be nothing you'll want to watch, and it will leave you more depressed than you already are.* For the past two nights, the only thing he had done was go through the methodical process of cleaning his pistol, checking its mechanisms, wondering how long it would be before he would have to use it.

He had to do something with his night hours, but he didn't know what. He started walking, but he had no idea where he was headed. There were people on the sidewalks, some happily jaywalking from one side to the other. They were in small groups, talking loudly, seemingly heading to a club somewhere, giving the impression that the evening's fun might just be beginning. But he had lost any sense of how to interact with other people. The last hint he had of human contact was watching the lights going out in Gina's apartment, as he imagined her long hands reaching up to turn off the switch.

Market Street cut at a broad angle that crossed the other streets. On the other side was a building with a cocktail glass in neon lights. He suddenly felt the need to be inside somewhere, drink in hand, soaking up whatever life he could get from a neighborhood bar. The doorway under the brightly lit Martuni's sign had been commandeered by smokers who were going through their rituals. The inside was dark and murky with a horseshoe bar that took up most of the main room. There was a smaller room off to the right where a piano was accompanying some off-key patrons who were trying to sing.

What was he doing there? He felt suddenly ancient, realizing that he was probably twenty years older than anyone else in the place. Despite the convivial crowd around him—or maybe because of it—he could feel the walls closing in on him from every direction. That feeling had been building for weeks, and now it was getting worse. His body's weaknesses were more pronounced. The sleeplessness, the lightheadedness, the recurring pains throughout his back and legs and chest—all of them were pinning him against a wall. And there was no respite from the opposite direction. His isolation from friends, family, and everyone else was pushing at him just as insistently. Illness seemed to have joined hands with loneliness to squeeze the life out of him.

The future was just another encroaching wall, squeezing in on him like the others. He was face-to-face with the realization that he had nothing to offer anyone. His current job was a hopeless joke, and he could see nothing beyond it.

And he couldn't escape into the past. That had been walled off as well, closing the box around him. In some ways, that was the hardest wall to deal with. As lonely as he was in San Francisco, it was nothing compared to the emptiness that had invaded his apartment in Indianapolis. His pictures, his memories, his artifacts—everything about his past was starting to suffocate him. If he was ever going to breathe, he had to get out of there.

His past life had been a fantasy that had deluded him for over forty years. Jimmy was…Jimmy was what? He was someone different from what he had thought. He would have loved him just as much if he had known. But he didn't know. And he couldn't blame his ignorance on those who hadn't told him. It wasn't Jimmy's fault. And it wasn't Carolyn's fault either. It pained him to see that poor woman going through such anguish over something he should have already known. What hurt the most was that he hadn't seen it himself. He'd missed every opportunity to know Jimmy in the way that he really was. Now, there was just a big empty space inside him where everything had disappeared.

◆◆◆

"Did you ever find a book you wanted?"

It took a second to realize that someone was standing beside him talking. He turned and saw a man standing at the bar who was almost his own age. He struggled for a second to recognize him.

"You probably don't remember, but I'm the one who tried to sell you that book the other day over at the bookstore."

He suddenly remembered the face.

"I never did get anything to read. I probably should have."

"My name's Morrie, by the way. What's yours?"

"Davey."

He thought for a second about giving him a phony name, but why bother? The Perini woman already knew his name. Why keep it from this guy?

"Are you from around here?"

Was this guy coming on to him? Anything was possible. But maybe he just wanted to talk.

"No, I'm from Indiana."

Morrie laughed. "That's kind of a coincidence. We just brought on a young girl from Indiana who is working for us part-time at the store. Her name's Alexi—I love her enthusiasm."

"Did she tell you anything about herself before she came out here?"

Morrie shook his head. "No, and I didn't ask her. I figure it was none of my business. I think she's a niece of our manager, Gina."

That little bit of information caught Davey's attention for a second, but then he realized it must have been a cover story that Gina had concocted.

"Did you meet Gina when you were in the store?"

"I think I saw her."

Morrie wanted to make chitchat. That was fine. He didn't mind talking.

"Are you from around here?"

"Yeah, I have a house out on the avenues. My wife and I lived there for twenty-three years before she died a few years back. I thought about moving after that, but I just never got around to it. It's convenient, though, for my bookselling job. I just take the N-Judah train on the Muni line, and I'm right here. I get to work with the younger kids at the bookstore, and I love it. Gina has me organizing reading groups for children. Do you have any children or grandchildren?" Morrie asked.

The question hit a bit of a nerve. "Yeah, I have a daughter. She's pregnant, so I guess I'm about to be a grandfather."

"You're lucky."

He didn't feel lucky. The idea of Mandy having a child was just an abstraction—something from another world. He wondered if she would even bother to tell him when the baby was born.

"I didn't mean to be too personal, but these kinds of things mean a lot to me. Our only child, Eric, was killed in Iraq by a sniper's bullet about eight years ago, so Brenda and I missed the entire experience of grandchildren. Now, with her being gone, too, I'm a little envious of people who have that opportunity."

"I guess it's good that you're able to work with children."

Was that the right thing to say? He didn't know if anyone in Morrie's situation would want to hear something like that. The conversation had meant nothing to him at first, but as they kept talking, he couldn't help admiring Morrie's determination to move on despite the bad luck he'd been dealt. He was beginning to like the guy.

"Let me buy you another beer." He reached around to catch the bartender's attention, but when he looked back, Morrie had a look of shock on his face.

"What's the matter?"

"There," he pointed at his chest, "inside your coat. Is that a gun you're carrying?"

He winced a little, not wanting to make too big a thing of it. Obviously, his shoulder holster and gun had taken this guy by surprise—and not in a good way.

"Yeah, it's the pistol that I carried years ago when I was a cop. It's no big deal. I've just gotten into the habit of wearing it. It doesn't mean anything."

But Morrie was up off his stool, his hands in front of him in a defensive position.

"I'm sorry, but I just can't be anywhere if there's a gun around."

"Look, I'm sorry." He tried to tone things down a bit so the others in the bar wouldn't overhear what they were saying. "I'm not planning…"

"It doesn't make any difference what you're planning,"

Morrie's voice wasn't loud, but his words had a soft, intense bite.

"If there's a gun somewhere, sooner or later it will go off. Somebody will be hurt or killed. It may be me—it may be you—it may be someone else. But that doesn't make any difference. It will kill someone."

"It's just a form of protection."

He repeated that line almost by rote. Did he mean that? He tried never to think about why he carried the gun, but he knew it was something more than just warding off attacks.

"My son was killed by gunfire." The emotional level in Morrie's voice was building. "I think I already told you that."

He nodded.

"But you also need to know what happened to my wife."

He didn't expect that, and it hit him like a slap to the face.

"Four years ago, the ex-husband of one of Brenda's coworkers walked into the insurance office where she worked and shot his wife. But he didn't stop at that. He shot three other women in the office, and then he shot himself. Everyone knew he was mentally disturbed. He shouldn't have been released from the hospital, and he shouldn't have been allowed anywhere near a gun. Nevertheless, he went to a gun show and bought an assault rifle. No questions were asked, nobody did a background check—he just gave the seller his credit card and walked out the door with his killing machine. The man who sold it to him had some remorse, but not very much. He later told the police that 'gun owners have rights.'"

Morrie paused for a second.

"But what I think he really meant to say is that guns have rights. When that attack was over, there were five bodies lying on the floor of the office. They were all dead, but the gun lying next to them was still working fine. It was full of life, probably ready for its next appointment."

There was nothing more to say. Morrie was already at the door, heading out into the street. There was a sudden chill in the spot where he had been standing.

◆◆◆

HE DIDN'T LOOK AT the clock, because he might never get back to sleep. But he knew he was in the dead zone—too early to wake up but too late for his heart to stop pounding. He was sticky with sweat. He threw off the wet sheet and blanket and then flipped over the pillow to find a drier side. His T-shirt was drenched. But he knew he'd have to cover himself with something warmer in a few minutes when the sweating began to turn into shivers.

Would it be life or would it be death? The dark thoughts were building up inside him, trying to grab a foothold. What did he have to fight with? His pistol was over on the dresser where he'd left it. Was it still his faithful companion? When he unstrapped the holster from his shoulder, he'd been afraid to touch the weapon itself. Morrie's words had shaken him. Did the pistol have an existence of its own? Had it been following him around all these years, ready to spring to life at a moment of its own choosing? Maybe it was capable of creating death on its own terms and then lying amidst its handiwork, getting ready to serve—or be served by—another owner.

What was it to be? His underpants were as wet as everything else from his midnight battles, but he kept them on. The moistness suddenly felt good, as he let his hand roam around on its own for a few moments, feeling whatever it wanted. It wouldn't last; it never did. But for the moment that sad bit of pulsing life diverted his attention from the fears that were trying to force their way into his head.

Was he flirting with life or with death? The pills that almost killed him warned that he had to be "healthy enough to engage in sexual activity." Was he "healthy"—or maybe "healthy enough"—to do what he was doing? And could anything that lonely and pathetic be thought of as "sexual activity?" And if it was going to kill him, so what? Whatever it was that was going on, he found himself in a place where he hadn't been for a long time, and he was frightened.

His fumblings had somehow become longer and more sustained. But after each pang of pleasure, he checked his body for signs of an impending disaster. The threat to his heart would probably be greater as he got closer, but at a certain point he ceased to care. He needed to get there. Memories emerged and were discarded. Faces came and went. Some images—like the pictures back in his apartment—were too toxic to touch. But he kept going. As he got deeper into the almost forgotten rhythms of his body, he kept searching for something. Finally, he seemed to find it, as a pair of long, gentle hands emerged from his subconscious and pushed his own hands aside. And seconds later, there was a voice that was talking to him and urging him to follow the rhythm of those hands. It was a low, melodious voice that he found intoxicating until…until he began to recognize it. Sadly, he wished he hadn't heard that voice at all. After a twinge of regret, he drifted back to the empty place where he had started.

◆◆◆

HE HEARD ONE SHARP crack and then another. It sounded like a pair of gunshots, but he wasn't awake enough to be sure. The noises could have come from the tail end of a dream, but he worried they might have come from outside the building. Light was pouring in around the edges of the blackout curtains in the hotel room. He could tell that he had overslept, but he didn't realize how late it was until he looked at the bedside clock and saw that it was 10:30 a.m. *My God,* he thought, *I haven't slept that late since I was a teenager.*

Then he heard a siren. It seemed to be the distant wailing of an ambulance that was several blocks away, but then he realized it was heading north in his direction. It was followed by another siren—this one had a different pitch that he recognized as a police car. The two sounds seemed to be converging about a block to the south of his hotel room.

His body started moving before his mind was fully engaged. He was sure the sirens were coming somewhere in the vicinity of Hayes Street Books. The gunshots and the siren could have had nothing to do with the store, but his mind didn't believe that for a minute. He pulled himself up from the bed, searching for the clothes he had scattered around the room. Within a few seconds, he was out the door heading down

Gough Street toward the intersection with Hayes. He reached the corner, and all his fears came roaring to the surface.

Two police cars were already blocking the street, and an EMT vehicle was parked in the middle of the block. The cops had put up a barricade across Hayes Street, forcing cars to turn down toward Market. The barrier at the other end of the block had been moved aside long enough to let an ambulance through, and it was easing its way down the street to where the EMT vehicle was parked. The police were holding people back on the other side of the street, while trying to get them to move in either direction away from the mid-block area. On the north side of Hayes Street—the side with the bookstore—the sidewalk had been cleared completely. Some of the people who had been there were walking toward him.

He found a kid in his twenties who had just been pushed back into the intersection.

"What's going on?" he asked.

The kid had a look of confusion on his face.

"Everyone's saying that there was shooting at the bookstore and that someone was killed."

Alexi

MORRIE WANTED HER TO play a few children's songs during the weekly story time, so she carried Gina's guitar downstairs. She loved playing it again, and the chords for the children's songs came back to her pretty quickly. She felt so good sitting with it in her lap that she convinced Gina to take a picture of her holding it and send it to her mother.

Gina poked her head around the bookshelves and told her she need to talk to her. But the way she said it was odd. She had just been talking with Gina a few minutes earlier, and there was nothing unusual in her voice. But now there was a look on Gina's face that she'd never seen before. The two of them walked outside and headed up to the apartment. Gina had a couple of sheets of paper in her hand that probably had something to do with what was bothering her.

They never got all the way up the stairs. Gina stopped at the landing and said maybe they could talk there. She sat on the top step, thinking she wasn't going to like whatever it was Gina was going to say.

"I talked to your doctor this morning, as a follow-up to when we saw her. Something came up, and she wanted to double-check it. Anyway, I had her send me the report." Gina hesitated for a second. "Alexi, this is going to be okay. We'll deal with it just like we've dealt with everything else."

Gina read her the last part of the report, and then she looked back up at her. She thought there might have been a tear in Gina's eye, but at that point she was crying so heavily herself that she couldn't see much of anything.

"We've got to talk about this and decide what to do. We'll have to tell your mother."

She nodded yes to everything, but within moments she thought that the room and the hallway were starting to close in on her. She had to get out of there—if only for a few minutes.

"Gina, can I have that?" She reached for the report that Gina had in her hand. "I've just got to take a walk or something. Would that be okay?"

Gina nodded yes and gave it to her. As she started down the stairs, she was so unsure of her footing that she almost stumbled. When she reached the door to the street, she turned right and walked past the bookstore without going in. She couldn't stand the idea of talking to any of her new bookseller friends at that moment. She kept going for several blocks, heading up Hayes Street past the point where it began climbing the hill. She stole a look at the medical report sticking out of her shoulder bag, thinking any moment it might burn a hole in the fabric.

She felt stalked. For the first time since she left Indiana, she thought she could feel him behind her, gaining on her no matter how fast she climbed the hill. She could hear his voice, his phony prayers, his awful whisperings, and she couldn't get away. She was panting heavily by the time she reached Alamo Square at the top of the hill. She sat down for a second on the cement wall around the park and just tried to think. The unfairness of it all threatened to overwhelm her.

She started walking again, first down Steiner Street and then turning left on Haight Street, knowing that would take her back to where she started. She couldn't run away from this, so she'd have to deal with it. Somehow it was going to work out. Five blocks later she was at Octavia Street, just a few blocks from the store. Some residents had installed a community garden near the spot where an old freeway had been demolished. It had become one of her favorite spots in the city. She found a bench near the sidewalk where she could sit down. She opened the report and tried as calmly as she could to read it.

A van came screeching to a stop at the curb next to her.

"Get in the back!"

She was startled by his words. But the muscular man with the shaved head who had just jumped out of the passenger side of the van didn't wait for her to respond. He grabbed her by the elbow and forced her into the back, slamming the door behind her. He got back quickly into the passenger's side, as the van sped off. Her shoulder bag was thrown against the seat as she hit the floor. She got up as far her knees and started screaming as she tried to pull on the side-door handle.

"Don't bother trying," the man in the front yelled at her. He turned around just enough to shove her back into the seat. "It's locked from up here, so don't waste your effort. Now shut the fuck up!"

She squirmed out from under his arm and started to yell even more. She tried to reach down for her shoulder bag, but he grabbed it out of her hand before she could get a grip on it. Then he tossed it on the floor in front of him.

"Let me out of here!"

He had a weapon now—a gun with a long muzzle that he swung around and held up to her cheek. His eyes were staring right into hers.

"I told you to shut up, and I mean it."

The fat man who was driving the car gave an ugly laugh. He stared at her through the rearview mirror. "You better do what he says, kid. He's been itching to fire that thing. If you're not careful, he might use it on you."

She climbed up onto the back seat and shoved herself into a corner. Her pulse was beating rapidly, as she tried to figure out what was happening to her. Who were these men? She thought she may have seen them somewhere around the church back in Indiana, but she couldn't be sure.

The man driving the van was asking questions of the other one.

"Which way do I go?"

"Go up to Grove and turn right."

"Should I turn on Franklin?"

"No, you want Gough, which is the street right before that—Franklin's one-way in the wrong direction. Just ease up a little when you turn on to Hayes. Let's see if we can get this done in one pass-by."

"Do you know what you're looking for?"

"I've seen the picture enough times. I know what she looks like."

What were they doing? Her sense of alarm grew as they got closer and closer to the bookstore. She eased herself over toward the window on the right side, worrying that at any moment the bald man might reach over and slap her back into her seat.

They were three doors away from Hayes Street Books. Through the window of the van she could see Gina talking to one of their regular customers on the sidewalk just outside the door. The customer moved away, and Gina turned to her right, facing them, as she started to head into the store.

"That's her," the driver said.

"I know. I've got her." The bald man pushed on the button to lower the window and brought the gun up so that it rested on his shoulder. His cheek was down against the stock, as he eased the muzzle out the window.

"Gina!"

The word came screaming out of her mouth before she even had a chance to think about it. At the same moment, she stuck her arm over the passenger-side seat, trying to reach the gun. Just as her hand touched his arm, she heard a loud, deafening crack. The noise stunned her. Then she heard the same sound again, as the gun was fired a second time.

"Okay, hit it! Let's get out of here."

As the driver sped up and turned sharply at the next corner, she was thrown against the side of the back seat. Images of the neighborhood went flying by the window, and she realized they had crossed Market Street and turned on to the freeway. Within minutes they had merged into another freeway heading south with the rest of the traffic. She stayed huddled in the corner, quietly shivering as she wondered whether either of the bullets had hit Gina. And if they missed, what else did they hit?

The bald man reached around and grabbed her by the arm until he had her face wedged up between him and the driver's seat. He slapped her hard with his free hand. "I ought to kill you now, you little shit." His breathe was so close she could almost taste it.

His cell phone rang, and he let go of her to answer it. He plugged in his headphones to listen.

"Yeah? Who said that?"

He listened again intently for a few seconds. "I don't think they know what they're talking about. I was there, remember, and there was no newscaster anywhere around."

The person on the other end was talking loudly, but she couldn't quite hear it. "Yeah." The bald man was in an argument. "Yeah, I hear what you're saying."

"I just know that I had a good aim. If anything went wrong, it was because this Goddam kid hit my arm. You know what I'm saying?" There was another pause while he listened. "Yeah, I hear you."

The driver turned off at the next exit and started driving down the city streets. As the fat man drove, the bald man grabbed her shoulder bag off the floor in front of him and began rummaging through it. He pulled out a sheet of paper that had caught his attention, and he began reading it. As he did so, he broke out into a short laugh. He picked up his cell phone and hit the return button, waiting as the person on the other end picked up the call.

"You're going to love this." He turned to the driver to let him in on the joke. "It turns out that the little bitch is pregnant."

Davey

THE FOG HAD COME pouring over the Hayes Street hill without warning, and it was unrolling itself down the street, bringing with it a cold that blanketed the shops in a drizzly mist. That cold was nothing compared to the icy chill that had settled in his soul. He should have been asking people around him what happened, but that would have meant opening his mouth and trying to utter words—or at least some meaningful sounds. He could barely function. All of his systems were turning themselves off one by one.

He could watch, and maybe listen—for the time being; he was capable of that. Even someone who was empty inside could do that much. He wandered the perimeter around the police lines, trying to piece together what had happened. Rumors were everywhere, many of them incoherent. There were a couple of people who claimed to have seen the shooting, and the police were talking to them. A pair of ambulances blocked the view of the store from most angles. He tried to peer around them and saw that one of the store windows had been shattered. The glass was strewn everywhere. Books that had been on display had apparently been tossed into the air and had landed on the sidewalk as the window exploded. The door itself had been split, and the EMT crews had yanked the rest of it off its hinges so that they could get their rescue gear through the doorway. A stretcher was loaded onto one of the ambulances. Then it pulled away. The siren got louder as it reached the intersection.

The forensic team was sifting through the debris in front of the store, hoping to find something. He knew how futile that could be. If it was a drive-by shooting, there would be no clues lying around—a couple of bullet casings, a possible skid mark, but that was about it. But like good police officers, they'd dig through the debris, bucking the odds, hoping something might show up. That was their job. That was what they were paid to do. But if they were burnt-out cops—like him—they would have no illusions. Maybe they would know that they were at the end of their rope.

A van with the logo of a local news station came through one of the barriers, and the driver parked it in the center of the street behind the police vehicles. As soon as the van stopped, a young woman jumped out and headed straight over to the officers who were handling the investigation. They apparently knew her, because they began talking to her and gesticulating toward the bookstore. Finally, they let her through the police line. She pushed her way into the store with her cameraman in tow. After a few minutes, she reemerged and motioned for her cameraman to set his equipment up at an angle where she could use the bookstore as a backdrop.

This is Cheryl Lopez reporting live for KPIX news.

I'm standing in front of Hayes Street Books, a popular meeting spot in the Hayes valley, where a drive-by shooting this morning has left this neighborhood in a state of shock. Witnesses say that two men in a van drove by the store less than an hour ago. As they got near the building, they appeared to slow down while one of the occupants fired two shots into the store, killing one person and wounding another. Police are still trying to piece together a motive for the shooting.

As you can see from these images taken inside the building, the shots did quite a bit of damage. There are books strewn everywhere. This picture shows a guitar that had been propped up next to a bookcase. It was apparently shattered by a ricochet from one of the bullets.

In addition to the gunshot victims, the police are investigating the disappearance of a fifteen-year-old girl who worked in the store, and they're trying to determine if it was related to the shooting. There's at least one witness who saw what he described as a young girl in the back seat of the van wrestling with the shooter at the time the gun went off. Other witnesses described the shooter as a muscular bald man, while the driver was described as a man who appeared to be quite overweight. No one got the make of the van, and the license plates appear to have been covered. So the police don't seem to have much to go on.

The names of the victims have not been released. But as I talked to the very shocked employees, I got a strong idea of who they were. The injured woman is the general manager of the store and a well-known figure in the community. The man who was killed was a widower in his late sixties who ran the store's popular children's reading program.

◆◆◆

IT WAS CALLING HIM, and as he got closer he could hear it screaming.

It kept repeating his name, saying over and over that it was no longer going to be denied. The hotel room was just a few yards away, and he knew it was sitting on his dresser where he left it as he ran out of the room. It was waiting for him, insisting that he come back, demanding that it be allowed to finish the job that had to be done.

"*A widower in his late sixties who ran the store's popular children's reading program.*"

Somehow Morrie knew this would be his fate. The minute Morrie had stumbled into his life, his death was just around the corner.

"*The general manager of the store, a well-known figure in the community.*"

Gina had been shot because of him—there was no other way to explain it. If he hadn't been so determined to find her and expose her, she wouldn't be fighting for her life in an ambulance right now.

"*A fifteen-year-old girl who worked in the store.*"

He had set out to find Alexi, but thanks to him she might be lost for good.

"*A muscular bald man.*"

Curly.

"*A man who appeared to be quite overweight.*"

Slim.

No one mentioned John Blaiseck, the man who must have set everything in motion.

But it was he—Davey Fallon—who was the agent of disaster. He'd pinpointed the store, documented everyone's movements, forwarded the pictures, and gave Blaiseck everything he needed in order to do what he had done. If it hadn't been for his own toxic intervention in things, it never would have happened.

He had gone from being sad, to being lonely, to being useless. And now, finally, he'd become destructive. He could no longer tolerate himself. He couldn't just sit and wait any longer while those walls closed in around him for the last few inches.

The pistol was where he left it. He pulled it out of the holster, as it kept screaming at him not to resist. It turned itself around, demanding that he let it do what it had to do.

The pistol and he stared at each other.

Gina

I AWOKE TO THE sight of a doctor looking down at me. He was still in his blue surgical cap as he hovered over me for a few seconds more. The stencil across his gown said University of California Medical Center. I had to blink a couple of times before I could remember where I was.

"You did fine," he said. "The bullet missed your vital organs. We got the pieces out of your shoulder, so there should be no permanent damage. If all goes well, I think we can send you home tomorrow."

Send me home.

As I thought about that, I wondered what was left of my home and everything else.

As the drug wore off, the vision of the shooting crept back into my head. I remembered a few things—they were confusing and terrifying but still vivid. And I also remembered other things that Sylvia told me when I was half awake and heading into surgery. My head was a collage of facts, pain, and paranoia all wrapped into one awful narrative. But one thing was certain: my life had fallen apart, and I didn't know if I had the energy to put it back together.

I knew Morrie Richards was dead—that dear, sweet man didn't deserve to be dragged into any of this. How did the others at the store tell the children what had happened? Some of the kids were probably walking up to the bookstore, just a few doors away, when he was gunned down. Sylvia didn't want to tell me about Morrie—not as I was being wheeled down the hall on a gurney, heading into the operating room. But one of the nurses who walked by let it slip. *Is this a patient from that shooting downtown—the one where someone was killed?* I saw Sylvia wince. I knew what she was thinking: now that I knew someone had been killed, it was better that she tell me who it was. She didn't want me to go into the netherworld of anesthesia with that question bouncing around in my brain.

And I knew Alexi was missing. As chaotic as that scene was in front of the store, I would have known if she were there. By the time Sylvia arrived at the hospital, I had to blurt out what my intuition was telling me: "They took Alexi, didn't they?" Sylvia hemmed around her answer a bit, conceding that Alexi was missing but not willing to admit that she'd been kidnapped by the people who shot me. By the time I was out of surgery, however, Sylvia had more information. But it wasn't anything she was happy to pass on to me. The police found a witness who saw a girl matching Alexi's description being forced into the back of a van similar to the one seen on Hayes Street minutes later. The police hadn't yet confirmed her identity. But I didn't really need any more proof of that, because in my heart I already knew she was in the van. The last thing I remember before the bullet hit me was Alexi's voice. It was muffled, but still she was screaming my name at the top of her lungs. I turned to see where she was, and that slight movement allowed me to avoid a direct hit from the bullet. In that moment, Alexi had saved my life.

An orderly wheeled me from the recovery room back into the room where I would be spending the night. It had a partial view of Twin Peaks, but I didn't feel like looking at the scenery. Sylvia was there when they brought me in, and she helped the nurse get me off of the gurney and onto the bed. I thought then, as I've thought ever since: What the hell would I do without her? She made herself as comfortable as she could in the room with her notebook computer in her lap and her cell phone next to her on the table. Sylvia wasn't in her go-to-court clothes, but she still looked very good. As stupid as it was at that moment, I was envious of what she was wearing.

Sylvia said she had news about the investigation into the God's Children Foundation. She promised she'd spell it out for me when I felt up to hearing it. From the look on her face, I guessed it was something important. But she wanted to give me a few more minutes to clear my head.

I had a long list of worries. My fears about Alexi were at the top, and they were getting worse by the minute. There was no hint of where they'd taken her. The longer it took to come up with a solid lead, the colder the trail might get. The future of the bookstore didn't rise to that level of anxiety, but it was a worry nonetheless. What was going to happen to it? The store had been closed since the shooting, but the staff was planning to open it the next day. Miriam called and left a message, telling me not to worry about anything because they would take care of it. I didn't see how they could. If my memory of the shattered glass lying on the sidewalk near my face was any indication, the front of the store would have to be boarded up. I could only imagine what the inside looked like. I wouldn't have been a bit surprised if the owners resurfaced and fired me, once they realized that the shooting was prompted by someone out to get me.

Why did the reverend and his pals try to kill me? It had to have been them. If it had been anyone else, why would they have kidnapped Alexi? Sylvia and I had expected the reverend to go to the police, but I guess I shouldn't have been too surprised that he and his friends would take the law into their own hands and just grab her. There was a certain kind of logic to that from their point of view. The reverend would get Alexi back and keep the police out of the case entirely.

But why did they decide to shoot me? Once they had Alexi, was I still that much of a threat to them? I couldn't figure it out. I didn't know anything about them other than what Alexi had told me, so it was all secondhand information. Did the idea of shooting me come from the reverend or from those around him? Either way, it didn't make much sense. The only hint I had about what they might be doing was when that sad-eyed investigator stopped me at the Ferry Building and asked me about Alexi. Did he have a role in this?

◆ ◆ ◆

I THINK I MUST have dozed off. I don't know how long I was out, but it could have been a few minutes. As I fell asleep I'd been thinking about that investigator who had tracked me down and about our conversation out by the ferry terminal. And for that reason, I guess, I was startled out of my wits when I woke up. I had to blink a couple of times to make sure I wasn't dreaming. That same man with the same doleful eyes was standing there in the doorway of my hospital room, looking like a ghost of himself.

"Can I come in?"

"What are you doing here?"

I almost barked out the question. There was enough debris from the medications and congestion in my throat to make my tone sound harsher than I intended. Still, it was frightening to see him there.

"Please, I just want to talk to you for a minute."

His tone and his gestures were as abject as he could make them.

Sylvia sat up in her chair in alarm, as she looked from him to me and then back at him. She seemed ready to pounce.

"Gina, who is this?"

"It's the man I told you about. He's the one that approached me at the Ferry Building and asked me all the questions about Alexi."

Sylvia was out of her chair in an instant, heading toward him. "How did you get in here?"

She turned and reached for the call button. "I'm going to get security in here. I can't believe they let this guy past the nurses' station."

"Don't, please. I'll go soon, but there's just something I need to tell you."

I'm not sure why, but I was willing to listen to him.

"Sylvia, let him stay for a few minutes. Let's hear what he has to say."

Sylvia looked at me skeptically but then relented. I motioned for him to sit down in the empty chair near the door. I wasn't just being hospitable. He looked so frail that I was afraid he was going to fall down.

"Tell me your name again."

"It's Fallon. Davey Fallon."

"This is Sylvia—she's my best friend and lawyer. She's afraid to have you anywhere near me, and I can't say I blame her. But I'm willing to listen."

He nodded slightly, giving the impression that he knew his presence there was hanging by a thread. If I didn't like what I heard, I was going to call security myself.

"I understand." He glanced back and forth between us as he spoke. "The reason I need to talk to you is that I think I know the names of the men who shot you."

Sylvia's reflexes took her to the edge of her chair. "Who are they?"

"The two men I'm talking about fit the descriptions that I've heard about from the witnesses, and they always seem to travel together. They work for the God's Children Foundation in Indiana. I don't know whether they have any formal arrangement with that group or not. But they do jobs for them. Around the office, they're known as Curly and Slim, but I can give you their real names."

Sylvia had her phone out and was already pressing the record button.

"I want you to repeat what you just said and then give me everything you know about these two guys, including the full spelling of their names and anything else you might know."

Davey nodded okay.

"And do you understand that I'll be forwarding this immediately to the SFPD along with your name and all of your contact information?"

"I know what you have to do. I'm a former cop."

Sylvia kept the recording device in motion as Davey told her what he knew about the two men. She interrupted him a couple of times with questions—mainly to find out the connection between the killers and the people they worked for. It was hard to be sure, but I thought he was telling us everything he knew. If it was an acting job, it was a good one.

But when she got to the most important question, he had to admit that he had no more information than we did. He had no idea where they'd taken Alexi.

When she had what she wanted, Sylvia snapped the phone off.

"I'm going to step out into the hall where the phone reception is better and forward all of this to the investigating officer on the case." She looked at me. "Are you going to be okay in here alone with this guy while I go make my phone call?"

I told her I would be.

◆ ◆ ◆

"I BLAME MYSELF FOR what happened to you."

Davey Fallon hadn't moved from his spot near the door. He looked uncomfortable—probably thinking he might need to get up and leave at any minute, if things didn't go well.

"I followed you around for days and kept a record of everything you and Alexi did. I took pictures and sent them to the office at the same time I was sending them to Susan Wilder. I'm sure that's how the people at the foundation knew who you were and where to find you. It was a terrible mistake."

"I didn't see you doing any of that."

He shrugged. "I kept out of sight. I can be pretty good at that. What happened to Morrie Richards has hit me hard. He was a nice man—someone who could take life in stride and make the best of it. I talked to him the night before he was killed."

That surprised me as much as anything. I wanted to ask him where that happened, but I didn't want to interrupt what he was saying.

"I know it might not make that much sense, but I feel responsible for what happened to him."

His head was drooped. There seemed to be more that he wanted to say. His voice was low—at times tentative.

"Without me, they wouldn't have known how to find you."

He was repeating himself. He seemed to have a need to go over and over what had happened.

"If it hadn't been for me…" He paused, his mind off somewhere. "Sometimes I think that if I had never been…" His eyes were moist. "It's been a hard feeling for me to overcome."

"I'm glad you decided to tell me."

He nodded.

"I've always had a bad feeling about the foundation, but I couldn't put my finger on it. I haven't talked to anyone from there in several days. The only one I've spoken to is Susan Wilder."

He looked up at me. "I don't know what anyone else has done, but you have to believe that Susan is a good woman. She really cares about Alexi."

"I've known that all along. And I know that Alexi loves her and misses her." I felt a need to reassure him. "I never wanted to keep her away from her mother."

Davey nodded slightly. He seemed to appreciate that.

"I didn't know what to expect when I caught up with you. I figured out how it happened—that you'd met up with Alexi in Indianapolis and drove her with you to the West Coast. But I didn't know why—I still don't. When I started investigating you, I was expecting to find someone with some sort of criminal connections. I thought it might be drugs, or kidnapping, or child molestation—anything at all. I wasn't sure. But after watching you for days, I realized how wrong I was. Alexi seemed to be free to come and go when she wanted. I'm not sure how to describe it… She just seemed happy around you."

"She is—more than I had hoped for."

Davey allowed himself a small smile. He seemed to be getting comfortable talking to me.

"I don't know why you got involved."

He shrugged a little, probably hoping I would give him an answer. When I didn't respond, he just continued his own line of thought.

"I've been trying to work backward from what I know. There had to be some reason why you went to all that effort. My only guess is that she was probably being abused in some way at home. Was that it?"

"Yes."

"Was it Reverend Wilder?

I nodded. "It was pretty bad."

He sat quietly for a few minutes, probably trying to come to grips with what I had just confirmed.

"But I still didn't know your connection with Alexi. I'm thinking that it must be something going way back that I don't know about. Otherwise, why would you have done it?"

"That's all true."

I knew he wanted to hear more, but I wasn't ready to go into my relationship with Alexi—not just then. That would have taken our conversation way off course. Right now, he was talking, and I wanted to listen. But he was starting to fade a bit. He rubbed his left arm, like it was in pain, and I could see that he was perspiring. He looked pretty bad.

"Are you okay?"

"Me?" He seemed surprised that I might be concerned. "I think I am—but I'm not really sure. I've had a rough couple of days, and…I guess I'm just lucky to be here."

He paused for a second, looking like he was trying to decide whether to tell me something else—something more personal.

"I had a heart attack a few years ago. And when I get a pain or anything like that, I always worry that I might be having another one."

"Well, if you need a heart specialist, the UC Med Center has some of the best in the world right here in this building." I made a grand gesture with my arms, forgetting for a second about the trauma in my heavily bandaged shoulder. I winced from the pain.

"How's your shoulder? Are you going to be okay?"

I told him what the doctor said, and he nodded. "Gunshot wounds can be tricky, so be careful."

"That's what I'm learning. Did you ever have a bullet wound?"

"Once, but it wasn't when I was a cop. It happened years before that when I was in Vietnam. It was a serious wound, and they had to medevac me out of there. It almost killed me."

There was more to that story. There seemed to be things that had been bothering him for a long time, and I could sense that he needed to talk about them. He hardly knew me, but sometimes it's easier that way. There've been times when I've been too fearful or embarrassed to say something important to a friend, but then I found myself blurting out the same thing to someone I hardly knew. Davey had reached that point.

"It's not just the bullets. It's the war itself that can kill you—it gets into your soul. You end up with the kind of wounds that can never heal."

He looked up at me, but his eyes seemed to be focused somewhere else. "You're lucky if you never went through that."

In fact, I did. I'd had my own war. But I wasn't prepared to talk about it.

"When I think about what happened, I sometimes feel it would have been better if I had died right there instead of spending my whole life trying to figure out what went wrong. I've been hiding from myself ever since and denying what was eating me up inside."

He had one more thing to say.

"I lost my best friend, Jimmy, that night. He was lying just inches away from me when the attack happened. I don't think I've ever loved anyone as much as I loved him."

◆ ◆ ◆

SYLVIA CAME BACK INTO the room, and she sensed that the atmosphere was emotionally charged, giving me a look of concern. "Is everything okay in here?"

I told her I was fine. Davey had composed himself enough to shake his head in agreement.

Sylvia was still wary. Her attitude toward Davey Fallon hadn't softened nearly as much as mine. Still, she managed to thank him for the information.

"The police were happy to get that. That's the only solid lead they have. Right now, they're checking all the auto rental agencies to see if they can find a van rented in the name of either one of those two."

Sylvia pulled her chair up to the only free table in the room and opened up her notebook.

"Gina, do you feel like going over this report?"

I was starting to fade a bit. The pain medication was wearing off, but I told her I wanted to hear what she had to say rather than putting it off any longer. She started peeling through a series of screens, looking for the one she wanted. She also had some printed pages that she pulled out of her briefcase.

"It's the report I was starting to talk about when he walked in."

She nodded her head toward Davey. Seconds later, her eyes followed, as she stared at him. I knew what she was thinking. She wanted him to leave. But Davey just sat there. He wasn't being obstinate. He was probably just too lost in his own thoughts to take the hint.

"Unless there's something confidential in there," I said, "I think Mr. Fallon can stay."

Sylvia shrugged. "Whatever you say—the report's not confidential anymore, because I've already sent a copy to the police."

Sylvia turned back to the screen on her notebook.

"The investigators had just put the finishing touches on the report and were walking into my office when we got the word that you had been shot."

Davey squirmed. Sylvia probably intended that comment for his benefit.

"What it shows is this: the God's Children Foundation is currently under investigation by the Justice Department as a front organization for a group that smuggles children into the US for sexual abuse. In many cases, the abuse is being committed by their so-called adoptive parents."

Davey looked shocked. I'd suspected something like that was going on, but for him it seemed like something out of the blue. But according to Sylvia, the child abuse was even more extensive than I had guessed. There hadn't yet been any indictments, but the entire ring was being investigated by at least two federal grand juries. The foundation had arranged some legitimate adoptions over the years—enough, apparently, to satisfy their big supporters and garner some favorable press coverage. But those adoptions, it appeared, just served as a cover for the more lucrative sex trafficking of minors. The church was under investigation as well because of its close ties to the foundation, but so far the investigators hadn't tied the church to any specific case.

Sylvia stopped for a second and looked at me. "When we give them what we have about Allen Wilder, that information will probably cement their case against the church."

There was more to the report. Sylvia didn't have the actual names of the men under investigation, but she did have the aliases that had been assigned to them by the DOJ. There were "John Does" all over the country that had been benefitting from this sex ring with preteen and teenage girls—as well as a few boys. The report referred to them as "International Johns," and they included several accountants in St. Louis, a group of real estate executives in Atlanta, and as many as five lawyers New York. The list went on and on— there were three suspects in San Francisco, including a local doctor. The Reverend Wilder wasn't named or identified on the list, but from the look on Sylvia's face, I could see that it would only be a matter of hours before that was rectified.

Sylvia stared at Davey, apparently trying to assess his reaction to what she'd said.

"As shocking as this is, it probably shouldn't come as a complete surprise. The signs were there. The International Labor Organization estimates that there are as many as one-point-eight million children sexually trafficked worldwide. That background information is included here in the report." She stabbed at the page in front of her. "UNICEF reported in 2006 that the number was closer to two million."

Davey was shaking his head from side to side.

"You have to believe me that I had no idea this was going on."

"I'll accept that for now," Sylvia said. "But I want to know more about the people you worked for. You said you worked with John Blaiseck?"

"That's the man who hired me, the one you could say I reported to."

"Well, I don't want you to guess at anything. Do you know anything about his background? According to the information we have from the DOJ, he's one of the main people behind the whole sex ring. He's been masterminding an operation to get kids out of orphanages, war zones, or anywhere else where they might be vulnerable and them matching up with pedophiles. Most of his clients have been in the US, but there are some in other countries as well. He's apparently been doing it for decades."

"I don't know anything about his background." Davey was almost pleading. "I never had any reason to look into it. I don't know where he's from. He has an Eastern European accent, and I always assumed he was Russian."

"Well, he's apparently Bosnian, and he's operating in the US under a fake identity. Reading between the lines on this, it appears that he's also a wanted war criminal."

There was a sick feeling in the pit of my stomach, and it kept growing as they talked. The painkillers were wearing off, but it was more than just that.

"Sylvia, do you have a picture of this Blaiseck person?"

She shook her head no. "There are no photos in the report."

Davey spoke up. "I might have one." He pulled his cell phone out of his pocket and flipped through the files. "Here's one of him standing in the hallway of the foundation office, talking to Reverend Wilder."

He gave the phone to Sylvia, and she handed it over to me. My hand was shaking so badly, I almost dropped it. It took only one glance at the phone, and I knew I was right.

"Sylvia, he's the one I told you about—the one from back in the war days."

Sylvia had heard my story enough to know immediately what I was talking about. "Good God," she muttered under her breath.

Davey was looking at me in confusion.

"I knew this man in Bosnia during the civil war back there in the nineties."

Davey said, "I never knew..."

"I'm sure you didn't," I interrupted. "I first saw him when I was growing up in an orphanage and then later on when he headed up one of the Militias. At the time, he was simply known as the *Komandant*. He had a brother that everyone knew as the *Hijena*—the Hyena—who was as sadistic as he was. The man you know as Blaiseck is a vicious killer, and I'm sure he's the one who ordered his thugs to kill me."

Davey still couldn't make the connection, and I could understand why.

"He wants me dead because I killed his brother. It was something I had to do. If I hadn't shot him, he would have killed me and Alexi's mother."

Davey looked speechless. I could see him trying to put together a question, but he couldn't figure out what to ask. Sylvia, for her part, seemed to be caught up in a rapid thought process, probably playing out in her head all of the possibilities of this new information. Me, I was exhausted.

"I need to be alone for a while, okay? Sylvia, could you ask the nurse to come in for a second on your way out? I need some more of the pain medication."

Sixteen years had vanished in an instant. For a few moments I was back in Bosnia, trapped in a cellar with the *Hijena* and Anja. The walls seemed to be tightening around me. The troubles from years earlier had finally found their way back to me.

Davey

SYLVIA KAPLAN CONFRONTED HIM as they left the hospital room. She acted like she wanted to talk to him, and she motioned for him to follow her down to the waiting room at the end of the hall. He stood there in that room for a second, not knowing what to expect, and then he finally sat down in one of the chairs. Sylvia pulled out a chair and sat opposite him, staring at him for a few moments. There was a time when that might have bothered him, but at the moment he just waited for whatever it was she had to say.

She finally shook her head a bit and settled into a frown. "Why are you here?"

He'd been asking himself this same question for the last twenty-four hours.

The gun barrel stared at him, and the voice told his trigger finger how easy it would be. Why are you waiting?

Why?

That was the question he couldn't answer.

Drowning in his failures, that question kept interrupting him. Why?

Why was he alone in that miserable room? Why had things gone so wrong and caused so much harm? Why had he spent his whole life trying to deny what was destroying him? If he ended it now, he'd never know the answers.

Why? It was the detective's question, and it saved his life.

He dropped the gun and fell back on the bed, sobbing out loud, with no idea of how he would make it through the next few moments. His heart was pumping madly, and he wondered if a heart attack would finish what he had just stopped himself from doing.

He lay there for hours until daylight gave way to evening. Each thought brought with it the same realization—he had no right to be there. The same brain that was contemplating each new speck of an idea could just as easily have been spattered on the walls, leaving those thoughts nowhere to go, no place to be born. As the night wore on, he realized that the images coming into his mind had been reclaimed out of nothingness.

◆ ◆ ◆

WHY? HE COULDN'T ANSWER her question.

The only answer he could think of made no real sense— maybe he'd been rejected by death and sent back to live his life.

Sylvia finally dropped her glare. She'd apparently decided she'd get more out of him if she talked to him in a more businesslike tone.

"Well, if you can't answer that, just tell me why I should trust you."

"All I can say is that I wouldn't be here if I didn't want to help."

Sylvia gave a short grunt, seemingly taking at face value what he had just said to her.

"Gina's kind of taken with you. I can see that. But I just want you to know that I'm not nearly as convinced as she is that you won't screw things up again. I only have your word that you're not in touch with those people. Do you understand what I'm saying?"

He nodded yes. He didn't want to get into an argument.

"So let's just say this—as far as I'm concerned, you're on probation."

She pulled out a business card and wrote something on the back. Then she handed it to him.

"That has my cell phone number on it, and I want you to call me if anything comes up—anything at all, okay? Will you promise me that?"

"I'll do whatever you want."

Sylvia allowed herself a smile. "Good, then I know we'll get along."

"There is one thing I need to tell you, however. Susan Wilder is flying into San Francisco tomorrow. I'm supposed to meet her at the airport. We arranged it a few days ago, and I don't want to change it."

The frown was back on Sylvia's face.

"What's that all about? Is she working with them on this?"

"No, I'm sure she isn't. She hasn't talked to her husband in days, and I doubt if she has talked to Blaiseck at all. She may not even know about the shooting and Alexi's disappearance. I doubt any of this even made the news in the Midwest. Either way, I need to talk to her."

He was dreading the prospect. He had no idea how Susan would react to everything that had happened in the last twenty-four hours.

"Maybe you should just tell her to stay home. If she comes here, she'd be in the way. We need to focus on finding Alexi."

He shook his head no. "I can't do that to her. I'm worried about what she might do if she's left alone. She hasn't told me all the details of what she suspects about her husband, but I know it's pretty serious."

"Well, if she suspects something about her husband, she's very right."

Sylvia put her notebook computer on the table and faced it toward Davey.

"Let me show you what was going in that house. Alexi kept a journal—it was apparently part of a whole series of journals. She had the current version of it with her when she got here. Here are some pages that I scanned. They're pretty devastating."

He looked at the pages until the descriptions became too brutal. "I had no idea this was going on."

Those pages answered a lot of questions. The last time he had talked to Susan, she had just found some of the earlier journals in Alexi's guitar case, and they were probably just as sordid as the pages Sylvia just showed him. Those descriptions must have torn her apart. And she was probably even more devastated when she read what else Alexi had been saying. He couldn't understand why Susan had been telling him, "We failed her." But now he understood. The explanation was there in Alexi's own words. In the journal, she kept asking the question, "Why can't my mother see what's going on?"

"There's one other thing you need to see," Sylvia said. "Gina flew to Indianapolis to get Alexi out of there right after Alexi sent her this. Take a look."

He thought he was beyond the point of being shocked by anything involved with the case, but the video was making him sick. It was so explicit that he found himself darting his eyes from side to side, hoping that there was no one else in that public waiting room watching him as he looked at something so awful.

"Now do you see why Gina did what she did? You're an ex-cop. You know the risks she was running. I knew them too, and I told her so. But she just had to do the right thing. I say that, so you'll know what kind of person you're dealing with."

◆ ◆ ◆

THE NURSE CAME INTO the waiting area and told them that Gina was awake. She wanted to see them.

As they got back near Gina's room, Sylvia took him aside one more time. "Okay, I'm going to trust you in all this. So don't let me down. I love Gina dearly. And if anyone hurts her, I'll come after them."

He nodded that he understood.

At the doorway to the room she stopped him again.

"There's one other thing you need to know so that you won't make a fool of yourself. Gina is transgender."

Alexi

SHE REFUSED TO GET out of the van. When they pulled into the parking lot of the motel, she kept sitting in the back, screaming when they tried to touch her. Finally, the fat man grabbed her and held her as the bald man tied a rope around her wrists. They pulled her out of the back and dragged her into the motel room. She wished there were someone in the parking lot who could see what they were doing, but the lot was empty. There were a couple of cars in the parking spaces, but there were no people.

She didn't know where they were, but it seemed to be somewhere in the industrial part of the city. There was a major street just beyond the intersection, but the cars were too far away for the drivers to see her. They couldn't have heard her no matter how loud she yelled. Even the motel office was out of view around the corner, and she couldn't see anyone who was running the place. The only thing visible was the sign that said "Sands Motel" sticking out from the side of the building.

She yelled that they were hurting her wrists. The bald one slapped her and told her to "shut up," as he pushed her down on the bed. The fat one just laughed. There was nowhere she could get away from them in that tiny room—one of her two kidnappers was with her at all times. A doorway connected that room to the adjacent one, and when they switched positions, they came and went by that door. When she told the fat one she needed to use the bathroom, he smirked and pointed her toward the bathroom door. She wanted him to untie her hands, but he wouldn't do it. And he refused to close the door. He just sat outside with the door half open and made snickering noises.

When nighttime came, she lay on the bed in the dark, wondering what they were going to do with her. The next morning she tried to prop herself up, but she couldn't do much more than stare at the curtains, wondering where she was. She knew the name of the motel, but that was all she knew. She had to find a way to get out of there, but she had no idea how to do it.

The connecting door opened, and another man walked in. She hadn't seen him before. He was tall and thin with brownish-gray hair. He had a weird moustache that curled around the corners of his mouth. He walked over to the bed and stared down at her. Then he grabbed one of her wrists and worked his hand under the twine that was tying them together. He appeared to be trying to take her pulse, but his touch gave her the creeps. Then a second man stepped through the doorway. This one had funny eyes and a mean look on his face. He looked like he might be the guy in charge. He stopped and said a couple of words to the bald man, and then he walked over and stood behind the one who was hovering over her. She thought for a second that she recognized him. Then, when she heard his raspy voice, she was sure of it. He was someone who hung around the church. And he was a friend of the reverend.

The thin man leaned farther over her bed and acted like he wanted to examine her body. He tried to lift her skirt, but she flailed around with her legs to try and stop him. Finally, the man with the raspy voice grabbed her legs, pinning them down harshly to the mattress, while the other man pulled down her underpants and felt around her lower abdomen. He finally backed off and said something about needing to go get his kit. She kept squirming, but the man in charge gave her a short slap with the back of his hand that got her attention. She found his finger poised at the tip of her nose, eyes glaring down at her. "If you know what's good for you, you'll lie still and shut up."

The thin man came back a few minutes later with a black satchel that he opened up. He pulled a syringe out of the bag and hooked it up to a small tube of liquid, pushing down on the plunger a couple of times to see if the liquid would squirt out of the tip. She tried to wiggle away, but it was useless. The second man had her in a tight grip that kept her immobilized on the mattress. She started screaming, but they ignored her.

The thin man took a deep breath.

"I think it's ready to go."

"Do it. I can't hold her down forever."

"It won't take effect immediately. It'll be few minutes before she's sedated, so you may have to hold her for a while."

"Then we need to get started."

The thin man looked uncomfortable. "Are you sure you want me to do this? These aren't the most ideal conditions, you know."

"What the hell are you talking about? You've done it before, haven't you?"

"Once—several years ago, but that was in a hospital. This is different. You've only given me an hour's notice."

The other man was right in the thin man's face. "I told you to get busy, so listen to what I'm telling you. If this thing blows up, you're in as much trouble as anyone else. So if you don't put in that syringe, I'm going to do it myself."

She felt the needle go into her arm, and after a few minutes the men started to back away. She tried to move her arms and legs, but she could feel them getting heavier. Although she was woozy, she could hear men's voices coming from the connecting room. The man who had given her the shot said he was stepping outside for a second while he waited for the anesthesia to take effect. Although her hearing was getting foggier, she could hear that the other one was talking to someone else in the adjacent room. She recognized a voice that terrified her. It was the reverend.

"Does he know what he's doing?"

"He's a doctor. He'll be okay."

"But is this his specialty?"

"What the fuck do you want me to do then? Do you want me to write a letter to the medical association for a recommendation?"

His voice was getting louder, as he seemed to be getting annoyed with the reverend's questions.

"But do we know anything about him?"

"We know all that we have to know. We know that he has the same taste for little girls that you do. And we know that if he doesn't do this, you're both going to be in deep shit. Now, do you want us to drive her down to some fancy new clinic, fill out all their forms, and give them all your personal information? How long do you think it would be before the police and the newspapers got their hands on that?"

She felt herself losing consciousness. The reverend's voice was starting to fade, but she could still hear the man with the loud raspy voice.

"What are you talking about killing? Nobody's killing anybody."

There was a pause. She strained to hear what the reverend said, but she couldn't make out his words. But the other man had apparently heard him, as he yelled out an answer.

"What is this? Are you telling me you're concerned about killing a fetus? Is that what has you all worked up?" He let out a huge laugh. "What is it with people like you? It's okay to bonk your teenage daughter, but it suddenly becomes sinful when you try to clean up the mess?

"Now, will you just shut the fuck up and let us get on with the job?"

◆◆◆

THE DRAB WALLS AND the frayed curtains were the first things she saw, as she fought her way back to consciousness. For a second she couldn't remember why she was there, but then the whole awful story hit her. She felt a gathering nausea and weakness that seemed to penetrate her entire body. Her clothing was ripped in a couple of places, and when she looked more closely she could see blood stains on her dress and legs. She tried to move, but that only triggered a pain that stretched across her stomach.

She lay there for several minutes, fighting a sense of panic. She still thought about escape, but that seemed hopeless. And if she didn't have the strength to get out of there before this happened, she would never be able to do it now when she felt a lot sicker and weaker. She was starting to despair, until she suddenly realized something. She was alone in the room for the first time since they kidnapped her.

The door to the adjacent room was still open, and she could hear the voices of the men. They were all in there. The man with the raspy voice was telling the men who had grabbed her off the street they had to leave.

"What's the big rush?" one of them asked.

"Someone identified you. It was on television a few minutes ago. The police released both of your names, and they've got a manhunt on for you."

"How the hell did that happen?"

"How the fuck am I supposed to know?"

Their voices seemed to be moving away, and she guessed that they were headed to the outside door of the other room—maybe even out toward the van. As she listened to them talk, she looked over at the corner of the room near her bed. Her shoulder bag was still lying in the place where they'd thrown it when they forced her into the room.

This might be her only chance. She eased herself over the side of the bed until she reached the floor. The pain in her stomach got worse as she did so, but she forced herself to crawl across the carpet, inch by inch on her back until she reached her bag. Her cell phone was still in the pocket. Although her wrists were tied together, she managed to maneuver the phone out of the bag and into a position where she could manipulate the keyboard with her thumbs. She typed the letter "G" on the address line, and Gina's cell phone number popped up. She thought for a second and then typed "M" as well. Her mother's cell phone appeared. She heard noises from the other room, and she sensed that they were coming back in from the outside. The message had to be quick: "Help Sands Motel."

She dropped the phone into the bag and tried to crawl back to the bed. She got halfway there and blacked out.

Gina

SOMEONE HAD PLACED A picture of Morrie in a handmade frame on the sidewalk outside the store under the boarded-up window. The photo was one that Miriam had taken of him reading a story to a little boy. He always said it was his favorite picture. People from the neighborhood had come by and put flowers next to it—an intimate gesture that might not have been expected in this young, hip, urbane neighborhood. That alone would have broken me up, but next to the flowers were several small piles of children's books that had been arranged in loving fashion. Kids had apparently been coming by in a steady stream to leave books for their favorite storyteller. I started crying so heavily that Sylvia and Cristina had to usher me over to a place where I could sit down to try to regain my composure. It took a little while.

Marco, Sylvia's paralegal assistant, had parked the van in a temporary spot in front of the store when they let me out. Sylvia wanted me to head upstairs to my apartment to get some rest—the bookstore could wait for a day or so until I got my strength back. But I told her no, I couldn't do that. I had to make an appearance downstairs. The booksellers who worked there were a pretty resilient group, but I needed to show them—and show myself—that this kind of thing wouldn't intimidate us. We were in business to stay no matter who attacked us.

I was still worried about Alexi. Even as I put on my bravest face and walked through the store, I had to fight a sense of panic. There'd been no developments in the case. The police had taken Davey's information about the kidnappers and released it to the news stations, but there were still no leads. I kept telling myself that she was still alive, because they had no reason to kill her. I was pretty sure it was just me they wanted to kill. Oddly enough, I found that comforting.

The store showed all of the damage that two high-caliber bullets fired through a plate-glass window can do. The front, of course, was partially boarded up, waiting for the glass repair company. In the meantime, we would simply have to live with the large pieces of plywood that were blocking out the light from the street. A couple of local artists had taken it upon themselves to paint some impromptu murals on the boards. That was fine with me, as long as they kept them respectful. Inside, a few of the bookcases had been splintered and were looking rather forlorn. There were a lot of damaged books as well. Some of them had to be thrown out, but others had been put on a shipping cart that someone had placed near the door. Miriam or someone had added a handwritten sign that said, "Buy a book and prove the murderers wrong."

Good wishes, I was told, had been pouring in from everywhere. The mayor's office had called to give us the city's condolences. City Hall was only a few blocks away, and the mayor planned to visit the store the following afternoon. The former mayor, who had an apartment down near the Ferry Building, had already been by to show his support. The American Booksellers Association called to ask how we were holding up and said they had sent out a special bulletin about the shooting. *Shelf Awareness*, the book-business trade journal, was planning a story about the shooting and had posted an in memoriam for Morrie. *Publishers Weekly* called and said they wanted to interview me when I felt up to it. The NCIBA, our local trade association, was already arranging a special benefit in Morrie's honor to raise money for the Law Center to Prevent Gun Violence—an organization on Bush Street where Morrie volunteered. Most poignantly of all, the staff had rearranged the children's section to find space for a permanent memorial and a new name: "Morrie's Room." Most of this was unexpected, and I was overwhelmed by it.

Sylvia stayed with me, as I walked around the store, trying to get reacclimated to my little world that had been so suddenly violated. I heard my cell phone buzz, indicating a text message. The phone was in my purse, but it was hard for me to reach it with my bandaged shoulder. I asked Sylvia if she would grab it. I could see from the look on her face that it was something important. "It's from Alexi."

Help Sands Motel

◆ ◆ ◆

MARCO BROUGHT THE VAN around as quickly as he could and double-parked in front of the store. Cristina jumped in the front seat. Sylvia got in the back. As she did so, she tried to convince me to stay put and not go with them.

"You need to take care of your injury," she said. "I'll keep you posted about what's going on, but you should stay here. With your shoulder all bandaged up like that, you can't do much anyway."

That was all perfectly logical, but she was dealing with me. So she knew she was going to lose that argument. I managed to crawl into the back seat and sit next to her, even though I could feel the pain curling down my back as I did so. I told Sylvia I had to go with them. She just nodded. Cristina had already located the Sands Motel on her iPhone map and was giving Marco directions. It was down in the Bayview District just off Third Street. It wasn't the swankiest part of San Francisco by any means, but I guess it was just the right place if you're paying a couple of hired killers to head into town to kidnap someone.

Finding the place wasn't the issue—the real problem was what to do when we got there. Was Alexi still there, or had they moved her? And if she was still there, who was there with her? Was it just the two men who kidnapped her, or were there more of them? And how about Blaiseck—the *Komandant?* Was he there too? All of my instincts said he was, but that may only have been my fear factor kicking in. What could we do against a potentially armed camp? Sylvia called the police while we were driving, urging them to send a squad car—several squad cars, for that matter. But what would happen if we got there first?

As Sylvia hung up her call to the police, she found a text message waiting for her. She read it and got a deep frown on her face. She tapped her leg in frustration. That was her sign that she wasn't happy.

"A complication—that was a message from Davey Fallon."

She took a deep breath and let it out grudgingly. "He just picked up Susan Wilder at the airport. And as they were getting into a cab, she got the same message on her phone from Alexi."

"What are they going to do?"

Sylvia shook her head that she didn't know. "I just hope they stay out of it for a while."

But we both knew there wasn't much chance of that. I knew what I'd do if I were Susan. They were on their way to the same motel.

We were a block away when the sign for the motel appeared. As we got closer, we saw only a few cars in the parking lot. There was no sign yet of the police. Marco pulled into a spot on the street just outside the lot. The office was around the corner out of sight. There was no sign of anyone.

He turned the engine off, and we sat there for a few seconds. My nerves were frazzled, and I could see that the rest of them were just as jumpy as I was. I was anxious to do something, but I knew we had to talk things over. There was only one entrance to the motel, and we were parked where we could keep an eye on it. The consensus of the others was that we should stay right there until the police arrived. I objected at first, but they convinced me it was best to wait. Since I had only one arm that was functioning at that moment, I was in no position to argue that we should barge right in.

◆ ◆ ◆

WAITING GAVE ME TIME to think—maybe, too much time to think.

As I watched that cheap motel, swallowing another of my pain pills, I had an eerie feeling that the resolution to our little drama was going to be played out on that oil-stained parking lot. I couldn't predict what anyone would do. Anything could go wrong. Someone might make a quick exit, or the wrong person might walk in at the wrong moment. Another might miss a cue or make a tragic misstatement. And what would happen if someone did something wildly out of character?

Two characters left the scene immediately. Minutes after we arrived, two men walked out from the shadow of the motel rooms and got into a van parked in the lot. The sight of them raised alarm bells in me. One was definitely overweight; the other was completely bald; they were driving a van—what more did I need to know? I couldn't prove they were the two who shot me, because I'd only caught a fleeting glimpse of them as my face hit the sidewalk. Still, I was sure they were the killers.

But knowing who they were didn't mean we could do anything about it. They seemed to be in a huge hurry to get out of there. The van sped out of the lot, slowing down just barely as it crossed the sidewalk, and then it made a sharp right turn into the street. Cristina had the presence of mind to record their quick exit on her phone camera, and by the time their van turned at the next corner she was already forwarding the video—along with the photo of their license plate—to the police. I was angry about losing them, but Marco pointed out that with them gone it might be easier to free Alexi from her captors. He was right, but I still wanted them—badly. As it turned out, they were gone from the scene but not from the story. We learned later that their vehicle had been picked up on a vid-cam in a parking lot at the San Francisco Airport. That led to a police scramble that finally caught up with them at one of the airline counters. They surrendered without a fight. But that was later, and this was now. The story at the motel was just beginning.

Another person walked in from the wings. He was a tall, thin man with an odd moustache. He walked hurriedly out of the parking lot, heading for his car, carrying a small black bag. As he got closer to our car, he appeared to see us. He was already a bundle of nerves, but after he saw us, he started walking even faster. He got into a car parked behind us and pulled out of the parking space as quickly as he could. Cristina once again had her camera ready and snapped a picture of his license plate as he went by. She passed her phone to the back seat so Sylvia and I could both see it. One thing on his bumper jumped out at me, and I could see Sylvia had noticed it too. It was a decal showing that he was a physician.

"Sylvia, we have to get in there right now. Alexi could be in serious condition, and we can't waste a minute."

Sylvia tried to slow me down, but it wasn't working.

"Gina, we don't know what room he came out of. We don't even know which room Alexi is in. This could be totally unrelated."

"You don't believe that any more than I do. That guy had 'back-alley abortionist' written all over him. We've got to do something."

The argument would have continued, but Marco interjected.

"Are those the people you were worried about down at the corner?"

Sylvia and I took a quick look to where he was pointing and saw Davey and Susan getting out of a cab. Sylvia muttered "oh shit" under her breath.

"Where the hell are the cops? They should be here by now."

Davey had stopped to pay the cab driver, while Susan had begun walking up the slight hill toward the motel. He tried to catch up with her, but she was already near the entrance to the parking lot, peering over the short brick wall to see if she could see anything. I'm not sure I would have recognized her. Even from a distance I could see that her appearance had changed. There was no brightly colored suit like she wore around the church. She was dressed almost completely in black in a somewhat shapeless dress. Her hair no longer rested on top of her head in a styled hairdo. Instead, she wore it straight down without any pretense or purpose, letting it fall wherever it happened to be. As she got closer, I thought I could see lines on her face that I hadn't seen before. It hadn't been that long, but she looked like she'd gone through a lifetime of changes.

It made no sense to wait in the car any longer. Now that Davey and Susan were there and walking into the parking lot, we couldn't keep our presence a secret. Sylvia got out of the car and quickly caught up with Davey, apparently trying to convince him to hold back since the police should be there any minute. Davey looked at Susan, and I could hear him urging her to stop as well. Susan stood there without moving, seemingly waiting for someone to tell her when she could move again.

I was a little slower getting out of the car. But I was finally steady enough on my feet to walk over to Susan. I dreaded the thought of talking to her. What could I say? I'd rehearsed what I thought should be the first words out of my mouth, but none of those words came to mind. All I could do was apologize.

"I'm so sorry for this. I really am. I had no idea that it would come down to something this terrible."

Maybe I should have said something more, but my voice faltered. I waited to see what Susan would say. Anger, sadness, sympathy—any of those reactions might have been normal in that situation. But for several long seconds there was nothing. She simply stared at me with blank eyes. I was beginning to squirm.

"You sent me pictures."

That was all. She kept staring at me as she said it. Was she thanking me, chastising me, or what? I didn't know. Even now, I'm still not sure. All I know is that she was in the grip of a deep emotional wound.

◆ ◆ ◆

"THERE THEY ARE."

Cristina saw them first, as the motel room door opened, and John Blaiseck stepped out. Reverend Wilder was a step behind him. Blaiseck had his body half turned, trying to help Wilder drag Alexi through the doorway. She was resisting everything they did. They saw us a couple seconds after we saw them.

What happened next? It depends on which version you want to hear.

I've ended up telling the story so many times—to the police, to hospital admission, to the press, to lawyers—that each time it comes out slightly different. Each version is the truth, as far as I knew at the time I said it. But storytelling can sometimes leave your head in a daze. All I know is that everything happened quickly—although, oddly, at that moment it felt like time had slowed down. I remember the whole scene as having been played out over a chorus of approaching sirens that got louder and louder. It almost certainly would have ended differently if the vehicles with those sirens had arrived a few minutes earlier.

Blaiseck saw us approaching and barked at Wilder. "Get her in the car so we can get out of here."

Wilder tried to push Alexi in the side door, but she broke away momentarily from his grasp. It was enough for all of us to see that her wrists were tied together. There was a haggard look on her face and bloodstains on her dress.

"What have you done to her?"

Those words erupted as a deep, anguished scream from somewhere behind me. I could feel the power of Susan's voice as it sailed past my head. When I turned, I saw a different woman. The blank stare was gone, and her eyes were on fire. Sylvia had her by the arm, trying to calm her down.

Blaiseck kept staring at the rest of us, seemingly unmoved by Susan's outburst. "Get her in the car," he repeated to Wilder, this time a little more forcefully.

Davey started to approach Blaiseck, urging the rest of us to stay back for a moment.

"John, this isn't going to do anyone any good. The police are going to be here in a few minutes, so you need to do the right thing and let her go. Her mother needs to take care of her."

Blaiseck glared at him. "Mind your own fucking business, will you? Her father's taking her out of here, and you're not going to stop him."

Davey tried again to get him to stop, but Blaiseck ignored him.

"Look, John—"

As Blaiseck turned toward the van, Davey reached over and put his hand on his arm. Blaiseck erupted. In one movement, he pulled an assault rifle from off the front seat and smashed it across Davey's face, forcing him back against the side of the van. Davey started bleeding as he sank to the ground.

Blaiseck turned and looked at the others. His eyes moved from face to face as the barrel of the rifle trailed along with his gaze.

"Does anybody else want to try anything?"

I'd seen that look before—years earlier. Blaiseck, when he was still the *Komandant*, had calmly walked up to one of his soldiers and shot him in the side of the head. I had no doubt he would do that again, if anyone challenged him.

Davey tried to get up from where he had been thrown against the van, but he could only move a few steps. He seemed to be ignoring the bloody wound on his face and instead was holding onto his chest. He fell down again just a few feet from where I was standing.

"I think I need help," he said. His color was pale, and his voice was so weak I could hardly hear him. "I'm having a hard time breathing."

I knelt down next to him and motioned quickly to Cristina to help me. "We need another ambulance." She'd already phoned for an emergency vehicle moments earlier when she first saw Alexi. Now, she nodded at me, as she sent off another emergency message.

"He can't breathe. We need to get his jacket off and open his collar."

I was having a hard time doing that with my one good hand. Cristina stepped over and pulled off Davey's coat and unbuckled his shoulder holster. While she ripped open the buttons on his shirt, I put the gun and holster in a pile with his clothing. For some reason, I remember thinking at that moment that Davey had never attempted to reach for that gun during his confrontation with Blaiseck.

The sirens were getting louder, and I was praying that there were a few ambulances along with the squad cars. Susan was still extremely upset, but Sylvia and Marco were trying to convince her that we couldn't do anything by ourselves. We just had to hope the police would get there in time.

Then Alexi made one more attempt to break away, swinging at Wilder with her tied-together fists. But she fell down near the back of the van.

Wilder leaned over her and said, "Come on honey, let's go back home. When we get there, everything is going to be exactly like it was. We'll be just like we were before."

And there it was.

They were just words, but they were words that made all the difference.

Which word was it that caused things to explode? Was it "exactly"? Or maybe it was "everything"? Most likely, it was the phrase, "just like we were before." Whatever it was, the reverend never had a chance to take those words back.

I heard another, deep-throated sound.

"No!"

It was a scream so loud that I will never forget it.

Then I heard a loud crack. And as I turned my head I could see Susan with Davey's pistol in her hand leveling a second shot at Wilder. He had already staggered back from the first bullet while twisting slightly to his right. When the second shot hit him, he fell flat on his face. Blaiseck reached for his rifle as soon as he heard the first shot, but he reacted too slowly. Susan shot him once in the head and then once more in the stomach as he turned around.

◆◆◆

MOMENTS LATER, THE SCENE was covered with flashing lights, squawking radios, and uniformed officers with pistols. But the most important people were the ones with the stretchers. Those who needed their attention were scattered throughout that dingy parking lot in little piles of humanity.

Cristina sat on the ground next to Alexi, doing what she could to make her comfortable. Marco and Sylvia had wrestled Susan to the pavement when she attempted to turn the pistol on herself. Now they sat on either side of her, trying to hold her, while she sobbed uncontrollably. I sat with Davey as I tried to keep him calm and ease his mind about his chest pains.

Wilder and Blaiseck were both lying apart—each in a pile of his own.

PART FIVE

Two Weeks Later

Alexi

SHE WASN'T GOING TO say anything unless she absolutely had to. Sylvia and Cristina had coached her earlier and cautioned her to be careful. Jail walls have ears. She didn't know if they were being recorded at the moment, but she didn't want to do anything that would make the situation worse. Without Sylvia there, she would have been lost. Sylvia seemed to know everything about the place. Even the sergeant at the front desk softened up when she talked to him, especially when she asked him about his family.

At one point, the guard even looked over Sylvia's shoulder and smiled at her. She wanted to smile back, but she was too caught up in her own worries to do anything other than just nod in response. The hardest part was still ahead. She was afraid she might break down completely when she got to the visitor's room and saw her mother.

◆ ◆ ◆

SHE WANTED TO SHUT everything out of her mind. From the day she was released from the hospital to the moment she walked up to the front of the jail, she tried to keep herself busy with other things, hoping to take her mind off the worst of it. The day before Sylvia arranged to meet her at the jail, she spent several hours with Gina looking at local music stores and checking websites, trying to find a replacement for the guitar that had been destroyed. Gina had a newer, smaller bandage on her shoulder that allowed her to move around better, so they could actually get out of the house. She tried to think about almost anything other than what had happened, but her mind kept coming back to that day. Even talking about the guitar opened a door in her head that brought in bad memories.

When she woke up in the hospital, Gina was holding her hand, stroking her fingers slowly, focusing on each one of them. There was a tube taped to her arm with a bag of some sort hanging on a pole near the bed. Gina told her later that a container of blood had been attached to her arm and pumped into her while she was sedated. The doctors had done a good job, Gina said. They saved her from all the complications she could have faced as a result of the forced abortion. The word "abortion" cut through her like a knife, but after a while it had become mingled with all of the other awful thoughts she was trying to deal with. She didn't know what the doctors had done, but she was sure that it was Gina's long, slow massage of her fingers that made the difference. The feeling worked its way up from her hand into the rest her body. "*You're going to be okay,*" Gina kept repeating. After a while, she began to believe it.

She still wasn't sure what had happened. From the time she sent the text message, until she came out of the fog in the hospital with Gina sitting next to her, reality and hallucinations had become one big jumble. She remembered a struggle in the parking lot. When she had tried to pull away from them, she was in so much pain that she had collapsed.

As she was losing consciousness, she thought she heard her mother's voice yelling at them to let her go. But was her mother really there? She remembered trying to ask Gina that question when she was in the ambulance. But there were so many things going on at that moment—with people sticking things into her body and shouting commands—she wasn't sure that Gina had heard her. She was beginning to think she might never see her mother again. But at some point Gina had answered her: yes, her mother was there.

She learned the rest of it later. She thought she remembered something that sounded like gunshots, but she was only semiconscious. It could have been anything. But piece by piece, as she lay there in her hospital bed, she found out what had happened. The shots were real. They had hit their victims, and both were dead. It wasn't until she was out of danger from her injuries that Gina finally told her everything that had happened. She explained it as gently as she could, but there was no way to make it any easier. The two men were dead, and her mother was being held for murder.

She kept reliving what happened. She couldn't erase it from her mind. There always seemed to be one more part to it—one more awful piece—that she hadn't dealt with. Several times she broke down crying, and Gina would just sit down next to her and hold her. She started to blame herself for everything, but Gina put a stop to that in a hurry.

"Don't think like that," she said. "You did nothing wrong."

And in the midst of that, she made a decision. She had to go see her mother as soon as she could. Gina thought she should wait a few more days and not rush it. She'd only been home a short time. But she wanted to do it as soon as possible. Gina relented. Then she poured a pot of tea and brought it into the living room, making it clear that she had something she wanted to tell her. As she sat on the couch, Gina pulled up a chair so they could talk face-to-face.

"Alexi, your mother's very depressed. She may dig herself out of it, but I can't be sure. We're doing everything we can to help her."

She guessed something like that might be happening. She wanted to know everything Gina was telling her, but it was painful to hear.

Gina said that Sylvia had been trying to talk with her, hoping to get her cooperation. If she would just work with the lawyers, they might be able to develop a good defense—or at least get the charges reduced to something they could live with. But they weren't getting any cooperation.

Gina shook her head slowly, like she was having difficulty explaining it. "She just keeps saying she wants to take whatever punishment they give her."

That last statement brought on the tears.

"I thought about not telling you any of that, because I knew it would be too painful. But if you're going to talk to your mother, you need to know it. Maybe it would help if she could just see you."

Gina stared at her for a few more seconds.

"I know I told you not to blame yourself for any of this, but the truth is I've gone through a lot of that myself. I probably could have done things differently."

"Don't say that!"

As she rushed to console Gina, Gina forced a slight smile.

"You have a home with me as long as you want it. You know that. But I never intended this to be permanent. In my heart, I always hoped that it would work out for you to be with your mother. I just hope someday we can make that happen."

◆◆◆

BY THE TIME THEY got to the visiting area at the end of the hall, she was starting to shake. Sylvia gave her a reassuring squeeze on the arm as the policewoman opened the large metal door. Sylvia said she would be just outside if they needed anything, but she would try to leave the two of them alone as much as possible. She appreciated that, but she knew her meeting with her mother wasn't going to be all that private. The two of them would be separated by a thick glass wall.

Her mother's appearance shocked her. Gina had warned her that she would look different, but it was still a surprise to see how much she'd changed.

"Hi, Mom. Are you all right?"

Her mother didn't seem to know why she was in that room. She hadn't focused on the glass wall until she heard a voice. Then she looked over and started crying.

"Oh, Alexi, are you okay? I knew you were in the hospital, and I was worried sick about you. But my lawyer, Sylvia, says they took good care of you. Are you really okay?"

"I'm fine, Mom."

Her mother was still standing at the back of the room. She seemed reluctant to get any closer to the glass.

"Can you come up near the window, Mom, where I can see you better?"

"Oh, Alexi. I look frightful. I don't want you to see me this way."

"I just want to see you. I don't care what you look like."

"But it's not right for you to have to come into a place like this." She turned her head away for a second. "This isn't at all what I wanted for you."

"I don't mind. Really, I just want to see you."

Her mother was quiet for a moment before saying anything. "Davey Fallon told me about Gina, and he said she's been taking good care of you."

"She has, Mom."

Her mother just shook her head slowly. For the moment, all of the emotion seemed to have been drained from her. "That's good, Alexi, because I'm going to be in here for a long time."

"It doesn't have to be that way."

But her mother continued with the same thought. "I killed two people, and that's a terrible thing. They may never let me out. So I don't think you should plan to come here very often to see me."

"No, Mom, no." She was getting more and more upset about the way the conversation was going. "You've got one of the best law firms in town working on the case."

Her mother shrugged.

"You can't just roll over and die. They have a plan for helping you, but you have to cooperate. Sylvia says that they have a strong case for something called 'temporary insanity'—maybe even a claim for self-defense."

Her mother gave a sad little laugh. "Is that what they're saying?"

"Yes. There are all kinds of things they can do to help you, if you'll only let them."

Her mother was silent for a few moments. And when she began again, she was off on another line of thought.

"I failed you, Alexi."

Those dark days at the church sprang into her head, but she had concluded that it wasn't her mother's fault. She was asking too much of her. She should have found a way—any way at all—to let her know what was happening.

"You didn't fail me, Mom. Don't say that!"

"Yes I did, sweetheart. I should have seen what was going on."

"You didn't see it, because I didn't tell you."

"But you said yourself I should have seen it." She paused for a second. "I've read your journals. There were signs, and I missed them all."

"I didn't come right out and tell you. I don't know why—maybe the reason was that I didn't want to hurt you… I don't know, it could be you were doing the same thing. Maybe you just blocked out the signs, because you knew how much it would hurt me if it were true."

Her mother shook her head and attempted a smile.

"Do you realize what you're saying? You're telling me I ignored the real story in order protect the fantasy one. Someday when you're a mother you'll realize that's not good enough."

The logic of the conversation was getting all twisted. She had to break through it somehow.

"Mom, forget all that. I need you. I need you right now!"

The tears were coming now, and she didn't do anything to stop them. She leaned up against the window with her mouth against the microphone, as she kept repeating, "I need you."

Her fingers were spread against the glass as she started to pound against the window. She stopped when she thought she might get in trouble with the guards. Instead, she just leaned into the glass and wept.

After a few seconds, she realized her mother was leaning up against the window on the other side. She had placed her hands against the glass and spread out her fingers, matching them one to one against her own. Her mother was leaning into the mouthpiece, and she was weeping along with her.

Gina

I HAD ONE PILLOW fluffed atop the other, and the reading lamp that I'd purchased at a secondhand shop on Market Street was angled just right. I had on a new nightgown, which was a treat I gave myself after the bandage on my shoulder was removed. The scar on my shoulder was still tender at times, but my new nightie had a full top that covered it up. I was in my favorite reading position, and I was ready to dive into a group of advance reading copies of books lying on the covers next to me.

All of the books were soon to be published, and I'd promised the sales rep that I'd write a comment for some of them. I planned to leave them for Alexi when she got back. At the moment, she was staying with Sylvia while they worked on her mother's bail motion. I wasn't sure when exactly she'd return, but that might depend on how the hearing went. Since Alexi had a pretty broad interpretation of young adult fiction, I wasn't going to object if she delved into something that publishers might think was beyond her age level. After what she'd been through, she could read anything she wanted.

There was a light tap on my bedroom door, and I told him to come in. It had to be Davey, because he was the only other person in the apartment.

"I saw your light. I thought you wouldn't mind if I stuck my head in for a minute."

He stood there, looking a bit unsteady. I told him to sit down.

"You can throw that stuff off the chair or just sit down on the end of the bed, if you like."

"If you don't mind, I'll just ease myself down here." He sat down at the foot of the bed, and I moved my feet over to accommodate him.

The pajamas were his own, but the robe was one that I picked up at a shop on Gough Street when I realized he was about to be released from the cardiac care unit and had no other place to go. He still wasn't able to button the pajamas, because the bandage underneath was so big that the cloth wouldn't stretch. That's what happens when you have open-heart surgery—you get a bandage that stretches from the top of your sternum all the way down to your stomach.

"Are you feeling okay? I know you've been eating better."

He nodded. "I'm getting better. I'm pretty sure of that."

"Good."

He sat there for a second with a thoughtful look on his face. "I hear you've been looking for a new guitar for Alexi."

"Yeah. My old one has a bullet hole where the fret board used to attach to the sound box."

He nodded as I explained what happened.

"Well, you don't have to buy her a new one. There's a wonderful old guitar sitting in my closet in Indianapolis. It's a classic model. I'd like Alexi to have it."

"That's very nice of you."

Davey shrugged. "I can't let it sit there forever. It's not doing anyone any good where it is."

He stared down at his feet. "It was Jimmy's guitar. His sister gave it to me." He looked over for a brief moment. "I told you about Jimmy, didn't I?"

"A little bit. I'd like to hear more, when you're up to it."

He nodded his head a little, but he was back to staring down at his feet. I wasn't sure where the conversation was going.

"I never really thanked you for being there with me when I was going into surgery."

"You don't have to thank me. One of my unwritten rules of life is that no one should ever go into a hospital without having someone there to look out for things."

"I know you were going through a lot." He looked up as he said it.

"Everyone was going through a lot at the time. But at least you were in the same hospital as Alexi. It wasn't much extra trouble for me to go up a few floors to see you."

He tried to laugh a little. "It's just something I won't ever forget."

He sat there for a second, gathering his thoughts. He was back to staring down at the floor.

"I was pretty scared. It made all the difference in the world that you held my hand when I was being wheeled into surgery."

He gave a little smile, but it wasn't directed at me—he was still looking at the floor. "You have very reassuring fingers."

I smiled at him, but he wasn't yet watching.

"Did you have any trouble getting in there with me?"

"No. I told them I was your wife."

"You did?" That got him to turn around and look up. "It might have been more believable if you had said you were my daughter."

I shrugged. "No one checked. I guess I must have looked the part."

Since I had his attention, I had one more thing to tell him. "Speaking of daughters, I had a nice conversation with Mandy."

"You talked to my daughter? How did you even know about her?"

"I was posing as your wife, remember? The nurse handed me your wallet and everything else. I looked through your address book for names and numbers that I might have to contact, and I found her listing. Since you were having open-heart surgery, I thought she ought to know about it. So I called her."

He shook his head in disbelief. "I haven't talked with Mandy in about eight years."

"She said it was more like ten." I gave him a smile to keep his attention. "But she's planning to call you tomorrow."

He was still skeptical. "Why after all this time does she want to talk to me?"

"Maybe it's because I told her how heroic you were in trying to rescue Alexi and how you've been through a lot of things and come through them pretty well."

I had to give him my biggest smile after that.

"You're going to be a grandfather, did you know that? Mandy's having a little boy—due in about two weeks."

"I heard about that."

"I got the feeling she would like to talk to you about it."

He smiled for a moment, but it faded. There was still something bothering him, but I didn't know what it was.

"Did she tell you why she picked tomorrow to call me?"

"No."

"It's because it's my birthday. I'm going to be seventy."

I took a quick look at the clock. "It will be midnight in about twenty minutes. We'll have to celebrate."

He shook his head. "I don't need to celebrate. I just need to get through it."

"What do you mean?"

He took a deep breath and let it out slowly. "My life has been so empty in recent years that I vowed that I wouldn't let it drag out past my seventieth birthday."

He was looking me straight in the eye now.

"The gun I always carried around? It wasn't really for protection. It was for me. I always knew that I would turn it on myself—maybe sooner than today, but today for sure."

I reached over to grab his hand. Our fingers intertwined for a few moments.

"I guess it's a good thing that your pistol is locked up in an evidence locker somewhere down at the Hall of Justice."

"I guess so."

But I realized that wasn't enough.

"What I really meant to say is that even if that pistol were sitting right here in front of us, we'd be strong enough to beat it. I think we would look right down the barrel and say, 'That's over. We're moving forward.'"

Davey squeezed my hand a little tighter.

"Thank you." There was a tear in his eye.

He made a move to get up. "I've bothered you enough for one night. It's time to get back to bed."

"Why don't you just stay right where you are? Just turn around a little and lean back. I'll throw one of the covers over you."

"Are you sure it's okay?"

"I'm sure. Here, let me get the books out of the way."

He stretched out, trying to get comfortable, as I reached over to turn out the light.

"Is that you down there?"

"Yeah, am I too close to you?"

"No, it's fine."

"Well then, try to get some rest."

"Okay. Good night."

I squeezed his hand a little. "Good night."